MAN AND WIFE

Lord, but she was lovely in the candlelight. Justin wished that he might take her in his arms. Yes, and why should he not? After all, she was his wife. Therefore, he took her hand and drew her to her feet. "I wish that you would call me Justin. Why do you look startled? It is my name, after all."

"Thank you . . . Justin." Would he kiss her now?

If only he dared kiss her! But in this moment his bride seemed to trust him a little bit, and he did not wish to frighten her away. "We have had a great many misunderstandings between us, I think. Permit me to clear up one of them. When I said I did not wish my wife to associate with Conor Melchers, I did not refer to Magda. It has been a very long time since I thought of Magda as anything other than a curst nuisance."

Elizabeth was encouraged. "Magda is a trifle unconventional perhaps."

"Magda has an abominable inclination to meddle. If I may say so, as I should not, I say so to my wife, and nothing that we say or do together may be considered improper, Elizabeth." Ruefully, Justin smiled, and raised his hands to cup her pretty face. Elizabeth's eyes were open wide, her lips slightly parted. She looked infinitely kissable.

Well, then, he would kiss her . . .

Books by Maggie MacKeever

CUPID'S DART

LOVE MATCH

Published by Zebra Books

LOVE MATCH

Maggie MacKeever

ZEBRA BOOKS
KENSINGTON PUBLISHING CORP.
http://www.kensingtonbooks.com

ZEBRA BOOKS are published by

Kensington Publishing Corp.
850 Third Avenue
New York, NY 10022

All Kensington titles, imprints, and distributed lines are
available at special quantity discounts for bulk purchases for
sales promotions, premiums, fund-raising, educational, or
institutional use.

Special book excerpts or customized printings can also be
created to fit specific needs. For details, write or phone the
office of the Kensington Special Sales Manager: Kensington
Publishing Corp., 850 Third Avenue, New York, NY 10022.
Attn: Special Sales Department. Phone: 1-800-221-2647.

Zebra and the Z logo Reg. U.S. Pat. & TM Off.

First Printing: December 2003
10 9 8 7 6 5 4 3 2 1

Printed in the United States of America

Chapter 1

*"Marriage is a thing of the utmost consequence.
Especially marriage to a duke."* —Lady Ratchett

Along the Bath Road bounced an elegant closed carriage, attended by outriders and liveried footmen, drawn by a team of four beautifully matched grays. The well-sprung coach gleamed black with great yellow wheels. A ducal crest was blazoned on its doors. From his high seat John Coachman, reins in his left hand and blackthorn whip in his right, held the spirited horses to a sedate pace. Ordinarily he would have enjoyed a gallop as much as they, but not on this steep, winding road and with these passengers. 'Twas not every day that Justin St. Clair, the Duke of Charnwood, took himself a bride.

The interior of the carriage was as elegant as the exterior, and as comfortable as money could have it made, with locking shutters, a secret compartment for valuables, three lamps, a compass and a clock, and a crimson velvet décor set off with gold braid. The carriage's owner lounged on one plush seat, long legs stretched out in front of him, broad shoulders propped against the lushly upholstered squabs. On the seat beside the duke sat his tall top hat. On the seat opposite perched his new duchess, who wore a carriage dress of blue and a bonnet elaborately trimmed with ribbons and roses. The lady was more slender than was fashionable, her hair dark blond streaked with lighter strands, her eyes a warm brown; and if no fault could be found in her fair complexion, her features remained slightly irregular. The duke's cool gaze rested on lips a little too full for perfection, a nose well-shaped but a trifle long, a chin that hinted his new duchess might not be quite so docile as she looked.

Justin realized that he was assessing his bride as if she were a filly up for sale at Tatt's. His eyes moved to the traveling clock. Theirs was a marriage entered into for the sake of duty, the duke's duty to get himself an heir, and his bride's duty to make a brilliant match.

That the duke was a marital prize of the first order, the duchess was well aware. She could hardly fail to be aware, so frequently had her mama pointed out the fact. *How* she had brought this paragon up to scratch neither Elizabeth nor Maman had the faintest notion, for the duke had been one of the *ton's* most eligible gentlemen, and Elizabeth had suffered so profound a shock on discovering he had offered for her that she hadn't recovered from it yet. Secretly, Elizabeth had hoped to receive no offers. She especially had not wished to receive an offer from a duke. Now she would have to spend the rest of her life being properly duchesslike.

Her bridegroom was paying her no attention. Through lowered lashes, she stole a look at him. Dispassionate gray eyes; chestnut hair cropped short yet still long enough to curl. An athletic figure that showed to advantage in sky blue coat, striped waistcoat, buff-colored breeches; dazzling white linen, a flawlessly tied cravat, and highly polished boots. He looked every inch the duke, with sun-gilded skin, aristocratic features, a stern cast of countenance.

He also looked bored. For whatever reason the duke had chosen Elizabeth, he wasn't smitten with her charms. Thus far during their journey Charnwood had fidgeted with his watch fob, cane, and ebony snuffbox, and was at the moment drumming his fingers on his knee.

The coach bounced and swayed, jolted over a particularly vicious bump. Elizabeth clapped her hand to her mouth and moaned, "Your Grace!"

The duke's cool eyes moved to his bride's face, which had turned a familiar shade of sickly green. He stifled a sigh and rapped on the roof. The coach swayed to a stop. Without awaiting assistance from either footman or bridegroom, the duchess grabbed the door handle and tumbled out of the carriage.

The duke waited for his footman to lower the step, then descended onto the rough stone roadway. As far as the eye could see stretched hill upon lovely undulating hill, covered in green foliage, dotted about with occasional clumps of cows and sheep.

Justin did not dote on sheep or cows, or even lovely scenery, of which he had already seen a great deal this day. His servants hovered silently about, trying to pretend that it was not unusual for the ducal conveyance to be parked alongside a busy thoroughfare while carriages and coaches and drays rumbled and thudded by. Certainly it was not unusual today.

The duke raised an eyebrow. John Coachman gestured toward the shrubbery. "I believe Her Grace is, ah . . ."

The shrubbery was thick with thorns. Justin pushed his way through the prickles and found his bride bent over a stone wall, trim blue-clad derriere pointed up in the air, hem hiked up to reveal more than a glimpse of white silk stockings and half boots of kid. Shapely white silk stockings, unexpected in so slender a female. What other surprises might hide under that unflattering dress?

Ungentlemanly musing, perhaps, but the lady *was* his wife. Who was now wiping her face with her handkerchief and muttering to the shrubbery. Justin moved closer. A twig snapped beneath his boot.

The duchess jumped bolt upright. The back of her head collided painfully with the duke's face. "Damnation!" she gasped, and then clapped her hands to her mouth. Though she frequently *thought* profanities, Elizabeth seldom gave them voice.

Justin winced and clasped his nose. "There you are, my dear," he managed. "If you are through taking your, ah, constitutional, perhaps we might continue on our way."

The wretched man was bleeding. Elizabeth fumbled for her wilted handkerchief, and stifled an urge to give his injured nose a sharp tweak. Not that she disliked her bridegroom, but she didn't like him either, and blamed him entirely for the butterflies that had taken up residence in her tummy. "I am so sorry," she fibbed. "I did not mean to damage you, Your Grace."

Justin stood stoically while his bride ministered to him, and tried not to contemplate the previous uses of the bedraggled handkerchief being applied none too gently to his nose. If only they hadn't stopped at that inn for refreshment. The squab pie had been a mistake.

The duke pushed back through the thorny shrubbery. His duchess trailed behind. Poor lass, the coachman thought; she looked as if she wished the earth would open and swallow her right up. Begad, was that *blood* on the handkerchief the duke held to his face?

Justin ignored his servants, who were all trying very hard not to gape at him. Elizabeth was still green. "Take deep breaths," he said, around the handkerchief. "Relish the fresh air. Lord knows we're surrounded by enough of it. You should have told me that you suffered from *mal de mer*."

Elizabeth was tall for a woman. Standing by the duke's side, her eyes were on a level with his chin. She stared at that elegant and somewhat imperious article as she obediently inhaled. "I didn't *know* I got travel-sick. I have never ridden so far in a coach before. Maman does not approve of jauntering about. I feel much better now."

She looked better. Her color was less green. Justin handed his lady back into the carriage, then swung himself up beside the coachman. "A word, John, if you will. On roads such as this even the best-sprung of carriages must sway. We will proceed onward at a snail's pace. Look on the bright side. You might even set a record for the longest time ever taken to arrive in Bath." The coachman grinned and touched his hat in acknowledgement of the command.

Gingerly, Elizabeth sat down on the carriage seat, and prayed that her blasted stomach would behave. How Maman would scold when she learned that Elizabeth hadn't even got to Bath before disgracing herself. Not that Elizabeth meant to tell her, but someone surely would.

Justin climbed into the carriage and settled on the seat opposite. "You're still bleeding," Elizabeth observed. "If only we had some ice. Lean your head back. Yes, like that. No one has ever bled to death from a bloody nose, Your Grace. Although I don't think we may be so hopeful about your poor cravat."

The duke dabbed cautiously at his injured nose. His

bride was taking an almost ghoulish pleasure in the sight of his blood. At least she wasn't missish. "I have other cravats."

"Quite a few, I should imagine," Elizabeth murmured. "Keep your head tilted back so that the bleeding will let up."

The chit knew her bloody noses. Perhaps she went about assaulting all her *beaux*. Not that Justin was a *beau*, precisely. He knew practically nothing about his new duchess, other than that her bloodlines were unexceptionable, and her dowry handsome. The future mother of his children, or so Justin had been promised, was a good biddable girl with a proper way of thinking, who would be easily trained to suit; she would think and do what she should, and cause her husband not a moment's unease. Damage to his person hadn't been mentioned. Cautiously, he lowered his head, and contemplated his travel-worn bride. Her carriage dress was rumpled, her bonnet askew. She twisted a little pink reticule in her lap.

The carriage hit a bump in the road and jolted roughly side to side. Both the duke and duchess held their breath. Elizabeth relaxed. "Not this time!" she said, and looked her bridegroom right in the face.

He blinked. Her eyes were not simply brown, as he had thought them, but flecked with gold; her eyelashes amazingly thick and long. They were, in short, quite lovely eyes.

Even as the duke was digesting that startling revelation, Elizabeth looked down at her lap. "You must tell me if you begin to feel unwell again," he said. " 'Tis no great trouble for the coach to stop."

What a poor thing he must think her. Elizabeth gripped her reticule. "I doubt there will be any further reason to stop. I must surely be too empty to—" She couldn't think of a duchesslike turn of phrase. "I think the bleeding has stopped, Your Grace."

Justin removed the blood-soaked handkerchief from his face and regarded it with distaste. What did one do with such an item? He could hardly return it to its owner. Nor did he care to put it in his pocket. He solved his dilemma by dropping the handkerchief on the carriage floor. "I perfectly take your meaning. The phrase is, 'cast up your accounts.' You need not be so formal. We *are* married. Try and see if you can call me St. Clair. I wish you'd tell me why you're on pins and needles. I am hardly an ogre, Elizabeth."

Blast! Now she'd insulted him. Elizabeth had been warned—countless times!—that her bridegroom was high in the instep. "I'm not afraid of you. It's just that everything happened so quickly. Not that I regret it. Maman was the one who longed for St. George's, Hanover Square."

Justin had expected that his bride would try to reassure him that he was not an ogre. He had *not* expected that her tone of voice would make him wonder if she had wanted the ceremony to take place at all. "Poor puss. Has your mother been lecturing you?" he asked, with one of his rare, enchanting smiles.

How very handsome was the duke when he wasn't being stern and forbidding! Elizabeth was amazed. "I will not put you to the blush, My Grace. Maman has made sure that I understood perfectly how I am to go on." Damnation, now she'd admitted to the highest of sticklers that her character was so lacking that she needed instruction in such things.

His bride was very young, thought Justin, for so eighteen must seem to a man of thirty-two. "Indulge my curiosity. Just what *did* your mother tell you?" He was amused by the notion that Elizabeth had ever in her short life put a foot wrong.

Which of the many things that Maman had said would bear repeating? Elizabeth smoothed her battered reticule. "I'm to appear amiable and accomplished. To demonstrate dignity and gentle seriousness and a modest reserve. I'm *not* to display unbecoming levity, or bother you with nonsensical notions, but to be at all times sunny-tempered, and exhibit great good sense. I'm probably also not to repeat this sort of thing to you, but that wasn't mentioned. You look astonished, sir. You *did* ask. To behave in any other manner would bring dishonor on my family."

"I'd no idea I wed such a paragon." If this was a blatant taradiddle, Justin wished merely to set his bride at ease. "Must I remind you that I am your family now? No, don't poker up! I didn't mean to scold. The first thing I would have you do to honor *me* is to forget everything your mother said. You are my duchess, and need answer to no one but myself."

Silently, Elizabeth pondered this remarkable suggestion. Not that she imagined her new husband would be any easier than Maman to please.

Justin studied his bride's averted features. There had been no kisses during their courtship, nor any of the other nonsense so beloved of young misses. He had never seen or spoken with Elizabeth without a chaperone. The duke found himself curious about the disheveled young woman in the opposite seat.

He leaned forward to touch her hand. She shrank back. Even through her gloves, her fingers felt ice cold. "Elizabeth!" he said, so sternly that she started. "Surely you weren't forced into this match."

Would Charnwood consider being locked in her

bedchamber as coercion? Elizabeth wished he would let go of her hand. "No, Your Grace."

She looked like she wished to leap out the window. What a clunch he was. Heaven only knew what misapprehensions so young a chit might cherish about the marriage bed. How best to soothe his bride's maidenly terrors? The duke patted the hand that he still held. "My dear, you need have no fear of me. I promise that I don't mean to misuse you in any way."

Elizabeth didn't expect that her bridegroom meant to feed her on bread and water, or lock her in her room. And if he did, what of it? 'Twas not as if she had never been locked in her room before. There were other things a husband could do, however. Very nasty things, the precise nature of which she could only guess. "I am glad to hear it, Your Grace."

He had not convinced her. She perched stiff as a broomstick on the velvet seat. "We shall have a great deal of time in which to grow comfortable with each other, Elizabeth."

What, exactly, made up "a great deal of time"? Maman had been very definite on the topic of gentlemen and their needs. Elizabeth was to climb into the marriage bed, and close her eyes and clench her teeth, and think herself elsewhere. Lust turned even the most proper of gentlemen into slavering beasts.

Elizabeth wished herself elsewhere now, even though her bridegroom looked considerably less forbidding with battered nose and blood-spattered cravat. "As you wish, Your Grace."

As he wished? Justin thought not. Else he would not be having this extremely awkward conversation with his bride. "St. Clair," he said, as he released her hand and leaned back in his seat. "Or I shall start calling *you* 'Your Grace,' and we shall 'duke' and 'duchess' each other into a rare tedium. I hope that you will enjoy our stay in Bath."

Relieved that he was no longer clutching her, Elizabeth glanced out the window. "Maman didn't approve of watering places. She says Bath is overrun with all sorts of rabble, and that she'll never set foot there."

"In that case perhaps we shall stay indefinitely in Bath. Tell me, is there anything of which your mother *does* approve?"

Elizabeth turned her head to study her bridegroom. "She approved of you, Your Grace."

Of course Lady Ratchett had approved of Justin. He was a duke. "The Charnwoods have been visiting Bath since the days when Prince Bladud cured his leprous pigs in a reed-grown spring. Our current residence is in the Royal Crescent. I trust it will meet with your satisfaction, Elizabeth."

The duke didn't *look* like a lustful beast. Not that Elizabeth was entirely sure what a lustful beast *should* look like, save that Maman had pruned up her lips and shuddered when she said the words. "Oh yes," fibbed the duchess. "I'm sure I shall like it of all things."

Chapter 2

*"No woman of understanding can marry without
infinite apprehension at taking such a monstrous step
into the unknown."* —Lady Ratchett

The elegant Charnwood carriage was only one among
many vehicles to arrive in Bath this day, as could be at-
tested by the small pageboy stationed at the city's outskirts to sound an alert when the ducal conveyance
came into sight. The hour had considerably advanced
when that event at last took place, and the duke had acquainted his bride with all manner of details about
Bath, from Prince Bladud's leprous pigs to the earlier
rumors that the city was about to be invaded by French
troops, a matter which need not overly concern her
now that Bony's attentions were directed elsewhere;
and she had thus far managed not to further disgrace
herself, although the bouncing of the carriage, the
rumble of wheels and thud of hooves had given her a
blinding headache, and caused her butterflies to turn
somersaults, and she had only managed to withstand

further disaster by counting the regularly spaced milestones all along the road. Still, Elizabeth was curious enough to gaze out the carriage window and enjoy her first sight of the city, an elegant sprawl of terraces and squares and crescents built in the native cream-color freestone, set in a valley with the River Avon running through it. Now, at almost twilight, wreaths of faint mist rose in the cool evening air. "Oh! It's beautiful!" she breathed.

How young she looked, peering out the window. Were it not so unladylike, his bride would probably have her nose pressed to the window glass. "It won't be much longer now," said Justin. "Despite Lady Ratchett's objections, I believe you may enjoy your visit here. The city offers amusements of all sorts. Shops as fine as London. Assemblies and soirees. The Pump Room and the Baths. You might like a walk to Beechen Cliffs, or a visit to the Abbey. Or perhaps you might care to inspect the superbly modeled bronze head from the Temple of Sul Minerva that was found under the cobbles of Stall Street some seventy years ago."

What Elizabeth would have liked was to get out of the blasted carriage. Her body felt like one great bruise, and the stays of her corset pressed into her flesh. The hills surrounding the city were crisscrossed with paved manicured streets, interspersed with circular arrangements of buildings and spaces for promenades, so mathematically precise that the town might have been cast all at once into a mold. Lights twinkled in countless windows. Despite her discomfort, Elizabeth was charmed.

The carriage rattled through the cobbled streets that led to the Royal Crescent, halted on the pavement before a great curving sweep of tall white-pillared houses standing shoulder to shoulder behind a stately array of Ionic columns with angular Roman volutes. "There are one hundred and fourteen columns," Justin said, in response to his bride's bemused expression. "I counted them one day." He stepped down from the carriage, and then turned to grasp Elizabeth by the waist and swing her to the pavement.

'Twas a strange and not particularly pleasant sensation to be swept off her feet. Elizabeth clutched her reticule and her bonnet and hoped that she might not throw up all over her bridegroom's shiny boots. When the duke set her down, she stumbled. Elizabeth's posterior had gone numb several miles back. She winced as she straightened up.

Busy issuing instructions to his coachman, the duke did not notice his bride's discomfort. He turned back to her. "Our luggage will have arrived before us. All should be in readiness for our arrival. Come and I will introduce you to the staff."

Elizabeth brushed at her wrinkled skirts, adjusted her bonnet, and allowed her bridegroom to take her arm. His servants would judge her, of course, and whisper about her when they thought she was out of earshot, just as Maman's servants had. She thought wistfully that it would be nice if some of them liked her just a little bit.

The Palladian facades of the thirty stately town houses blended together into the appearance of a single great mansion, approached by dignified arrangements of steps guarded by exquisite railings and lamp standards. In the doorway of St. Clair's rented house hovered a slender middle-aged man with thinning hair and pinched lips and, at the moment at least, a nervous tic. "Welcome, Your Grace," he said. "If I might have a word—"

The duke escorted Elizabeth up the stairs. "Contain yourself, Thornaby. Elizabeth, this is my valet. He is so eager to greet you that he has met us at the door."

"Your Grace." The valet bowed, then blanched at sight of the duke's bruised nose. "Oh, sir! You have been damaged! His Grace will require a cold compass, Mrs. Papplewick. At once!"

The walls were painted pale peach, the floor was marble, and the cornice carved. A circular stone staircase with bronzed iron balustrade and mahogany handrail led to the upper floors. Lined up in the hallway were the duke's servants, all staring—though they tried not to—at their master's blood-spattered person and damaged nose. Chislett, the butler, a most superior individual with bushy white eyebrows that matched the color of his hair. Mrs. Papplewick, the housekeeper, a sharp-faced woman with shrewd dark eyes and a brisk capable air. Liveried footmen in white cloth jackets with turned-up cuffs and pocket flaps of red plush that matched their knee breeches. Housemaids wearing pristine white aprons over dark stuff gowns, and starched caps on their heads.

One housemaid scurried off to fetch a cold compress. Another was sent flying in search of a fresh cravat. Thornaby pushed his slipping spectacles up his nose. "Your Grace, it is most urgent—"

"With Thornaby, you will find that it is always urgent," Justin said to Elizabeth. "Stop hovering, man! I have it on good authority that no one has yet died of a bloody nose."

The duke appeared to be sublimely oblivious of the servants bustling around him, removing hat and gloves and brushing off his coat. The duchess was politely relieved of her bonnet and coat. Each and every one of the servants blamed her for the damage to their master's person, she thought.

Another woman stepped into the hallway. Past her first youth, she shared the duke's chestnut locks, drawn back in long ringlets, and gray eyes beneath sharply defined brows. There the resemblance ended, for her elegant features were marred by discontent. Thornaby murmured, "Lady Augusta arrived several hours ago, Your Grace."

Lady Augusta might as well have worn mourning black as that blue muslin, thought Elizabeth, who had met Charnwood's cousin once during their brief courtship. The woman was used to acting as the duke's hostess. Apparently she wasn't prepared to give up that position easily, despite the circumstance that he now had a wife.

With a gesture, Justin dismissed his servants. Only Thornaby remained behind, and the liveried footman at the door; the little housemaid who skittered into the hallway bearing a cold compress on a silver tray, and another who appeared with a fresh neckcloth. Elizabeth wished she might have departed also. Little as she might know her husband, it was clear to her that he was furious.

"Augusta," he said coolly, as he removed the compress from the tray and applied it to his nose. "What catastrophe has brought you to Bath? The house burned down around your ears? The servants decamped with the silver plate, perhaps?" Reverently, Thornaby took the neckcloth. The housemaids exchanged a glance, and hastily withdrew.

St. Clair's irritation made little impression on his cousin, who continued walking toward him until they stood almost nose to nose. Or nose to chest, because she was considerably the shorter. Her pale eyes flicked over Elizabeth. "How typically selfish of you, Justin, to think of no one but yourself. You might show some consideration for your bride. Bad enough you married her in such a clandestine manner. You might as well have eloped to Gretna Green. People will think that you are ashamed of her. There *is* a considerable disparity in your stations, no matter how handsome a dowry she brought."

Elizabeth made a soft little noise. The duke glanced at his bride. Surely she hadn't just said what he'd thought she said. No gently bred young lady should know such a vulgar word. Unfortunately, there was some truth in his cousin's spiteful statements. Justin had been so eager to have this marriage business done with that he had given scant consideration to how the world would view his haste.

How to remedy his thoughtlessness? "The world will think what I tell them to think," he said. "Hear me, cousin. *You* will inform anyone who asks that ours was a grand romance, and that we wed quickly not out of expedience but desire."

Two pairs of eyes fixed skeptically on him, one gray, one gold-flecked brown. "I credit your nose was bloodied in a fit of passion," murmured Lady Augusta. "How unfashionable, to be in amours with your wife."

Justin had already embarrassed his bride by marrying her so quickly. He would not shame her further by explaining the circumstances of his damaged nose. "Cry pax, cousin. You overstep yourself."

If so, Lady Augusta would never admit it. "No matter how you wish it, your marriage will be a matter for conjecture. Not that it is for me to censure your conduct. However, someone must appear to support you in this folly. As well as show the girl how to go on."

Certainly he did his bride a disservice if he saddled her with his angry cousin. Justin opened his mouth to speak. Then he closed it as Elizabeth stepped forward, her chin thrust out in a challenging manner, her cheeks pink instead of green.

Not for nothing had Elizabeth spent eighteen years

under her mother's roof. She drew herself up to her full height and looked down her long nose. "I wonder which one of us the world would say is behaving badly at the moment, Lady Augusta. I assure you *I* know perfectly well how I am to go on. Unless you think there is something I might teach *you*—proper manners, perhaps?—you needn't tarry here on my account."

So his bride had a temper? Justin almost smiled to see Augusta gasping like a fish. She glanced at him, as if for assistance. Damned if he would come to her rescue this time. "We will talk of this later," he said sternly, and indeed they would, because this conduct was outrageous even for his cousin, and he was very curious as to what had prompted Augusta to interrupt his honeymoon.

Lady Augusta's expression changed. She looked sly. "I rather think that later you will have other things on your mind. At which time you might recall what you said to me about catastrophes."

Before Justin could respond to this statement, Thornaby nervously cleared his throat. "Your Grace—"

Came a commotion in the front doorway. A gentleman strolled into the hallway, an impossibly handsome man with guinea gold hair styled *à la Brutus,* and sideburns extending downward toward his chin. His cravat was tied in the intricate Mathematical style. He wore highly polished Hessian boots, kerseymore Unmentionables, a horizontally striped Marcella waistcoat, and a startling violet coat. So glorious was his appearance that he might almost have been an angel, except for the angularity of his beautiful features, and the mischievous twinkle in his bright blue eyes. In his arms, he carried the largest birdcage Elizabeth had ever seen.

"Thank God I've found you, Saint! Hallo, Gus, I didn't know you was invited on the honeymoon." Lady Augusta huffed and turned on her heel and marched out of the room. The gentleman smiled at Elizabeth. "Gus don't like me much. I can't imagine why. You must be Saint's bride."

Justin looked also at the gentleman, and the birdcage, and the high-perch phaeton waiting outside in the street. "It's too much to hope that if we ignore him, he will go away. Elizabeth, this is Nigel Slyte. He will try to tell you that he is my friend. Why the Devil are you hovering with that neckcloth, Thornaby?"

Mr. Slyte set down the birdcage and made Elizabeth a sweeping bow. "His *oldest* friend," he said cheerfully. "I'm the best of good fellows to have put up with him for so many years. I knew him before he became so high and mighty, so I make allowances. Saint, your bride is a solemn creature. Have you overwhelmed her with your consequence?" He winked at Elizabeth. "You've married a curst cold fish, Your Grace. I wish you joy of him."

This amiable stranger was certainly not puffed up with consequence. Nor was he offering to tell her how to go on. Since St. Clair had been distracted by his valet, who was determined to replace his soiled neckcloth, Elizabeth smiled and said, "Fiddlestick!"

Nigel clutched his lilac heart. " 'Fiddlestick!' Her Grace has spoke. And a lovely Grace she is. No wonder Saint wanted a private ceremony. He was afraid someone would try to steal her away. Saint, you didn't tell me you was to wed a Nonpareil."

Elizabeth suspected the duke's desire for a small wedding had been inspired by a well-founded dread of what Maman might do with a larger one. "That would be because he *hasn't* married one. Do you make it a habit of trying to provoke your oldest friends?"

Nigel staggered back a step. "A leveler, I vow! Dashed

if you didn't pop one right over my guard. Was it you that drew Justin's cork?"

Oh, Lord, was it so obvious? Elizabeth flinched. "It was an accident. And you must admit that your Nonpareil would have done nothing like that."

"I don't know." Nigel tilted his golden head to one side. "She might have. A good biddable girl, ain't you? Well brought-up young woman, innate sense of propriety, quiet demeanor, lack of artifice? A Nonpareil, in other words."

Elizabeth doubted Nonpareils went about casting up their accounts all along the Bath Road. "How very dull you make me sound."

"Bloodied Saint's nose, didn't you?" Nigel said comfortingly. "It's early days yet. Briggs, bring in that chest." A footman appeared in the doorway with a heavy wooden box.

An irritated mutter came from beneath the birdcage cover. Elizabeth's attention was caught. "Oh! Is it a poll parrot?" she asked.

Nigel shuddered. "Shush! Never use that phrase in her hearing, lest you wish to see her sulk for days. Yanks out her feathers, and flings them all about. Dreadful mess. You probably also should not mention that she is very old." He pulled back the cover. "Say hello to Birdie. At least *I* call her Birdie. Her real name is something unpronounceable. Although she don't believe it, she is a macaw. Birdie has been on the Grand Tour, met royalty, and had her portrait painted. It hangs in my aunt's house. Would that Birdie hung there also, but my aunt can't abide her. Nor can she get rid of the creature, because it belonged to one of her husbands, and is mentioned specifically in his will. Therefore Birdie lives with me. Spends the majority of her time dozing on her perch and biting anyone who comes within range. You wonder why I don't arrange a fatal accident? I've thought of it, I admit it, but Aunt Syb would have a fit. I'm obliged to keep on Aunt Syb's good side. A matter of financial practicality, you see."

Elizabeth saw that the duke's oldest friend was an incurable humbugger. She stared at the big scarlet macaw. Yellow feathers on its upper wings blended into blue. Its tail was a deep blue mixed with red, its cheeks a pinkish white. The bird clicked its great curved beak at her and stretched out one long wing. "How pretty she is!"

"That's the ticket!" said Nigel. "Empty the butter dish over her head and maybe she won't bite you just yet. Saint, it won't do you any good to ignore me! I hate to do anything to disoblige you, old fellow, indeed I do, but Aunt Syb requires my presence and I dare not leave that damned—dear!—old feather duster with my servants for fear they'll drop her into the soup pot."

Lord Charnwood turned away from his valet, who was trying very hard to discreetly impart disjointed tidings that seemed to have something to do with baggage arriving unexpectedly from France. "Lady Ysabella is ill?"

"Doubtful," retorted Nigel. "The last time she threatened to turn up her toes it was because the sawbones had said she was only to eat meat and plain boiled rice, and had forbidden her all wine. I expect to find her as fractious as usual. She'll threaten to cut me out of her will again, and feed me on boiled beef and cabbage until I wish to turn up *my* toes, at which point her health will improve exceedingly. Do say that you'll keep Birdie for me. You know she's monstrous fond of you."

Lord Charnwood glanced at the birdcage. "I know nothing of the sort. The last time you left her here she bit and abused everyone from Thornaby to the laundry

maid. Have you ever been shaved by a valet with a ban-
daged hand? I'm lucky he didn't slit my throat."

Nigel tsk'd. "Unfair, Saint. Look, Birdie already has
taken a liking to your bride."

Elizabeth knelt by the cage. Head tilted to one side,
Birdie contemplated her through one and then the other
gold-rimmed eye. "What you mean is that my bride is
too green to know chalk from cheese," Justin retorted.
"I doubt it is in that bird to take a liking to anyone."
Birdie squinted at the duke, and muttered irritably.

Elizabeth looked up. "May we keep her, Your Grace?
I mean, St. Clair! Maman does not approve of birds.
She says they are very dirty and make too much noise. I
have always wished to know a bird."

Nigel beamed. "And here's your opportunity! Damned
if I'm not heaven-sent!" Then his eyes widened and his
smile faded. "Mouse!"

This pronouncement caused considerable reaction.
The duke swore under his breath, while Thornaby so
far forgot himself as to clutch his master's sleeve. Nigel
strode swiftly toward the door. "I'd love to stay, indeed I
would, but I must be off! Aunt Syb awaits! Everything
you'll need for Birdie's comfort will be found in that
chest. Believe me, I shan't forget that I'm in your debt!"

What a fuss over a little mouse! Not that Elizabeth had
ever met a mouse, or any other rodent, due to Maman's
fiercely held dislike. But shouldn't everyone be jump-
ing about and flapping things, instead of standing as if
turned to stone? Elizabeth winced as she stood up from
her crouch. And then she turned to stone herself.

Not a rodent stood poised on the staircase, but a lusciously rounded woman of perhaps thirty years of age, a
very beautiful creature with a porcelain complexion,
short curly black hair, and startling emerald eyes. An
Empire gown of clinging floss-trimmed gauze left not

an inch of her lush person to the imagination. Her hands were pressed to her magnificent bosom. Around her slender neck hung a cameo. Pale green silk slippers adorned her dainty feet.

Dramatically she paused, savoring the moment. Then she opened her arms wide. *"Eh bien!* Saint! Your Magda has come home!" she cried, as she flung herself down the stairs and into the duke's arms.

Chapter 3

"Obedience is the indispensable virtue in a good wife."
—Lady Ratchett

"A good biddable girl," muttered Elizabeth, as she paced the bedroom floor. "Well brought-up young woman. Innate sense of propriety. Lack of artifice." She kicked at a tapestry footstool that was so foolish as to put itself in her way. "Damn and blast!"

The chamber was hung with puckered green satin that matched the window and bed hangings of rich damask, and furnished charmingly with a tallboy and writing desk, dressing table with an oval glass, upholstered chairs with overstuffed seats, satinwood-veneered wardrobe, and a great mahogany bed with delicately carved posts. Candles blazed on the mantelpiece, and a fire burned in the hearth. Elizabeth tossed her reticule on the floor. She might well have stomped on it had not her red-haired abigail Daphne entered the room, followed by servants carrying hot water in cans and a large hip bath.

Apparently His Grace had decided that his wife was to bathe. That, or the entire household already knew of the countless times she'd caused the carriage to pause along the road. Elizabeth glowered. Daphne snatched up the discarded reticule and set it out of harm's way.

The servants departed. The bath awaited. Elizabeth was alone with her abigail. Daphne helped her mistress out of the carriage dress and petticoat, then unhooked her corset. Elizabeth sighed with relief. "Thank you, Daphne. Perhaps you might see if you can find me something to eat."

Daphne curtsied. "As you wish, Your Grace."

The door closed behind her. Elizabeth untied her garters, stripped off her knitted silk stockings, pulled off her chemise, removed her wedding ring, and stepped naked into the tub. Maman would not approve of such immodesty, but Maman wasn't here. For that, at least, Elizabeth could be grateful. She sank up to her chin in the warm, soapy water. Lord, but it felt good. Elizabeth might have been grateful to her husband for his thought-fulness—if it *was* his thoughtfulness—had he not just banished her to her bedchamber as if she were an in-convenient child.

Elizabeth lifted the soapy sponge to her chest and smoothed it up and down her arms. The duke was a powerful man, accustomed to the gratification of all his wishes, and unquestioning obedience. Naturally he would expect the same obedience from his wife. Had not Maman warned her it would be so? Maman had also pointed out that when a gentleman married a damsel for her fortune, that damsel could consequently expect no rude awakenings. Which just showed that Maman didn't know everything. Although even Maman could have hardly anticipated that Elizabeth would find beneath her husband's roof not only one extraneous female, but two, one a relative and one definitely not, for to embrace a relative like the strange woman had embraced Lord Charnwood must surely be against the law.

The duchess applied the soapy sponge to one long leg. Charnwood's cousin didn't appear eager to do his bidding. Elizabeth found herself almost in charity with that disagreeable female. Not, however, with the exotic creature Mr. Slyte had referred to as "Mouse," Clearly, this Mouse was no stranger to either Mr. Slyte or St. Clair. Mr. Slyte, however, had not wished to closet himself with her. Unlike the blasted duke. Perhaps it was the long carriage journey as well as the various trying events of the day that had so overset Elizabeth's equilibrium. She could not recall that she had ever before wished so strongly to wring someone's—anyone's!—neck.

Daphne returned to the chamber, followed by a little housemaid carrying a tray. The housemaid set down her burden, curtsied, and withdrew. Daphne held up a great towel and wrapped it around her mistress as she climbed out of the bath. "Well, Daphne, we have become very grand," said Elizabeth as the abigail patted her dry, slipped a nightgown over her head, and seated her before the dressing table with its array of glass bottles and flasks. "What are they saying belowstairs?"

Daphne glanced at their combined reflections in the oval glass. She looked her usual practical red-haired self. Her mistress, on the other hand, appeared pale and drawn. "Very little that I've been able to hear, Your Grace. I'm unknown to them, so they don't care to talk in front of me. That Magda person was here when I arrived. She seems to be familiar with the staff. At least with the housekeeper and butler and cook."

That Magda person was better known to Lord Charn-

wood than was his wife. A pity he hadn't married *her*.
Elizabeth looked at the refreshment tray, on which sat a
pot of chocolate and a plate of digestive biscuits.

Digestive biscuits? Elizabeth scowled. The entire household *did* know of her adventures along the Bath Road.
After those adventures, Elizabeth would have liked to
enjoy a meal. A very large meal. Boiled salmon and
dressed cucumber with anchovy sauce. Roast loin of
veal. Artichoke bottoms. Perhaps a rhubarb tart.

Her tummy rumbled. Elizabeth swallowed. Perhaps the
digestive biscuits weren't such a bad idea. She picked
one up and nibbled at it gingerly.

Daphne had already seen her mistress's belongings
unpacked and stowed away in the tallboy and wardrobe,
had arranged the duchess's dressing chamber just so.
Now she unpinned Elizabeth's long hair and picked up
a silver-backed hairbrush. Lady Ratchett had been vastly
pleased that her daughter had made so illustrious a
match, as well as determined that the new duchess should
do nothing for which her mama might blush. Daphne
was to inform Lady Ratchett immediately if Elizabeth
made a misstep. There was nothing new in this; Daphne
had been frequently quizzed by Milady in the past. In
Lady Elizabeth's place, Daphne would have married the
Devil himself to get out of that house. Though Charnwood might be a duke of the first stare, he could only
be cast into the shade by Lady Ratchett when it came to
raking a body over the coals.

Gently, Daphne drew the brush through her mistress's long hair. The abigail knew which side her bread
was buttered on. She was handmaiden to a duchess now,
and they no longer dwelt under Lady Ratchett's roof.
Whatever Daphne told Milady—and she must eventually tell Milady something—she wouldn't do so just yet.

Soothed by the rhythmic brushstrokes, Elizabeth

closed her eyes, and wondered how long it would be before Daphne sent Maman a report. "No doubt there is some good reason for the woman's presence," she murmured. "I must not make a piece of work of it. It would never do for me to disoblige my husband. Maman has said so."

Daphne thought His Grace might benefit from a little disobligement. Not to mention Lady Ratchett. "You are very forbearing, Your Grace. Another lady might well have swooned from the shock."

Was her abigail baiting her? Elizabeth opened one eye. "Surely you don't think me one to kick up a dust over trifles?" she inquired.

Daphne wielded the hairbrush with considerable vigor. "It's not my place to think, Your Grace. But if I *was* to think, I think I'd want some explanations in your place. No true gentleman would have his ladybird under the same roof as his wife."

Now Elizabeth was gossiping with a servant. Maman would not approve. To the Devil with Maman. "Ladybird?"

Daphne set down the hairbrush on the dressing table and crossed her arms beneath her bosom. "Ladybird. High flyer. Bread and cheese and kisses. Bachelor's fare, Your Grace."

Elizabeth rubbed her aching temples. She might have felt better for a few hugs and kisses herself. Although not from her husband, because Maman had been very precise about what *that* led to.

No wonder Daphne thought she should have swooned. The abigail believed the duke had brought his bit o' muslin into the house. Amusing, to contemplate such outrageous behavior from so high a stickler. "Daphne, you have been reading too many romantic novels."

True, the abigail was fond of romantic novels, tales of damsels in distress who managed to preserve themselves, if not their virtue, in the bare nick of time. In Daphne's opinion, her mistress was in as dire a predicament as any fictional heroine, being powdered and perfumed in preparation for initiation into some wicked sultan's harem, while the brute amused himself elsewhere. Daphne was glad to be a mere servant. No one would ever expect *her* to sacrifice herself on the altar of parental dictate.

She pulled a bottle from her pocket. "Do you have the headache, Your Grace? A couple drops of laudanum should ease the pain." Meaningfully, she paused. "More than that and you'll fall fast asleep."

Elizabeth eyed her abigail, and then the little bottle. Maman had not approved of laudanum. "If you 'Your Grace' me one more time, I swear I shall throw this hairbrush at you, Daphne!" Oh Lord, now she sounded like St. Clair.

Daphne set the laudanum bottle on the dresser. A pity, she had rather enjoyed "Your Grace." Ah well, her mistress would grow used to it. As well as to other things. The duchess looked very pretty in her square-collared nightdress and dressing gown of fine lawn, her thick dark golden hair reaching almost to her waist. Daphne wondered if the duke had even noticed that his bride wasn't exactly platter-faced. He hardly *could* notice while he was amusing himself with someone else.

A knock sounded on the door. Two footmen entered the room, between them carrying Birdie's huge cage. Panted one, "Compliments of His Grace." Elizabeth gestured toward a mahogany table with graceful tapering legs. The footmen set down their burden. Birdie sidled across her perch, head feathers ruffled, hard hooked beak opened to bite. Quickly the footmen stepped back.

"You're bleeding," said Elizabeth. "Oh, goodness, you both are."

" 'Tis nothing, Your Grace." Already the footmen were backing out the door. With them they took the metal bath.

Elizabeth regarded the macaw. "You are very bad, Birdie," she scolded. The parrot ignored this inanity and displayed her bright blue rump.

Cautiously, Daphne approached the cage. "Angels defend us! Your Grace, Lady Elizabeth, is that great thing a *bird*?"

Birdie turned an acerbic eye on the abigail. Elizabeth said, "Don't get too close! As you have seen, she bites. Hand me the blue linen shawl. Perhaps she will be soothed by the color. We'll drape the shawl over the cage."

Carefully, the women placed the shawl over the back half of the great metal cage. Birdie gave no particular sign of appreciation, but neither did she damage them. "Thank you, Daphne. You may go. I'll have no further need of you tonight." Daphne gathered up the stained and rumpled carriage dress and bore it away.

Elizabeth sank into a chair beside the birdcage table. Birdie sidled along the rough wood perch, to which some bark was still attached, ruffled her feathers, and did a little dance. Then she spread out her wings and fanned her tail. "Biscuit?" the parrot inquired.

The creature talked! 'Twas the brightest moment in Elizabeth's entire miserable day. "Had you eyelashes, you would flutter them at me, you shameless thing. And for naught, because I ate the biscuits all myself. I suppose you are meant to keep me company while my husband occupies himself elsewhere. You're prettier than he is, at any rate." The parrot cast her a reproachful glance, then hopped down off its perch and began to forage in the bottom of its cage.

Elizabeth was inconvenient in truth, had Charnwood

his ladybird downstairs. Could Daphne be correct in her suspicions? *Was* the sultry Mouse a Fair Unfortunate? Elizabeth had never seen a fallen woman, or at least not that she knew of, although there *had* been an incident when Maman had called a lady a brazen piece, and cut her dead in the street.

That lady had been a good deal less outrageous-looking than this Magda. Elizabeth was sent to bed with digestive biscuits and chocolate while Charnwood did whatever it was that he was doing elsewhere in the house. Surely the duke did not think to have his fancy piece under the same roof as his wife.

Alas, the duke might have anything under his roof that he wished, and the duchess could say nothing about it. Or she *could*, but it would not signify. Charnwood was lord of all he surveyed, as well as a great deal that he did not. Even Elizabeth's fortune, left to her by her grand-mama, was no longer her own. "Had I feathers, Birdie, I would pull them out and strew them all about myself! To think that Maman said in time I might hope for some small return of mutual affection!" 'Twas enough to make a cat laugh.

A cat, and perhaps a parrot. Birdie cocked her head to one side and cackled, a raucous, grating sound. Elizabeth wondered if the macaw was laughing with her, or at her. Lord, but she was in a swivet, to worry about the partialities of a bird.

She stared at the bed, a great solid piece of furniture with curtains and canopies, cozily adorned with piles of pillows and blankets, and a green and white counter-pane. Tonight she would sleep there with her bride-groom. Doubtful that the fair Magda had ever closed her eyes and pruned her lips and counted a herd of sheep. Maybe things were different when a gentleman climbed into a bed that was not his own.

The duchess moved to the dressing table, studied the wedding ring that lay there, diamonds set in accent points among pearls in splendidly wrought gold. Gingerly, she picked it up and slipped it on her hand, then raised her eyes and looked into the glass. Ordinarily Elizabeth didn't spend much time contemplating her reflection, for she knew how short she fell of the feminine ideal. Still, she was not horribly bad-looking. There was nothing wrong with her face except for its shape and slenderness. Nothing wrong with her person except that she was tall and thin.

What would the duke think of her person? What would he *do* to her person? What was he doing to some other person now? St. Clair had mentioned Prince Bladud and his pigs. If only she could contract leprosy, she might sleep alone tonight. Her gaze fell upon the laudanum.

Elizabeth picked up the small bottle. Daphne had said two drops would quiet a violent headache. The duchess drank six, then crawled between the soft, monogrammed lace-trimmed sheets. If Charnwood chose to remove himself from his mistress long enough to consummate his marriage, she wouldn't mind it in the least, because she would be fast asleep.

Chapter 4

"A licentious style of dress is as certainly a token of like laxity in manners and conduct." —Lady Ratchett

Despite the opinion of at least two members of his household (or in reality just one, because the second wasn't entirely sure *what* she thought), the duke was not amusing himself with his unexpected guest. Or the *least* unexpected of his guests, because he might have anticipated that his cousin would try to interfere with his honeymoon, and that Nigel would descend on him with that accursed bird. Magdalena, however, he had not expected to see again in this life and hopefully not in the next, he having ever followed a conventional path that surely would not lead him into the fiery depths where a schemer such as Magda must surely come to eventually reside. But here she sat, in the book-lined library, curled up in one of the stuffed wing chairs, as at ease as if they were old friends, and he didn't trust her one inch.

The years since their last meeting had been kind. Magda remained one of the most beautiful women Justin had ever seen. As well as the best endowed. Naturally she wasn't wearing a corset under that flimsy gauze gown. Doubtful that she owned such a thing. She *should* have been wearing a corset, although only the most uncharitable of persons would have called her plump. Magda's face was thinner than he remembered, the bones more defined. With her high cheekbones and pointed chin and slanted green eyes, she put him in mind of a cat. The duke didn't care for cats. Cats were sly, deliberately charming, self-serving creatures who swiped against one's ankles and purred until you picked them up, and then when tired of being petted, unsheathed their sharp claws.

'Twas an apt description of the woman curled up in his wing chair. Justin regarded her without appreciation over the cold compress he held to his nose. "Well, Magda," he said. "I assume that is still your name."

She dimpled. "Unkind, Saint! Of course I am still Magda, Magdalena Delacroix now, Madame de Chavannes. *Zut!* I do not think I have ever seen you quite so angry. It is very bad of you not to at least pretend to be a little bit glad to see me, Saint."

"But I'm *not* glad to see you!" the duke retorted, impatiently. "I have just got married. How dare you come here like this and push your way into my house!"

Magda wrinkled her nose at this inelegant turn of phrase. "I didn't push my way in! Chislett recognized me immediately he opened the door. He must have thought he saw a ghost because he turned white as one himself. Then he whisked me inside before I could say a word."

Justin reminded himself to speak sternly with Chislett. "What devilment are you up to, Magda? You need not deny that you are up to something. I know you of old."

Madga stretched languorously, stood up, and crossed

the room to stand before him. "You were fond of me once, *mon cher,*" she murmured. "Have you forgot?"

Justin looked down into her exquisite little face. "I have forgotten nothing. Do not try and play off your airs on me, Magda. I am immune."

"Are you, I wonder?" Magda ran her fingers provocatively down the lapel of his coat. Justin caught her wrist and held her motionless.

She made a *moue* and twinkled up at him. "Very well! I shall stop toying with you, Saint, though I vow you provoke me to it, you are become so monstrous starched-up! The truth is that I wanted to come home. Impossible to make exact arrangements; I had no notion of when or even if I would arrive. When I did reach England, I had no place to go, and I thought immediately of you."

He doubted it. Justin wondered what, in fact, her first thought had been. "And Monsieur de Chavannes?"

Magda's piquant features sobered. She pulled away. "It is very off-putting to see one's husband's head atop a pole. I did not wish that mine might join his, so I fled. Come, Saint, do not look so disapproving. It is not unusual to take along a friend on the honeymoon, *n'est-ce pas?*"

She was beautiful, clever, and ruthless. And it would seem she had nourished some genuine feeling for her departed spouse. "A friend of the bride," amended Justin. "You are not that, I think. And now you will excuse me. Elizabeth waits."

Magda glanced back over her shoulder. "Your bride may wait a little longer. Can you not see the humor in the situation, Saint? I gather from that dreadful expression on your face that you do not! You have Gus here with you also. You shan't convince me that *she* is a friend of the bride."

Justin could hardly argue with this. He resigned himself

to a few moments' conversation. "Dare I ask *why* your husband lost his head?" he asked.

"Let us just say that Jules was indiscreet." Magda took up a position by the fire. "*Mon Dieu,* the rumors I have heard since I returned to England. General Bonaparte has under construction a monstrous bridge by which his troops will pass from Calais to Dover, directed by officers in air balloons. A Channel is a tunnel being engineered by a mining expert. The Corsican has disguised himself as a Brit and is patrolling English shores aboard a fishing smack. *Absurdité,* but you may be sure Bony hasn't given up his invasion schemes. Anyone who can defeat England will be master of the world."

Justin understood that there would be no more discussion of the Chevalier. "You still have an interest in politics."

Magda sank back down in the armchair. "Only a fool is *not* interested in politics. Revolutions are periodic outbursts following always the same curve from rebellion through chaos to dictatorship. History is a circle. Only a monarchy can restore order and security to France."

Justin's lips twisted wryly. "In other words, you support the Bourbons."

Magda toyed with the cameo around her neck. "*Mon cher,* I will support anyone who promises to return my husband's properties to me."

The compress was no longer cold. Justin set it down on the massive mahogany *secrétaire,* beside a table globe, quill pen, and Sheffield plate wax jack. He poured brandy from a decanter into a glass.

Magda looked pointedly at the decanter in his hand. Justin poured a second glass of brandy, and carried it to her. She smiled up at him. "Charnwood has taken a wife at last. Your affections have become fixed."

They had been nothing of the sort. Justin stared at the fire burning in the hearth. "Elizabeth is a good biddable girl with a proper way of thinking. She will make me a comfortable little wife."

Magda turned sideways in the chair, the better to observe him. "You danced attendance on her at least a little bit, I hope, my Saint. Stood up with her at balls. Sent her posies, made her distinguishing little attentions. Perhaps"—she looked roguish—"just a little kiss?"

Justin felt queerly guilty that he *hadn't* kissed his intended wife. It was Magda's damnable influence; he knew he had been most correct in his conduct toward Elizabeth. As it was Magda's fault he wasn't kissing Elizabeth right now. Still, he found he wished to speak with her, which was queer in him. "That is none of your concern."

"Of course it is my concern." Magda rested her chin on her hand. "Though you do not care to admit it, I am your friend. Come, Saint, tell your Magda everything."

She was not *his* Magda, thank God. "I began to feel mortal. One can't get an heir without first getting a bride."

"Some do," observed Magda. "But I perfectly see that you are not among them. When did this mortality come upon you?"

Justin drained his brandy snifter. "On my thirtieth birthday."

"And it took you two more years to screw up your resolve? My poor Saint. Oh yes, I recall perfectly your age. Nigel and Gus are a mere year younger than yourself, and I am two. *Tiens!* You picked out a good biddable girl with a handsome dowry, who will never allow passion to get the better of reason, or enact you dramatical high flights! Your proper little English miss will suit you well. Who knows, you might even come to care for her a little bit."

Justin frowned. "Don't push me, Magda."

She twinkled at him. "Ah, Saint, you have become so very sober. I remember when you were considerably more *fun!*"

Justin stood up. He didn't care to engage in a discussion of old times. "As you pointed out, I cared for you once. Because of that, and because I make no doubt you will revenge yourself on me if I refuse you, I will permit you to stay here for a time. But understand this, you will cause Elizabeth no distress. Moreover, you will not permit Gus to do so. I trust I make myself clear."

"Clear as daylight." Magda raised her glass to him. "I do not wish that there should be bad feeling between us. In case I have not said it, I wish you happy, Saint."

The hour was considerably advanced when St. Clair climbed the stairs, the matter of Magdalena having taken up no little time. He had approached his marriage in his usual reasonable manner; how had everything gone so wrong? Instead of gently introducing his bride to the realities of matrimony, he had been closeted in the library with the provoking Magda. Hopefully Elizabeth would be appeased by the presence of the bird.

Thornaby waited in the dressing room, where a cheerful fire burned in the hearth. The valet's expression, however, was mournful. "I fear, Your Grace, that the cravat could not be saved."

"Then I shall have to buy a dozen others, shan't I?" The duke sat down in a carved chair. "You will forgive me for putting you to the blush, Thornaby. It isn't every day that I take a bride."

For that, Thornaby could only be grateful. He laid his master's appalling appearance smack at that young woman's door. Never in all the years of his employment with the duke had St. Clair been so careless of his appearance. He saw the bramble scratches on His Grace's boots, and moaned.

"Not another word!" said Justin. "Or I'll have Mrs. Papplewick fetch the vinaigrette, and then think what the servants would say."

Thornaby was very aware of his superior position in the household. 'Twould not improve his credit to have a housemaid waving burnt feathers under his nose. Tight-lipped, he made no further comment as he wrestled the duke out of his tight boots and clothing and into his satin dressing robe, then departed, cradling the misused coat as tenderly as if it were a babe.

Of all times for Magda to choose to reappear. Justin's tête-à-tête with Magda had given him a new appreciation of his bride. He regretted having left Elizabeth so much to her own devices on their first night in Bath. Not that he would expect so well-bred a miss to stage a scene that shook the rafters. Still, she must feel something. He wondered how she would greet him. Justin found, somewhat to his surprise, that he was curious to find out.

The bedchamber was softly candlelit. A fragrant scent sweetened the air. Birdie dozed in her shawl-draped cage, head tucked under her wing, standing on one leg. Justin looked around with a certain anticipation for his bride. Then he saw the little lump huddled in the middle of the bed.

Had his reassurances been for naught? Was she hiding from him, foolish child, with the covers pulled up over her head? The duke had no previous experience with green misses, much preferring knowledgeable women of the world who could be trusted to enjoy his favors for as long as was agreeable to them both, and then

bid him an unemotional farewell. Not that His Grace
would be sufficiently lost to propriety or common sense
as to marry a woman of that sort, and had very rightly
left behind his mistress for the duration of his honeymoon.

Came a gentle snore from the bedcovers. The duke
moved closer, drew back the counterpane to gaze down
at his wife. She looked even younger in her sleep, her
features softer and more relaxed, her long hair in charming disarray, her nightdress slipped open to reveal a tan-
talizing glimpse of one sweet breast. Justin felt the
stirring of desire.

He would be getting no future children on his bride
if he didn't first persuade her not to fear him. Or he
could, but that would be the act of a knave. Then he saw
the laudanum bottle sitting on the table. Was the chit so
frightened of him that she must drug herself?

If not his bride, St. Clair had woken up Birdie. The
parrot sidled along her perch. "Biscuit?" she inquired.

Had Elizabeth no choice but to marry him? Was her
sense of duty so strong? Justin would not have his bride
behave toward him merely from a sense of duty. With
an odd pang of regret, the duke withdrew to his dressing room.

Chapter 5

*"A modest reserve is essential to the
perfection of feminine attraction."* —Lady Ratchett

Elizabeth awakened to a dreadful screeching, as if a monstrous hinge lacked oil. Perhaps she was still dreaming. Cautiously, she opened one eye. Green puckered satin, a mountain of lace-trimmed pillows, a bright parrot in a huge cage . . .

Memory returned. The blasted laudanum had left her fuzzy in the head. "Yes and good morning to you, Birdie!" Elizabeth muttered. "Now will you please hush?"

The parrot regarded her with one yellow-rimmed eye. "Biscuit. Biscuit, biscuit, biscuit!" she demanded, and then squawked as Elizabeth threw a pillow at the cage.

Elizabeth sat up and looked around. Had the duke joined her in the night? His side of the bed appeared untouched. *She* appeared untouched. Elizabeth didn't know whether to be glad or sad. Certainly she hadn't wanted her husband to touch her. But neither did she think that she wanted him to be touching anyone else instead. Was he with Magda still? Again? Was that where he'd spent the night?

A knock came on the door, interrupting Elizabeth's efforts to imagine how a slavering beast must look. A little freckled housemaid in a black gown and stiff white apron peered into the room. "Your chocolate, Your Grace."

Elizabeth eyed the tray. "And my biscuits. Yes, Birdie, you may have one. Set the tray over there, if you will. Katy, wasn't it? Not too near the cage, or she will have my chocolate too."

The maid set down the tray and grinned. "Aye, Your Grace. Ach, she's a pretty thing!"

Elizabeth wondered if the little housemaid would like to share *her* chamber with a parrot. "Pretty is as pretty does. Perhaps if we feed her she won't wake up the rest of the house."

"Me mither has birds," said Katy, as she edged closer to the parrot. "Though none so grand as this. Look at the bonnie great beastie, pretending to be starved. Dinna fash yourself, acushla, we'll soon have ye a bite or two to eat." She cast a guilty look at Elizabeth, and bobbed another curtsy. "It's that sorry I am, Your Grace. 'Tis such a pure wonder of a bird she is that I forgot meself."

Elizabeth climbed out of bed and moved to the other side of the cage. "Birdie *is* a great grand creature." She looked at the parrot languishing pathetically in the bottom of the cage. Birdie flapped a feeble wing. "Are you sure she isn't ill?"

"Ach, she's just malingering. Your Grace! Watch this." Katy crumbled a biscuit and opened the cage door.

"Wait!" cried Elizabeth. "That beak is wicked." But Katy had already thrust her hand into the cage.

Birdie opened one eye. "Biscuit!" she moaned. The

housemaid dropped the crumbled biscuit in the food dish, and removed her hand unscathed. Elizabeth watched with fascination as the parrot hopped up on her perch, picked up a chunk of biscuit in one claw, and began to dine. "Shameless hussy," she remarked.

Katy grinned. The duchess was a right one, despite all that was being said belowstairs about how she'd bloodied the master's poor nose. 'Twas even being whispered that himself had slept alone last night, for fear his bride would again pop his cork. "I'll warrant," said Katy, "that Herself would like a bath."

Thus it came about that St. Clair was awakened from his restless slumbers by a great squawking and splashing and what sounded like a not entirely successful attempt at song. What the devil was going on in the bedroom? *His* bedroom? In which he would have much preferred to sleep and was not entirely certain why he had not. Justin reached for his dressing robe and opened the door.

A startling scene greeted him. His duchess and one of the housemaids hovered on either side of the parrot cage, in which a large bowl of water had been placed. As he watched, Birdie perched on the edge of the bowl, then hopped into it, with a great splash and a flapping of wings and a burst of dissonant whistling. The housemaid whistled along with the parrot. Elizabeth was laughing. They were all three very wet. "I know that tune, I swear I do. But I can't think of its name."

Justin strolled into the room. "I believe it is 'Jack's Maggot.' A country dance. One envisions Nigel gamboling around his drawing room in an effort to keep the bird amused. That will be all, Katy."

The little maid curtsied. Elizabeth flushed guiltily. Yes, and well she deserved to feel guilty, because it was her fault that he'd passed a restless night. "You do dance, Elizabeth?"

His Grace didn't look like a slavering beast. Although he *did* appear a trifle wolfish with his hair untidy and that strange expression on his face. Elizabeth found herself staring at the expanse of chest revealed by his nightshirt. It looked like a very nice chest. Not that she had much—indeed, any—experience with such things.

Elizabeth swallowed. Her mouth had suddenly gone dry. What in blazes had he asked her? "Maman does not approve of dancing. She says it is vulgar and causes one to grow overheated." She felt more than a little warm herself.

"Maman does not approve of perspiration? A pity. There are any number of pleasant things that might raise one's temperature." He was doubtful that Lady Ratchett would approve of her daughter's very revealing wet nightgown. Elizabeth, though tall and slender, was very nicely formed. "Or perhaps Maman simply does not approve of pleasant things."

Elizabeth smiled. "It is certain that Maman would not approve of your saying so, Your Grace."

Her hair was lovely, loose like that, tumbling down her back. Justin's fingers itched to smooth away the tangles. "I believe this is the first time I have ever heard you laugh."

Elizabeth could not think clearly. Perhaps it was because she had never before seen a gentleman clad only in his nightshirt and robe. Was laughter now on the list of things she was not to do? "We have not had much time together, Your Grace. Either you and Maman were negotiating, or I was busy being ill."

Did she reproach him? Justin stepped closer. "Or you were busy sleeping. You must have been very tired, Elizabeth."

He had been in the bedroom last eve? Had not the fair Magda slaked his carnal appetites? Perhaps Daphne had been mistaken in thinking Magda the duke's mistress. Even Charnwood's oldest friend had called him a curst cold fish. Although Mr. Slyte might take back his words if ever he saw the duke tousled and unshaved and damnably handsome as he looked now in his dressing gown.

Lord, what was she thinking! Elizabeth stared at the birdcage. Birdie edged along the perch toward her. "Biscuit?"

"You have had quite enough biscuit, you greedy creature." Elizabeth crumbled another, all the same. Did St. Clair intend to claim the privileges of marriage to which he was entitled *now*, in the bright light of day? Privileges which according to Maman were at best revolting and at worst rather painful, but had to be endured, because such things were imperative for a gentleman's good health? Yet gentlemen were by nature perverted, and given half a chance, would engage in a variety of the most revolting practices, and Elizabeth must therefore beware. Since Maman hadn't gone into detail about what constituted a revolting practice, Elizabeth wasn't sure what she was to beware *of*. She suspected that her husband could explain it all to her, dared she ask.

Justin might have gotten a warmer response from Birdie, who was currently making a great mess with biscuit crumbs. Elizabeth appeared considerably more interested in that wretched parrot than in himself. He touched his bride's dark blond curls. "Do you make a habit of taking laudanum?"

Oh Lord, his hand was in her hair. "I had a headache, Your Grace."

Justin had two headaches. He did not think laudanum would make either go away. "You will not take laudanum again. It is not good for you. You may come to me the next time you have the headache."

Elizabeth lowered her lashes and wished that she might swallow an entire bottle of laudanum all at once, just because he said she should not. The warmth of his hands burned through her nightdress. Her very flimsy, wet nightdress. She must look positively Paphian. Was his lust being excited? Was hers? Did females experience lust?

Elizabeth was certainly experiencing something. She felt goose bumps all the way down to her toes. If only the duke would let go of her so that she could think. "As you wish, Your Grace."

As he wished? Nothing had been as Justin wished for several days. Certainly he had not wished to sleep on the cot in his dressing room, there to toss and turn and dream at last of his wife's shapely ankles, not to mention other things.

He had been too long without a woman. Elizabeth was not the type of female to ordinarily inspire him with such thoughts. Perhaps it had something to do with the fact that she was his wife. Who stood stiff as a marble statue beneath his hands. Well, not marble, perhaps, because her cheeks were pink, and her skin warm and soft.

He raised one hand from her shoulder to lightly stroke his knuckles along her jaw. She gasped and flinched away. Justin remembered Magda's hint that his courtship had perhaps been a trifle perfunctory. "Do you ride, Elizabeth?"

What had riding to do with his hands upon her body? Elizabeth was afraid she knew. "Horses are so very large, Your Grace. Maman was afraid I would fall off and get hurt."

Maman was probably afraid you would take to your heels, thought Justin. *Lord knows I would have.* "Since we are up so early, due to that accursed bird, we might as well take advantage of the morning. Get dressed and I will have the phaeton brought round."

He moved away from her at last and walked toward his dressing room. The door closed behind him. Elizabeth let out a great pent-up breath, and sank down in a chair.

Chapter 6

"Let your countenance be pleasant but in serious matters somewhat grave." —Lady Ratchett

Daphne threw up her hands at sight of the water and feathers and biscuit crumbs strewn all about the bed-chamber, and immediately rang for a bevy of house-maids to clean up the mess. Birdie's cage was borne off to the kitchen, where the parrot might enjoy the sun-light and new people to terrorize. Elizabeth was tucked into a figured muslin gown, cherry spencer, boots of embroidered silver cloth; hair drawn behind and held securely there with pins. Yorkshire tan gloves for her hands, a cloth of cherry-striped pink around her neck, a chip hat ornamented with flowers tied under her chin. "There!" said Daphne with satisfaction. "You'll do, my lady, indeed you will."

Do for what? Elizabeth wondered. She glanced in the mirror. All her finery aside, she remained a mere dab of a girl. Well, not a dab perhaps, because she was so tall, but still not of an appearance to compete with a woman of the world. Not that she *wished* to compete with Magda, or anyone else. But when had she ever been allowed to do what she wished? She screwed up her courage, lifted her hand, and knocked at the dressing room door. There came no answer. She opened the door.

The chamber was empty. Thornaby had outdistanced Daphne in the race to see whether the master or mistress would be quickest turned out. Odds belowstairs had been even. Whereas the duchess's long hair had to be dressed, the duke had to be shaved.

Slowly, Elizabeth made her way down the winding stair. She supposed she must be grateful to avoid facing fair Magda and sour Lady Augusta over the breakfast cups.

St. Clair waited in the hallway. He had dressed for the day—rather, Thornaby had dressed him—in doeskin breeches, striped waistcoat, a claret-colored coat. In one hand he held his leather gloves and a tall-crowned hat. His nose was less swollen today, though considerably more bruised. Elizabeth hadn't noticed his nose earlier. She'd been entirely too distracted by the glimpse of his bare chest.

He didn't *look* like a gentleman with a love of dissipation. Not that Elizabeth would know. Yes, and why should she mind so much that her bridegroom had perhaps taken his amorous inclinations elsewhere? Maman had said that he would do so, though not so soon. Maman had not explained how, *after* he had taken said inclinations elsewhere, Elizabeth was expected to act. She was still pondering that matter as she reached the bottom of the stair.

The duke smiled at her. "You are very fine today, my dear," he said as he offered her his arm. Elizabeth remembered the feeling of his hands in her hair, on her shoulders, against her cheek. How warm she'd felt, and how breathless. She supposed it would be highly improper in her to box her husband's ears.

The day was bright and sunny, the air a little chill. Dew sparkled on the grass. The huge sweep of the Palladian façade glowed golden in the bright light.

At the front door waited an elegant phaeton. The carriage was painted, varnished, and polished to a high degree of perfection; the horses sleek and black. Justin helped his bride into the seat, in the process enjoying a glimpse of a well-turned ankle and silver boots, then sprang up beside her, and took the reins from his groom. There was no coachman's seat in the phaeton, no place for a tiger behind. "I thought you might like to see Bath by daylight. You will tell me if you feel travel-sick."

His coat was not light-colored today, but dark. The duke was a cautious man. Or his valet was. "I am fine, Your Grace."

Justin glanced at her. "As I have already remarked. And you were to call me St. Clair." He flicked the reins. The phaeton clattered over the cobblestones.

Bath truly was a town of hills and trees. Hills and trees and fish ponds, bowling greens and clipped yew hedges; terraces and buildings and flights of steps enlivened with beautiful stone and bud vases and garden sculptures. The duke entertained his bride with stories of the city as the phaeton rumbled through the streets. Bath had been established as a town soon after the Roman invasion of Britain in A.D. 43. Even in Roman times, the town had been famous for its baths and the adjoining temples. For over two thousand years, the main attraction of the place had remained the same, the sulphurous waters that sprang out of the earth ready for use.

Modest Brock Street opened into the Royal Circus, a perfectly circular space divided into three segments of uniform houses, their separate identities indicated only by doors at intervals, for all the world, Elizabeth remarked, like an English version of the Roman Coliseum turned inside out. From there they progressed past the Assembly Rooms, the Baths, the Abbey—an Abbey in name only since the dissolution of the monasteries in 1530—with its pinnacled Gothic grandeur, and angels ascending and descending a ladder to heaven. Elizabeth was fascinated to observe that one of the angels was carved upside down. Then on to Pulteney Bridge, a three-arched structure with a Venetian window in the center, and domed pavilions at each end, lined both sides with shops. By the time the duke had finished explaining that in the 1600's the waters at Bath were so revered for fecundity that after one visit ladies often proved with child, even in the absence of their husbands, the streets were filling up with smart barouches and gentlemen on splendid horses and elegantly garbed women out for a stroll. Hoofs and wheels clattered, newsboys shouted, the muffin man's bell clanged. The duchess expressed a desire for a muffin. The duke fetched her one himself.

Justin brushed muffin crumbs off his coat. Elizabeth was happily devouring her treat, regardless of propriety or mess. Rather like Birdie with a biscuit. Had Elizabeth given her breakfast to the bird? Ah well, easy enough to have someone clean out the carriage. More important, what the Devil was he to say to her? Something, certainly, for he had delayed long enough.

"I wished to speak to you without interruption, Elizabeth. Which is deuced difficult in the house." At last he had her attention; she looked up from her muffin to glance warily at him. "I regret that Augusta has chosen to disturb our honeymoon. The Devil is in it that she must decide to go off on one of her starts just now. I'm sorry to say that I cannot trust her. There is nothing for it but that she must be with us for a time."

The Devil was in it that Lord Charnwood would *want* his cousin with them. Because the duke was of a disposition that if he did not want Augusta with them, then she would not be. Naturally he expected his wife to accept his decision. Elizabeth thought of his hands in her hair, and immediately lost her appetite. "Why is that, Your Grace?"

Surely she didn't question his decision? He must have misunderstood. At any rate, she had spoken, which she hadn't done for some time. "You know that Augusta is my cousin. What you may not also know is that her brother gambled away the family fortune, including her dowry, and then fled the country, throwing her to the wolves. She despises him for it, almost as much as she despises me."

No wonder Lady Augusta was as sour as a lemon. Elizabeth forgot briefly that she was annoyed. "I can understand why she is angry with her brother. But why should she be angry with *you*?"

Justin shrugged. "Augusta is angry at everyone and everything. Life hasn't turned out the way she expected that it would. Now she is dependant on me, and that stings her pride. I have restored her dowry, and make her an allowance, the majority of which she loses at the tables. She would gamble away even more, did I not keep a sharp eye on her. Augusta shares her brother's addiction to play."

First a Cyprian, now a gambler. St. Clair's household grew more and more strange.

"Augusta thinks she is of an age to do whatever she wishes. I think that she is not. And so, we are forever at odds. I had anticipated that the moment my attention was directed elsewhere she would head for the tables. I did *not* anticipate that she would follow us to Bath. You must not let her get to dagger-drawing. Augusta will go to any lengths for the sole purpose of creating a scene. However, Nigel will doubtless divert some of her spleen."

Perhaps Elizabeth would box Lady Augusta's ears instead. "Your cousin and Mr. Slyte do not like one another?" she asked.

Justin turned the horses down a side street to avoid a traffic snarl involving a sedan chair and a produce cart. "We all grew up together. Augusta was more amiable then. Nigel would have wed her once, I think, but she'd have none of it because he is a younger son."

Lady Augusta was not only a crosspatch and a gambler, but a pigwidgeon as well. Elizabeth imagined it might be very amusing to be wed to Mr. Slyte. A pity *he* hadn't married her for her fortune. Although it was doubtful Mr. Slyte would look as good as the duke in a dressing robe.

The duke was looking at her quizzically. "Um!" said Elizabeth. "And now?"

"And now Nigel takes delight in baiting Gus, for she is even poorer than he. I can hardly blame him for it. Nigel has considerable expectations from his aunt. You have not married into an easy family, Elizabeth. I trust in your great good sense to keep above the fray."

Elizabeth trusted her great good sense to keep her from saying something she should not. St. Clair had told her everything but what she wished to know. Who in Hades was Magda? Elizabeth would allow herself to be nibbled to death by rabbits before she mentioned the woman's name.

"And then there is Magdalena," added the duke, thereby sparing his bride that dire fate. "Whom you met last night."

Elizabeth hadn't met Magda, precisely; instead she'd been hustled off to bed. She refrained from pointing this out. 'Twould be very interesting to hear how St. Clair meant to explain the introduction of that exotic female into his household. She was intensely aware of the duke's muscular body, so close to her on the carriage seat.

Justin was intensely aware of his bride's silence. If only she were a little older, a little wiser in the ways of the world. Then he changed his mind, because he would not care to have her introduced to the ways of the world by anyone but himself. "Magda is an old friend who has lived most recently in France. The situation there grows daily more unpredictable and dangerous. She fled with little more than the clothes on her back."

Elizabeth remembered the lady's scanty garb. "In that case she must have been very cold."

Fortunately the city bells rang out just then, obscuring that unwifely—or very wifely—comment. Justin glanced at his bride. "What did you say?"

Elizabeth was not so imprudent as to repeat herself. "A desperate journey indeed, Your Grace. And so she fled to you."

Unless Justin was mistaken, and he didn't think he was, his bride's voice held an acerbic note. Not surprising that she might be a little miffed. " 'Tis an awkward situation, I admit it. However, I have a certain obligation which leaves me little choice."

Obligation, was it? Inclination, more like. If anyone had countless choices, it was the duke. Apparently the large majority of the misses in the marriage mart, not to mention Maman, had been holding a philanderer in high esteem. The duke *did* intend that his fancy piece take up residence under the same roof as his wife.

This, after all the lectures she had been given by Maman about what was proper and what was not. Up

until this very moment, Elizabeth had not truly believed Charnwood could be so wicked. She contemplated her gloves.

His bride remained silent. Perhaps Justin had not made
his position clear. "Magda's husband was beheaded.
She barely avoided the guillotine herself. I trust that
you understand, Elizabeth. Magdalena and I have a history. I was fond of her once. For me to fail and do my
duty now would be unthinkable."

Not a current ladybird, but a previous one? Who
would doubtless waste no time in worming her way back
into the duke's embrace. If she had not already done so
the previous evening, while the duchess slept alone. "Truly
I wish to please you in all things," Elizabeth said, without a smidgen of truth. "But I find I do *not* wish to
humor you in this, Your Grace."

The spirited blacks that drew the phaeton might have
turned their heads and spoken to him, so astonished
was the duke. "*Humor* me?" he said.

The Devil with duchessly decorum. Elizabeth lifted
her chin and returned her husband look for look. "You
will not like such plain-speaking, but I know no other
way to say it. I do not wish to share my honeymoon with
your blasted light o' love, St. Clair."

As a result of his bride's outburst, a number of
thoughts chased themselves through the duke's startled
brain. Surely the chit didn't mean to defy his authority.
He must have misunderstood. Yes, and didn't her defiance lend a most attractive animation to her features,
and color to her cheeks. She was atremble with her indignation, her bosom aquiver with outrage.

A nice bosom it was. No fit moment, this, to wish to
see his bride aquiver with an altogether different emo-
tion. Justin collected his scattered wits. "You are quick
to judge me, Elizabeth."

So she had been. Not that she regretted her outburst in the least. Elizabeth contemplated the passing scenery. "I beg your pardon. For me to question your judgment was a truly shocking thing. Naturally it is not my place to quibble about whomever you decide to include in your household."

Her tone was scathing. Although he had already discovered that his bride had a temper, the duke was not best pleased to find that temper turned upon himself. He pulled his horses to a stop and studied his bride's face. The stubborn chin was outthrust, her lips clamped tight together, her hands clenched in her lap. Justin had a horrid suspicion that at any moment she might burst into tears.

"Truly I am not the greatest beast in nature," he said gently. "You must trust me a little bit, you know."

Trust Charnwood? Elizabeth didn't trust herself to speak. What the duke mistook for tears was instead a very strong desire to kick him in the shins.

"As for Madalena, you are under a misapprehension," he continued. "Magda is not my ladybird, nor has she ever been."

Not? Go shoe the goose. "Forgive my presumption in asking, but just what *is* she, then?"

Definitely a temper. Those big brown eyes spit fire. "Your mama didn't tell you, I credit," Justin said dryly. "No doubt it didn't signify because I am a duke. 'Twas a long time ago, Elizabeth, and we were both very young."

Elizabeth's patience, such as it was, was wearing very thin. "Damn and blast! Maman didn't tell me *what?*"

Her eyes sparkled, her bosom heaved. Justin wished they were having this conversation somewhere more secluded than an open carriage, in the middle of Bath. "That Magdalena is my first wife, from whom I have long been divorced."

Divorced? Elizabeth gaped. "But how—"

Justin grew impatient. "I traded her for a horse! In the usual way, of course. I had not yet come into the title, and my father paid well to have the business quickly done with. Now let us have no more of this nonsense, if you please!"

Chapter 7

*"As a woman grows older, she should assume a
graver habit and less vivacious air."* —Lady Ratchett

The Duke of Charnwood's previous wife, who had
not been traded for a horse, or divorced on grounds of
temporary insanity on the part of her spouse (although
he had considered it), surveyed the interior of the
Pump Room. This was a splendid structure with great
columns, and curved recesses at each end, thronged already with visitors come to drink the first glass of water.
In their gallery, musicians played. Among the crowd were
professional men and philosophers and rakes; rheumatics, gout sufferers, people afflicted with unsightly skin
diseases; snobs, social climbers, and upstarts of fortune;
ladies, both respectable and not; invalids in wheeled
chairs.

With Madame de Chavannes was Lady Augusta, who
grimaced as she sipped the nasty-tasting water. "I don't
know," she muttered, "why you were so determined to
come here."

Cautiously, Magda sampled her own water. "*Zut!* It does taste very bad. Perhaps that London doctor made good his threat to cast toads into the spring." Augusta choked. Magda laughed.

"Damn you, Magda! You did that on purpose," said Augusta, when she could speak again. "I don't see how anyone can stomach three glasses of this stuff a day. And I shan't have a bath, no matter what you say."

Magda idly touched her cameo. "Never? You will eventually smell very bad, I think."

"*I* think you are being deliberately provoking. Which shouldn't surprise me. I'll make you a bargain, Magda. I'll go into the Baths when you do."

Magda had no intention of going into the Baths with Augusta. Or anywhere else, actually, which just went to show how easily one's intentions could be overset. "*Mais non!* The scandal of nude bathing has been removed, and along with it my interest. Do not just stand there scowling! Come along, *ma chere.*"

Madame de Chavannes threaded her way through the crowd, glancing with keen interest at the various faces around them. None were worthy of her attention. She cast a quick eye over the book designated for the registration of the city's more worthy guests.

Magda did not add her own name to those pages. Instead she turned to Lady Augusta, who trailed in her wake. Gus looked exceptionally well in her short robe of white muslin, trimmed round the neck with lace, worn over a striped muslin petticoat; her Dunstable hat was trimmed round with a narrow blue ribbon, across the crown a wreath of artificial flowers. Or she *might* have looked exceptionally well if not for her expression, which was fierce enough to frighten off anyone. "It is your own fault if you are unhappy. You insisted on coming with me, Gus."

Lady Augusta's elegant nose twitched in irritation. "Don't call me that," she said.

Magda returned her attention to her surroundings. "Better Gus than some of the other things Nigel has called you. I especially recall the episode of the hornet's nest. Poor thing, he was badly bitten. Unfair of him to blame you when we were all equally at fault. *Mon Dieu*, those were better days."

Lady Augusta emptied her glass and set it down with a thump. "For you, perhaps. I do not remember them so fondly. Nor do I think Nigel would wax nostalgic about being bit by hornets. May we please speak of something else?"

Her companion was as touchy as a bear with a sore paw. Not that it was difficult to understand why. Magda emptied her own glass. "Try and not be so dour, *ma chere*. The day is young, and we are in Bath, which I might point out was *also* your idea. And if the place does not delight you, it is a joy to me after France! Taxes upon tobacco, road travel, legal documents, windows, and doors. Domiciliary police visits and rigorous examination of travelers. Paris is a maelstrom of intrigue."

Augusta eyed her companion shrewdly. "And in the midst was meddling Magda. You can't convince me that you didn't enjoy yourself."

Magda looked into the distance. "With the fall of Robespierre, Paris followed the countryside in an intensifying reaction against the Revolution. In the springtime returning émigrés with a renewed hope of royalty congregated in *le petit Corblez* to hear the monarchial philosophies being preached abroad by Bonared, and de Maestres joined one of the countless counterrevolutionary groups, such as the Societe de Egaux—and then were allowed two weeks to leave the country or become intimate with Madame Guillotine. Ah yes, 'twas vastly entertaining to see poor Jules's head atop a pike."

Augusta could have bitten her bitter tongue. "I'm sorry. I didn't know."

Magda shrugged. "How could you? It is not an uncommon thing. I have been to *bals de guillotine,* where ladies who lost loved ones to the blade wore red ribbons round their neck. But I have escaped all that. Now I am determined to be gay."

Madame de Chavannes certainly looked gay enough in her long tunic of light muslin pulled in under the breast and trimmed with a Grecian design, bracelets around her ankles, rings on her toes, and Greek style sandals on her feet. At least she wore a shawl around her shoulders. And not, thank heavens, a red ribbon round her neck.

The crowd pressed close around them. Lady Augusta's nose twitched again at the smell of strong perfume and unwashed flesh. Apparently she was not alone in not wishing to bathe. It was said of Bath that here everyone met everyone else each day, and mixed with perfect equality. French Revolution or not, Gus was no great believer in *égalité.* "Do you think," she said faintly, "that we might go outside?"

Augusta was looking a trifle peaked. Magda glanced at the fine Tompion clock which marked the passage of the hours, then led the way past the statue of Beau Nash in the eastern alcove, through the elegant colonnade of the entrance, and paused beneath the Greek inscription which translated "Water! Of elements the best." "Are you feeling better now?" she asked.

Gus drew in a deep breath, which was perhaps unwise; the city, in its basin of hills, tended to retain bad smells. She huffed and made an acid comment on a passing lady's gown.

"*Tiens!* You are feeling better." Magda drew her arm through Lady Augusta's, and guided her past the sedan chairmen waiting in the courtyard. Along the busy street strolled more people with whom Gus did not wish to rub shoulders, cardsharpers and soldiers of fortune, ladies of the town and widows in search of husbands, the sick and not so ill. A stage doctor on an elevated platform covered by a ragged blanket extolled a nostrum designed to cure every imaginable disorder, and some that were not. Street sellers hawked cigars and walking sticks, spectacles and dolls, ballad sheets and shirt buttons, rat poison and whips.

A dapper fellow in a lemon yellow jacket tipped his hat and smiled, revealing a fine set of Egyptian pebble teeth. "A fine day, ladies. How d'ye do?"

Gus was having none of this classes-come-into-contact-with-perfect-equality-nonsense. She took firmer hold of Magda's arm. "We don't! Be on your way. I told you we should have brought a footman along, Magda. And you still haven't told me how you escaped from France."

There were a great number of things Magda hadn't told her companion, nor would she, because Gus had never been a marvel of discretion, but rather far too prone to let the cat out of the bag. Therefore, Magda repeated the tale she had told Justin of her journey via Rouen to Le Havre, and departure by way of a friendly fishing boat. In reality, the fishing boat had taken her only as far as a Royal Navy frigate, which had fetched her home along with Sir Sidney Smith. Not that Madga had received a hero's welcome, as had Sir Sidney, who was now embarked on frog-hunting in the eastern Mediterranean. Instead, she had entered the country without a passport, and would probably leave the same way. Among Magda's acquaintances she numbered William Wickham, head of a clandestine organization that had made espionage the most flourishing industry of Europe, due to the influx of British gold; Richard Ford, the chief magistrate of Bow Street; the Abbe Ratel; and a certain Louis Bayard, also known as *Crepin*, Louis Vincent, Franc, and a number of other aliases to the grand total of thirty-one, which was several more than Magda's own. All of which had led her to the conclusion that Royalists were as fragmented in London as in France, where each agent had a different Paris master, and everyone watched each other like hawks.

Not that Magda could be certain she *wasn't* being watched, due to her known connection with the Comitè Français, which was effectively a royalist government in exile. "*Ma foi!* Now I am hungry," she announced, and pulled Augusta down the street toward a coffee house. "Come along, *ma chere!* We shall refresh ourselves, and then inspect the shops, and see if we meet any of our acquaintances promenading among the fashionable crescents and squares."

For her part, Lady Augusta hoped she might not meet any of her acquaintances while in company with Madame de Chavannes. Not for Madame de Chavannes the traditional trappings of mourning. Rings on her toes, for heaven's sake.

Magda was up to something. Gus wanted to know what. She also wanted to delay as long as possible a further confrontation with her cousin, whom she must placate somehow. Gus followed Magda into the coffeehouse.

It was a coffeehouse for ladies only. Young girls were not admitted, because the conversation turned upon politics, scandals, philosophy, and other subjects not fit for their tender ears. The room was of a goodly size, the front window filled with coffee cups and pots and strainers of a dozen different designs, pint coffeepots ready by the well-filled antique grate, clean, polished floors.

A babble of voices filled the air, as the patrons read the latest newspapers, all of which had columns devoted to foreign news, and spoke of whatever they wished, which resulted in a great deal of good-natured joking, as well as rumor and gossip and talk of politics. Magda dropped coins into a brass box, then inspected the noisy room, and settled on a small round table placed near the back wall. A waiter brought two cups of hot steaming coffee in shallow delftware bowls. Magda requested a piece of almond cake. The walls were plastered with advertisements: Dr. Belloste's pills for rheumatism, Parke's pill for the stone, Daffy's elixir, Godfrey's cordial, Velno's vegetable syrup for the alleviation of venereal disease.

Venereal disease? Augusta's nose twitched. The waiter returned and placed a plate on the table. "Cake so early in the day? Magda, you are decadent."

Magda plunged her fork into the pastry. "I always was decadent, I think. But I didn't realize it until I lived in France. You have no idea how terrible it is to be an émigré. Living abroad in humiliating circumstances, properties confiscated, income stopped. You must not begrudge me my cake, Gus."

In truth, Augusta begrudged Magda nothing, unless it was that shocking dress. She knew what it was like to be penniless herself. Or if not precisely penniless, dependant upon someone else's goodwill. She stripped off a glove and applied one fingertip to a cake crumb that had fallen on the table. "Justin will tolerate no scandal," she remarked.

"Pfft!" Magda waved an airy hand. "You mean the divorce. Unlikely that anyone will recall that old business. Not after this long. And if someone does, I am a friend of the family, *n'est-ce pas?* The worst that may be said is that we are monstrous civilized."

In this setting, Lady Augusta felt monstrous civilized herself. Certainly she was a great deal more civilized than the people at the tables around them. She twitched her skirts closer to her chair. "I wonder why Justin married Elizabeth. She is but a girl."

Magda pushed the cake plate toward her. "You are mystified, Augusta? Allow me to explain. She is all that's proper, Saint's little bride. It is a marriage à la mode."

Augusta grinned. "She's your opposite, you mean. Saint may have gotten more than he bargained for. His proper little bride has already bloodied his nose."

If Augusta knew how attractive she was when she wasn't scowling, she would probably never smile again. Magda licked cake frosting off her lips. "You were always jealous, Gus."

Lady Augusta didn't dignify this accusation with a response. Not that it lacked truth. Considering her advanced age, and her circumstances, she was not likely now to make a match herself. Magda, on the other hand, had been married four times at last count. Perhaps five, including the unfortunate Jules, for whom she wore no mourning. *Better to have loved and lost?* Gus wondered if Magda would agree.

Lady Augusta picked up another larger cake crumb, and popped it in her mouth. "Elizabeth knows no one in Bath. She must not, because no one knows her. Justin will be off doing whatever it is that gentlemen always do. Elizabeth will be bored, poor thing. We cannot in good conscience abandon St. Clair's bride."

Magda sipped her coffee. "You mean that we cannot abandon the gaming tables. Do you think that here your luck will change? Saint will not like it if you expose his bride to such things, I think."

"Saint will not like it if you expose her to worse." Gus abandoned her good manners altogether and finished off the cake.

Magda regarded the empty plate. "As if I would do such a thing. You misjudge me, Gus."

"I *know* you, Magda. You always have an eye to the main chance. I wonder how you will manage to feather your nest in Bath." Augusta looked thoughtfully into her coffee cup. "Perhaps Saint had to have a fortune. The girl was well-dowered, from all accounts."

Magda chuckled. "You are of so many minds that you'll never be mad, *ma chere*. A pity that you are Saint's first cousin and could not marry him yourself."

Augusta choked on a mouthful of coffee. "Marry Saint? It's you who must be mad. Ah, but you *did* marry him, didn't you? A pity it didn't work out."

Magda's smiled faded. "I have thought so sometimes. Had things been otherwise—*Tout même*, that is water under the bridge."

Had things been otherwise how? Augusta was curious. Magda had changed considerably since her girlhood. For that matter, so had Gus.

Magda fell into conversation with the occupants of a nearby table. Lady Augusta picked up a copy of *The Lady's Magazine*, its frontispiece an elegant engraving showing Lord Nelson engaging two Spanish ships of superior force off Cape Saint Vincent, faced by a sketch of the national hero's life. She flipped the pages until she came to a fulsome ode to the late glorious hero. Her lips twitched as she read it. Mentioned were Neptune's heroes, Gallia's tarnished laurels, death-dealing thunder shaking oozy caves where hoary bellows crimsoned beneath a purple sky.

What nonsense. Gus was weary of politics. Naval mutinies, invasion scares—On display in Fleet Street were a

series of startling engravings showing the type of machine Englishmen might expect to see bearing down
upon their shores from France, a giant raft with four
windmills and a battlemented wooden fortress, batter-
ies of forty-eight-pounders at each corner. She studied
her companion, who was in rapt conversation about the
alarming aspect of affairs in Ireland. Could Magda be a
revolutionary herself, with a taste for republican senti-
ments and severed heads?

Magda finished her conversation, and her coffee.
Augusta set down her own coffee dish. "Saint will wish
to make known his presence in Bath. We shall give a
small entertainment. Soup à *la Reine*. A fillet of pheasant and truffles. Larded partridges. Woodcocks. Dantizic
Jelly. Lemon-Water Ice. Followed by a musical inter-
lude."

"And perhaps some cards?" Magda placed her elbows
on the table, and folded her hands beneath her chin. "I
do not mean to blast your schemes, truly I do not, *ma
chere*, but I must point out that Saint's bride is now the
lady of the house."

So she was. Augusta didn't begrudge her cousin his
happiness—if happiness he would find—but his marriage left her without a place again. She could hardly
live with St. Clair and his wife indefinitely. Unless she
made herself indispensable. "Elizabeth is not foolish.
She will allow herself to be guided by older, wiser heads."

Magda's brief impression of Saint's bride was not
that she was so malleable. The young lady had looked
quite able to spit fire. "Has it occurred to you that Saint
might wish to be private with his bride?"

Again, Gus grinned, causing herself to look several
years younger, and considerably less prim. "He's hardly
private now. *We're* here. A little effort on my part, and
we shall all rub along together tolerably well."

Unlikely, thought Magda. But if Augusta concentrated her efforts on the new Lady Charnwood, Magda would be left to pursue her own plans. Plans that would be much easier accomplished without Gus stuck to her like a court plaster. "*D'accord!*" she said therefore, as she got up from her chair. "And now let us survey the shops and perhaps spend some of Saint's new wealth."

Augusta's spirits rose. 'Twas one of her favorite things to spend money not her own. Not that she had money of her own *to* spend.

Perhaps she might even persuade Magda to purchase a corset. Justin would be grateful. In perfect accord, the ladies made their way to the shops on Pulteney Bridge.

Chapter 8

"A bride should always strive to appear accomplished and amiable." —Lady Ratchett

Dinner *en famille* that evening was not a comfortable affair. This had nothing to do with the excellence of the meal, for Cook had outdone herself in the preparation of stewed eels and sole à la normande, lobster pissoli, stewed celery, and roast beef, among other things; and the footmen stationed at the mahogany sideboard were assiduous in their attentiveness, quick to provide an additional spoonful of oyster sauce, or refill a wineglass. Despite all these good efforts, the food was consumed largely untasted, and the wine injudiciously drunk. Everyone seated at the vast mahogany dining table, where silver and crystal and excellent Staffordshire pottery gleamed in the soft candlelight, had other matters on his mind. The duchess brooded upon the perfidy of her mama, who had kept her in such appalling ignorance of her husband's marital history; the duke contemplated the odd circumstance that his bride thought so poorly of him that she believed he would introduce his fancy piece into the household; Lady Augusta pondered the relative merits of roast pheasant, boiled fowl with bechamel sauce, and galantine of veal. Madame de Chavannes, upon whose mind the most weighty matters of all might be expected to prey, was the most animated of the four, and had thus far discussed with great animation the Irish Rising, the defeat of the French at the Battle of the Nile, George III's repeated bouts of insanity, and the stubbornness of the citizens of Cairo, whose continued opposition to Bonaparte had resulted in ninety people shot in the Citadel, and seven others thrown in the Nile to drown, in one day alone. Currently she was embarked upon a slice of tipsy cake.

Madame de Chavannes was a prodigious eater. Elizabeth watched with fascination as she wielded her fork. Magda was dressed for dinner in a semitransparent gown with an astonishingly low-cut bodice, her curls in a Grecian style hairdo topped by an absurd peacock plume, her cameo nestled in the cleft between her breasts. She looked considerably more like a gentleman's *petite amie* than a previous wife. The lady was also older than she had first appeared, and rendered no less beautiful by cake crumbs on her chest.

Magda caught Elizabeth's gaze on her, and smiled. "*Alors!* You will call me Magda, and I will call you Elizabeth. Do not concern yourself that Saint and I are bosom bows, *mignonne.* He is a difficult man, this husband of yours. But Magda is here, and will tell you how you must deal with him."

Why was everyone so convinced she needed guidance? Elizabeth must appear a paltry thing indeed. Certainly her own dress of pale blue trimmed with satin roses could only appear missish in comparison with Magda's dramatic *décolletage.* As must Elizabeth herself pale in comparison. Still, she didn't think she wished guidance from this source. She peered around the fruit bowl in the middle of the table, a circular basket supported by three caryatids, each standing on the arm of a triangular base raised on satyr's masks with swags of fruit in between. St. Clair was deep in conversation with his cousin—Elizabeth heard oyster patties mentioned—and she returned her attention to the duke's previous wife, who was now being served with raspberry cream. "Magda," she said, "you have cake crumbs on your—um."

Magda twinkled as she brushed off her plump bosom. "You are astonished. My late husband used to say that I was possessed of the appetite of an elephant. *Quel dommage*, poor Jules! Never marry a Frenchman, *petite*."

Odd to be called "little one" by a lady who scarcely came up to her chin. "Unlikely that I shall, since I am already married," Elizabeth retorted. "To St. Clair."

Magda responded with a throaty chuckle, and a dismissive wave of her hand. "*Très bien!* I wish you joy of him. Saint! See how I am conversing with your duchess. We are all merry as crickets together, *n'est-ce pas?*"

For herself, Elizabeth didn't feel the least bit merry. Justin's cool gaze flicked over them, and away. Scant comfort in the fact that he regarded the fair Magdalena with no more enthusiasm that he did his bride. Elizabeth stared at a silver saltcellar. Dinner might as well have been a piece of boiled beef and cabbage for all the pleasure of it in her mouth.

The interminable meal finally ended. St. Clair lingered over his port. Lady Augusta requested that tea be served in the drawing room, and led the way to that lovely chamber, its walls hung with crimson Spitalsfield silk that complimented the gilded ceiling medallions of diamond and octagon shapes. On the floor lay a Moorfield carpet with large octagonal patterns of crimson and gold, brown and blue. Fine rosewood furniture was scattered around the room, various tables, a pianoforte, sofas and chairs drawn close to the warmth of the fire. Urns, candelabra, statuary, and porcelain figures were placed elegantly about. Oil paintings adorned the walls.

Near the pianoforte stood Birdie's cage. The parrot was balanced on one foot, inspecting her other claw. She looked up at their entrance, and let out a great squawk.

"What a discerning bird!" said Magda. "Or has she met you before, Gus?" She waggled her fingers at the cage.

Elizabeth and Lady Augusta waited, with mutual anticipation, to see if the parrot would bite. Instead Birdie fanned her feathers. Perhaps she recognized a kindred spirit in the peacock plume.

"That beauty wants more attention." With a last finger wiggle, Magda turned away.

"You speak parrot now, do you?" Lady Augusta took up a position behind the teapot, and began to pour.

Magda arranged herself upon a chaise longue covered in red velvet. "You might be surprised by the languages that I speak. Sugar, please, and cream, since you seem determined to do the honors, Gus."

Augusta twitched at this none-too gentle reminder that she had usurped the honors of the tea table. "I'm so sorry, Elizabeth. I didn't mean to presume. Would you prefer to pour?"

Elizabeth would have preferred to remain with St. Clair in the drawing room. Perhaps she might even have joined him in a glass of port. Not that she had ever tasted port. And not that he would have wished her company. She assured Lady Augusta that she had no desire to preside over the tea table, and instead sat down at the piano, where she began to absently practice her scales.

Augusta and Magda chattered away like the old friends that they were. Magda made an occasional effort to include Elizabeth in the conversation, which had to do with the shops they'd visited that day, toymakers and picture galleries and milliners. Madame de Chavannes had especially liked Sally Lunn's bun shop in Lilliput Alley. And though she had no intention of purchasing a corset, she did wish to visit the food markets, and to taste cheese. "Biscuit," said Birdie, plaintively.

How comfortable they all were together. Elizabeth felt like a stranger in her husband's house. Which in fact she was. Her fingers wandered over the piano keys.

Voices came from the hallway. "Don't bother to announce me, Chislett. I'm quite one of the family." Nigel Slyte strolled into the room. "'Pon rep! Saint's *ménage extraordinaire.* What have you done with him, ladies? Swept him beneath the rug, perhaps?"

Birdie squawked. Elizabeth swung around on the piano bench. Mr. Slyte was dressed for the evening in light brown coat, white waistcoat, buff-colored breeches buttoned at the knee with two gold buttons; yellow stockings with large violet clocks, bright yellow cravat tied in the Trone d'Amour, bright red watch fob, and decorative buckles on his shoes.

He paused so that the ladies might admire him, then opened the cage door. "Hallo, Birdie, did you miss me, you ungrateful fowl?" The parrot stepped onto his outstretched hand, ruffled her neck feathers and bowed her head. Nigel scratched her. Birdie closed her eyes. Had she been a cat, Elizabeth thought, the parrot would have purred.

"Hello, Mouse," Nigel said. "Nice dress, what there is of it. I must commend you on your timing. You always did have a special sense about such things. No, don't bother to pour me any tea, Gus. I prefer it without arsenic." Nigel sat down beside Elizabeth on the piano bench, Birdie perched on his shoulder now, and picking through his hair.

"Lice," he said, in response to Elizabeth's curious glance. "No, I don't have any, but Birdie don't know that."

Elizabeth smiled, grateful for Nigel's nonsense. "She likes you."

"Of course she likes me," Nigel retorted. "She's a female. All females like me. I'm irresistible." Across the room, Lady Augusta snorted. "Or almost all females. There's no accounting for their tastes."

Elizabeth glanced at Augusta, who looked very much the lady of the house, in a simple print gown with a deep V neckline trimmed with lace, long sleeves tight-fitted to the arm, a lace cap atop her chestnut hair. Clearly another house needed to be found for her if Elizabeth was ever to rule over this one. St. Clair had said that once Nigel would have married Augusta. Perhaps Augusta might be persuaded to be less off-putting. Perhaps Nigel might then be persuaded that they might still suit.

More likely that Elizabeth would go to her grave with Gus still presiding over the teapot. "You don't like females, Mr. Slyte?"

Nigel rubbed his cheek against the bird's soft feathers. "It ain't that I don't like them, I just know them too well. I've got a gaggle of sisters. Enough females to last a fellow a lifetime. No mystery left, you see."

Amused, Elizabeth struck a mischord. "Palaverer."

Nigel tilted his head to one side. "I must give you a nickname. Justin is so superior that I call him Saint.

Magda is Mouse because she ain't one. Augusta is Gus because it annoys her so. What shall I call you? Liz, Lizzie, Betty, Beth— No, simply Duchess, I think. It suits."

So little did the nickname suit her that Elizabeth had to smile. "Because I am not duchesslike, you mean."

Nigel returned the smile. "No, Duchess, because you've never been given a chance to be anything else. I'll wager you don't know *what* you'd like to be."

Other than not married? Elizabeth eyed her all-too-discerning seatmate. "I'm not entirely sure, but I think you just insulted me. That, or you're bamming me again, Mr. Slyte."

Nigel winced as Birdie took a strand of his hair in her strong beak and tugged. "Never shall I bam you, Duchess. My word on it. No, you shan't snatch me bald, you wretched bird."

The duke paused in the doorway. His expression was remote. His gaze flicked over Augusta behind the teapot, and Magda on the chaise, then rested on Nigel.

Elizabeth stared at her husband. He looked every inch the haughty aristocrat in his dark blue coat with flat blue buttons, the fawn pantaloons that displayed his muscular thighs. What a muddle she'd made of everything. Accusing him of libertine propensities. Condemning him for his shocking conduct, when in truth he'd done nothing untoward. Or almost nothing. The man *was* divorced. Still, there was no denying she'd pulled the wrong sow by the ear. Elizabeth dropped her eyes to the keyboard.

What a damned awkward business this was. His wife couldn't even meet his gaze. Justin walked further into the room. How could anyone think him capable of such domestic amusements as involved Magda and Gus? Both of whom were watching him, one set of eyes speculative, the other amused. "Hello, Nigel. Lady Ysabelle has recovered, then?" Adroitly, he sidestepped the parrot, which was fascinated by the tassels on his Hessian boots.

Nigel swooped up Birdie and set her atop a jasper-ware urn. "I threatened her with Daffy's elixir. 'Tis one of Aunt Syb's little pleasures to pretend to be on her deathbed and then make a remarkable recovery. There is clearly a malicious streak in the family."

If so, Nigel had not escaped it. Justin contemplated the parrot perched atop the urn. Birdie ruffled her feathers at him. "You've come to take the creature home."

"Not exactly." Nigel brushed feathers off his jacket, then draped himself against the piano. "You know how it is that Lady Syb only threatens to turn up her toes when she gets to feeling bored?"

Justin knew he wasn't going to like what was coming. "I am all suspense." He wished Elizabeth would look at him instead of the keyboard.

Nigel reached over the piano and played an arpeggio. "Aunt Syb dotes on you, Saint. So does Birdie. I would be green with envy if I was the jealous sort. Challenging you for alienation of affections. Pistols at dawn, that sort of thing."

"Fortunate for you that you're not jealous, then," retorted St. Clair. "Since I'm the better shot."

"There is that," admitted Nigel, as he picked out a lively upside-down melody. "I told Aunt Syb about your sudden marriage. And about Mouse and Gus. Had to tell her, didn't I? She was bound to find out, and then I'd have a peal rung over me for keeping her in the dark. Aunt Syb has decided that there's nothing for it but that now she must also come to Bath. Like some blasted knight in armor. Going to set us all to rights."

Nigel's tone was gloomy. Justin raised an ironic brow. "Does Lady Ysabella plan to take up residence with me also?"

Nigel scowled and abandoned the pianoforte. "No, she plans to stay with *me*. And Aunt Syb is very particular. She ain't going to like staying in a bachelor establishment. My valet will probably quit again. And the cook. I'll wish to go with them. Since I can't, instead I'll become a bedlamite. Much good her fortune will do me then."

Magda and Lady Augusta had been listening openly to this catalog of woes. "Poor Nigel!" Augusta said. "We'll all come to see you in that dreadful place. Perhaps we may make a party of it. We'll go into the city, and visit the lions in the Tower, and Nigel in Bedlam Hospital for the Insane."

"Don't think of it!" retorted Nigel. "The lions might eat you and then I'd be held to blame. Saint, I must beg you to keep Birdie with you awhile longer. Aunt Syb can't abide her in the same house. Although she'll probably wish to come visit to make sure I haven't done away with the fowl. Daresay she'd want to come and visit anyway. See what she can do about *your* household. Don't look so appalled, Duchess! You're probably the only one of all of us Aunt Syb won't wish to turn upside down and shake out."

"Ah," murmured Elizabeth. "Because I am such a pattern-card of respectability."

Nigel smiled. "You are, you know. And yes, I know I'm a humbug. You won't mind having Birdie a little longer. She likes you. Here, let me show you how to take off the top of the cage. There, now it's just a roost. She can't go far. Her wings are clipped."

Birdie didn't have to go far to cause trouble, as Justin well remembered. However, he also remembered his bride laughing in her damp nightgown. Therefore, he remained silent as Nigel explained parrot care to Elizabeth, and that Birdie liked to have her head scratched, and that one foot lifted signified a desire to be picked up. Strutting and fanning were courtship displays, however, in which case the bird was best left alone, or given a mirror in which to admire herself. Justin recalled a certain strutting and fanning episode involving one of his boots. Thornaby, unfortunately present at the time, had nigh swooned from the shock. Elizabeth was scratching the parrot's head. Justin wished she would scratch his head instead.

At this rate, he would soon be joining his old friend in Bedlam. "Very well! The bird can stay."

Magda offered a cup of tea. Justin suggested port. Nigel shook his head. "Must be off! Preparations to make."

The men walked into the hallway where Chislett presented Nigel with his coat and hat and cane. "I'll try to keep Aunt Syb busy, but you know how she is."

Justin had faint hope that the indomitable Lady Ysabella could be kept from meddling in his household. Ah well, he consoled himself, matters could hardly grow worse. "As for Birdie," Nigel added, "I am in your debt."

Justin glanced back into the drawing room, where Magda and Augusta had resumed their conversation, Magda considering the question of how London was to be defended if Bonaparte led his army to England, Gus more concerned with *croquettes de game aux champagne*. Elizabeth was coaxing Birdie to sit on her shoulder. "You are in debt to me for the rest of your life, at least."

Carefully, Nigel settled his curly-brimmed beaver hat on his tousled golden curls. "My life is bound to be longer than yours!" he said cheerfully. "I have only Aunt Syb to contend with."

Chapter 9

"It is our duty as gentlewomen to make sure we never succumb to desire and suffer its disastrous consquences." —Lady Ratchett

Restlessly, Elizabeth paced the bedroom floor, to the annoyance of her abigail, who was helping her to disrobe. Or attempting to help her. Daphne had a vested interest in the wager placed belowstairs as to whether the duke and duchess would share a bed this night. "Whatever is the matter, Your Grace?"

"I told you not to call me that." Elizabeth paused long enough to allow Daphne access to the buttons of her dress. "I don't suppose *you* were aware that Charnwood is divorced."

Daphne gaped. "Divorced? His Grace?"

"Then you weren't." Elizabeth sat down at the writing desk and picked up a quill. "I believe that I must inquire of Maman just how I am to *properly* deal with the inclusion of St. Clair's former wife in our honeymoon."

Divorced! Lady Elizabeth was indeed as sore beset as

any romantic heroine. Or maybe worse, because Daphne had never read about anything like this. Poor thing, married for her money to a man who had his previous wife in the house. Thornaby thought himself so superior. Daphne didn't see anything superior in being valet to a divorced man. Even if he was a duke.

"Mrs. Papplewick was talking about that Magda." Daphne peered over Elizabeth's shoulder to see what she had written. "Although she didn't say as they were wed."

Elizabeth set down the pen, to Daphne's relief. If Her Grace sent off that letter, Lady Ratchett would descend upon them like a whirling dervish—the abigail was partial to romantic novels of an Eastern flavor— and Daphne would have to explain why she hadn't kept Milady apprised of what was going on in her daughter's house. "What *did* Mrs. Papplewick say?" Elizabeth asked.

Daphne struggled with her conscience. Or rather, her sense of which side her bread was buttered on. Best her mistress knew the truth, even if she didn't like it. Which she wasn't likely to. "According to Mrs. Papplewick, Miss Magda was a gay, lively lass. Adored by servant and lordship alike. And though no one can say for sure what had happened between them, it is Mrs. Papplewick's opinion that it was himself as decided they wouldn't suit. A queer thing in and of itself, she said, since it was obvious to one and all that once Miss Magda had suited St. Clair to a cow's thumb."

As Elizabeth did not. Perhaps the duke might be persuaded to divorce a second time. In such a case, he would hardly return her dowry. Elizabeth had no desire to return to her mother's house. "Well," she murmured, "then that is that."

What *that* was, Daphne didn't care to inquire. She coaxed her mistress out of her clothes and into the sheerest of nightgowns, powdered her and creamed her and took the pins out of her hair.

Deep in thought, Elizabeth allowed her abigail to dress her like a doll. When Daphne was done with her at last, she walked toward the hearth. The Axminster carpet was soft beneath her bare feet. Daphne moved quietly around the room, fussed with the candles, plumped up the pillows on the bed, turned back the coverlet just so.

She picked up a scent bottle. Elizabeth waved her away. "I do not wish to be perfumed, Daphne! You may go!" The abigail doused her with scent, all the same. Elizabeth sat down in front of the fire and began to brush out her long hair.

No wonder Maman had been so insistent that Elizabeth be a model of all the virtues. The duke would also turn off Elizabeth, did she fail to suit. How could she help but fail, when even the glorious Magda had fallen short of the mark? St. Clair must have loved Magda once. She had, after all, suited him to a cow's thumb. Elizabeth wondered if perhaps Lord Charnwood still nourished a *tendre* for his former wife.

The door to the dressing room opened, and St. Clair stepped into the bedroom, for all the world as if Elizabeth had conjured him. He wore his dressing robe. His very lovely dressing robe of lustrous rich satin, a deep wine in hue. Did he wear anything beneath it? Elizabeth suspected he did not. For that matter, neither did she wear anything beneath her gossamer nightgown. Elizabeth wished she were wrapped in flannel. Perhaps the duke would attribute her reddened cheeks to the warmth of the fire.

How somber she looked. Elizabeth could hardly be blamed for holding him in low opinion—it was her wretched mother's fault, for not explaining things—but still, his pride was stung. Justin had ever conducted himself with the utmost propriety, especially toward his bride. He walked toward the hearth, where Elizabeth perched on a stool. The firelight caused lovely lights to dance in her long thick hair.

Warily, she watched him. Justin wondered if he might consider Birdie's absence from his bedchamber an encouraging sign. Indeed, the bedchamber looked very welcoming this night, the coverlet turned back invitingly, a floral scent in the air.

His bride looked considerably less so. "Good Lord, I won't eat you! Give me that hairbrush."

Elizabeth handed him the brush, uncertain as to whether he meant to apply it to her hair or to her rear. Yes, and why should the notion of being turned over the duke's knee cause her to squirm? At least her back was to him now, so she was spared further speculation upon what was or wasn't under that silky robe.

He said nothing, but drew the brush slowly through her hair. So slowly that goose bumps sprang up on her arms, and butterflies resumed their somersaults in her poor tummy, and Elizabeth longed to snatch the brush away from him. She refrained. Her behavior already left much to be desired.

Still St. Clair remained silent. He was angry, and no wonder. Elizabeth had accused that most proper of gentlemen with the most improper conduct. Although she didn't know what else she was supposed to think when no one had bothered to explain. But if Charnwood didn't have a *tendre* for Magda, then why had Elizabeth been left alone on her wedding night? Not that she minded. Elizabeth had taken laudanum for just that purpose, after all.

How quietly she sat beneath the brush strokes. How still. Her hair was thick and soft beneath his hands.

Lovely hair it was. As was her person in that gauzy gown. Here was none of Magda's lush excess, but rather an elegant landscape of slender valleys and hills. A landscape of which he had a splendid view in that flimsy gown, and which he was surprisingly eager to explore. With the fingers of one hand, Justin traced the contours of his wife's chin, and turned her face toward him.

St. Clair was looking at her with an intent expression. He wasn't thinking of Magda just now, at any rate. Elizabeth rather wished he were. He was standing, she was sitting. She could have easily reached out and satisfied herself as to what the duke did or didn't wear beneath his robe.

Her cheeks were flaming. The duke felt somewhat flushed himself. Doubtless it was because they were so close to the hearth. Justin didn't know when he'd experienced a fire so warm. Maybe the servants were using a different sort of fuel. He grasped Elizabeth's wrist and drew her to her feet. "My dear, we have got off to a bad start."

"Um." Elizabeth contemplated his bare chest. A very nice chest it was. St. Clair wore nothing beneath the robe on that part of him, at any rate. The duke was even more handsome *en déshabillé* than in his normal clothes. Thought of her husband in a state of even more extreme undress made Elizabeth's own heart hammer in her chest. She raised her gaze to his chin, and thought of Daphne's romantic novels, at which she'd sneaked several peeks. Slave girls and harems. Irresistible heathen sheikhs.

What would the sheikh do now? The duke, that was. Sweep her into his arms and kiss her? Fling her upon the bed and have his wicked way with her? Crush her against his manly chest?

His wife seemed fascinated with his chin. Justin was at a loss. What the Devil did one *do* with an untried miss? Maybe he should have asked Thornaby. Lord knew the man fluttered about him like a hen with one chick. Not that Justin would actually commit such a solecism as asking his valet for marital advice. He reminded himself of the vast amount of experience upon which he himself had to draw.

Draw upon it he would, and proceed slowly, and try not to frighten his bride further. As opposed to ripping off her nightgown and taking her right there on the Axminster rug.

Carefully, Justin placed his hands on Elizabeth's shoulders. So far, so good. Although her gaze remained glued to his chin, she neither shrieked nor shrank away.

Justin thought he might attempt eye contact. He slid one hand to her throat, and tipped up her face to his. The lovely brown eyes narrowed. "I have told you that you must not be afraid of me. Do you remember, Elizabeth?"

He stood so close that she could feel the heat of his body. Difficult to say which put out more warmth, St. Clair or the fire. Not that Elizabeth was exactly chilly herself. Who would have ever thought that so flimsy a gown could prove so stifling? "I doubt that I've forgotten any of the words you said to me, Your Grace."

Justin regarded her quizzically. "I'm not certain what that means. Have I been so neglectful? If so, I am sorry for it. Be patient with me, Elizabeth, Perhaps we may start with a light flirtation, although it seems very odd to get up a flirtation with one's own wife."

A flirtation, was it? Elizabeth swallowed. "I rather think we may be beyond that, Your Grace. Unless people get up to flirtation in their nightclothes. Although I suspect Maman would think it very indelicate of me to say so."

Justin trailed his fingers along her jaw. "Maman is not here. *I* think it adorable in you."

Adorable? Her? Elizabeth blinked. And then St. Clair lightly brushed his thumb across her lips, and the effect of that chaste salute sent tingles all the way from the top of her head down to her toes. Elizabeth wasn't at all certain that she cared for tingles. Or perhaps she did. St. Clair's proximity was wreaking havoc with her thought processes. She pulled away.

Justin counted to ten slowly. And then twenty. His bride was staring at him as if he had sprouted horns. "Good Lord, Elizabeth, was that so very dreadful?" he asked.

It had not been dreadful. Startling, perhaps, but not dreadful at all. However, Elizabeth could not help but hear Maman's warnings in her head. She had a horrid suspicion that the butterflies in her belly had something to do with all that lustful stuff. Perhaps Elizabeth was going to turn into a slavering beast herself. One of those feckless women ruled by the passions, like in Daphne's books. A brazen piece, to be cut dead in the street.

The prospect turned her perfectly sick. At least, she thought it did. She also wished the duke would touch her again. Perhaps he might even kiss her. Not that she would tell him so. A model of good breeding would hardly say such things to her husband. Elizabeth must be correct in her conduct. Display a well-regulated mind.

He was waiting for her answer. What had the question been? Elizabeth collected her scattered wits. "It was not dreadful, Your Grace."

But she had not liked it, either. Were he not holding her fast, she would probably take refuge behind the bed. Justin was at a loss. He could not remember that any lady had ever disliked his caress. Or perhaps they all had disliked it, and merely pretended otherwise. He was, after all, a duke.

The duke didn't look particularly formidable in this moment. Rather, he appeared perplexed. What must it be like for St. Clair to be always called starched-up, and high in the instep, and stiff-rumped? When all was said and done, Charnwood was just a man. A very handsome man. Wearing nothing more than a dressing robe. With a sash around the waist that she could have reached out and untied, had she dared. Not that she wished to. "Are you angry?" Elizabeth asked.

Justin lifted a tendril of hair off her forehead. "I will never be angry with you, so long as you speak the truth. This is all my fault. Had I not been so neglectful of my duties, we would not now be at this impasse."

Neglectful of his *duties*? He listed *her* among his duties? With a thump, Elizabeth came down to earth. The duke saw her as a chore to be performed, like bringing in a load of coal, or emptying the slops. "I realize that ours is a marriage of convenience, but I am *not* a chamberpot. And now if you will excuse me, I am very tired, Your Grace, and would like to go to sleep!"

Perhaps Justin might not be the adept that he had fancied himself in regard to caresses, but he was not so green as to think his bride wished him to join her in the ducal bed. Nor did he think her amenable to reason in that moment, or that she would care to explain what prompted her to compare herself to a chamberpot. "I will bid you good night, then," he murmured, and withdrew into his dressing room, and closed the door. Behind him came a thud. It sounded very much as if Elizabeth had flung her hairbrush against the wall.

The duke might have liked to throw something himself. How had he come to stick his foot so firmly in his mouth? Mulling over how he was to set up his nursery when his wife couldn't be convinced to let him in her bed—or *his* bed, which she had usurped—the duke went downstairs in search of a glass of brandy. The duchess, meanwhile, added another line to her letter to her mama. Not that she would post the missive, but there was some satisfaction in writing down her rage.

Chapter 10

"Few men expect to carry the elaborate homage and tedious forms of courtship into marriage." —Lady Ratchett

No laughter from the adjoining chamber wakened Lord Charnwood this morning. Nor did he feel inclined to invite his bride on a phaeton ride. Thornaby recognized the signs of a duke in a foul humor, and silently shaved and brushed and clothed his master before proceeding downstairs to report that St. Clair had passed another night in his dressing room.

Fortunately, Justin was not aware of the servants' interest in his sleeping arrangements—although had he thought about it, he should have been aware, for the servants knew everything that happened in a household, as well as what did not. Unlikely, however, that even then he would have guessed that wagers had been laid on the outcome of the marital impasse.

He walked into the dining room, where warm dishes had been set out on the sideboard, and footmen were lined up to serve. Justin contemplated smoked herring, grilled kidneys, cold veal pies; beef tongue with hot horseradish, sausages with mashed potatoes, grilled trout with white butter sauce. None of it appealed. He settled on hot coffee and a roll.

Nor did Magda appeal. That lady was already seated at the table, an empty plate before her, and crumbs scattered on the cloth. Today she wore another Grecian gown, pale green instead of white. Perhaps he would drape a napkin across her. Justin was in no mood to contemplate Magda's bosom across the breakfast cups.

Magda tossed a grape to Birdie, who was also on the table, and making a considerable mess of the fruit center-piece. The parrot caught the grape in her strong beak. "*Bien!* What a clever girl. You are up very early, Saint. Did you not sleep well?"

Justin sat down and reached for the marmalade pot. "Mind your own business," he snapped.

Magda, who was aware of certain wagers, tossed Birdie another grape. This time the parrot missed. The grape landed on Justin's plate. "*Zut!* Your nose is out of joint. It is your own fault for not properly courting your bride. Or have you forgot how to woo a lady after all those years of females throwing themselves at your feet? I see how it was for you. A handsome face, a title. Oh, yes, you are still handsome, even with that battered nose." She plucked off another grape. Birdie sidled closer. "All the ladies swoon for you. Except for Elizabeth."

Briefly, Justin was tempted to ask his former wife about the quality of his caresses. However, it had been many years since he'd caressed Magda, and he had no desire to do so again. "Cut line, Magda. I won't allow you to take a rise out of me."

Madame was impervious to snubs, at least snubs de-livered by her former spouse. She broke a piece of bread from the roll on his plate. Birdie edged forward, interested. Magda popped the bread into her own mouth. "Gus is very curious as to what prompted you to marry such a milk-and-water miss." She dimpled. "I told her it was because Elizabeth is my opposite. She *is* very tall."

Birdie edged ever closer to his roll. Justin moved it out of range. "There is people food, and there is parrot food. This is people food, and moreover it is mine." Realization struck him, and he glanced at Magda. "Gus brought you here to Bath."

Magda shrugged, severely challenging the confines of her bodice. "I encountered Gus in London. At the tables, *naturellement*. You must do something about that one, Saint. She needs a gentleman with sufficient wealth to stake her, and a skin thick enough to withstand her barbs."

"Even did I unearth such a paragon, I could hardly make her marry him." Justin glanced at his breakfast companion, and recalled his own bride's brief hesitation when asked if she'd been forced to wed. "You still have not told me why you've come here. And I don't refer to the breakfast table. Get out of my plate, you wretched bird."

"How suspicious you are grown." Magda diverted Birdie's attention from the ducal breakfast with an apple wedge. "Perhaps I merely wished to cry pax. *Vraiment*, I do not even recall precisely why we parted. You were jealous, I think."

The duke leaned back in his chair and looked saturnine. "If I was jealous, madam, it was not without good cause. As you have pointed out, I was very young. I would not be so foolish now."

Magda tilted her head to one side. "You are grown beyond jealousy, my Saint?"

Lady Augusta paused in the doorway. "What is that

thing doing on the breakfast table?" she demanded. The parrot shrieked. Magda tossed another grape. Birdie caught it with an elegant snap of her beak.

Justin swooped up the parrot. Birdie ruffled up and opened her beak. "Bite me and it's in the soup pot with you!" he said. She cowered dramatically away from him. He deposited her on the perch.

Lady Augusta chose rashers of bacon, and oatmeal with sweet cream. *Be conciliatory,* she told herself; much as it might go against the grain. Therefore she waited while a footman brushed parrot traces from the table, and summoned forth a smile. "Thank you, cousin! Not that I have anything against the pretty bird, but it did not seem appropriate to have her at the table. I trust you slept well?"

Justin regarded his cousin, who looked as if butter wouldn't melt in her mouth. "No," he said. "And if you step one foot inside Catterick's, I shall cut off your allowance for a year. You will have heard of Catterick's. It is a gaming hell."

Gus opened her mouth and closed it. "Tut!" said Magda. "Augusta only wished to speak to you further about the dinner party she is planning in honor of Elizabeth. "Soup *à la Reine.* A fillet of pheasant and truffles. Larded partridges, as I recollect."

" 'Twould be a charming evening." Gus toyed with her bacon. "The introduction of your bride to Bath society, Saint. The cream of Bath society, that is, not the encroaching mushrooms one encounters in the Pump Room and on the streets. I'll wager a pony—I mean, I am certain! That Elizabeth would like it of all things."

Justin studied his cousin. "You think so, do you?"

"Entrez donc!" said Magda. "Here is Elizabeth. Why not ask her yourself. Did you sleep well, *ma petite?"*

What a cozy group they made around the breakfast

table. Could Elizabeth have ducked out of the room without being noticed, she would have done so. However, Magda had seen her, as had Birdie, who let out a great squawk. Magda's *décolletage* every day dipped lower. Elizabeth wished that she might yank what little existed of that bodice right up to the lady's chin.

"I slept very well, thank you," she said coolly, and walked to the parrot cage, where Birdie was sulkily chewing on her perch. "Good morning, fuss and feathers! And how did *you* sleep?"

Birdie spread her wings and quivered. Elizabeth held out her hand. With the parrot perched snugly on her shoulder, she moved to the sideboard. A footman loaded up her plate with grilled beef and sausage, and a kipper for the bird.

Elizabeth looked as if she, at least, had enjoyed a peaceful night. The duchess also looked quite pretty in a pale blue long-sleeved gown. Birdie made an interesting accessory. Justin picked the grape up off his plate, and tossed it. Birdie caught it in midair.

Elizabeth looked startled. Magda laughed. "Your wife will think you are throwing food at her. Augusta doesn't like parrots at the breakfast table, *ma petite.*"

Elizabeth pulled out a chair. "A pity. I do."

Augusta looked at the duchess and her parrot, and bit down on her lip. When the pain let up, she said, "Magda exaggerates. Truly, I don't mind."

Justin could remain no longer at the table, lest he do something he would later regret, such as tumble his bride back among the china and throw up her skirts. He pushed back his chair. Magda's bright eyes twinkled knowingly. "You are leaving us, *mon cher?*"

St. Clair recalled that he disliked his former wife's sense of humor. "You will excuse me. I have business to attend."

"*Mon Dieu!* Poor Elizabeth will think you are all business. What can be so important as to interrupt your honeymoon?"

"It's quite all right, Magda." Elizabeth dumped a great deal of sugar into her teacup. "No one can expect St. Clair to dangle after his wife like a lovesick swain. Certainly I do not."

Nor would she expect her husband to empty the sugar bowl over her head. "How magnanimous. Tell me, *would* you like a party, Elizabeth?" the duke inquired.

She raised startled eyes to his. "No," she said.

Justin bared his teeth. "Then a party you shall have! Gus will arrange the business with Mrs. Papplewick. Just remember, cousin, that there will be no bloody cards!" He stalked out of the room. That had *not* been well done of him. In the hallway, he paused.

"*Merde alors!*" soothed Magda. "Justin is *très* dutiful. He was installed by his guardians with a strong sense of propriety at a very young age."

"That hardly explains why he married you!" said Lady Augusta, around what sounded like a mouthful of oatmeal. "Although it's true that Justin is a man of many responsibilities."

"You should know, *ma chere!* Since you are one of them. As I was saying, it would not occur to Saint that a honeymoon might interfere with his routine."

Elizabeth said, "Did it interfere with *yours?*"

"Magda didn't have a honeymoon," volunteered Augusta. "They eloped to Gretna Green."

"Damnation!" said the duchess.

"Biscuit!" Birdie croaked.

"*Tiens!* We shall go shopping," interjected Magda. "I saw the prettiest hat one could ever imagine, and wish to visit it again. Also, I require to taste a cheese. Never fear, Elizabeth! We shall not allow you to become bored."

"You will find us considerably better company than Saint, at any rate," said Gus. "The older he gets, the more ill-tempered he becomes."

The duke recalled the adage that eavesdroppers heard no good of themselves. His cousin made him sound like a crabbed old geezer teetering on the brink of the grave. Quietly, he left the house.

The air was chill, the sky overcast. The gray day perfectly suited Justin's mood. A brisk ride in the hills did little to improve his frame of mind, nor an encounter at the White Hart Inn in Stall Street with his man of business, who had brought an armful of papers for him to peruse and sign. Papers that could very well have waited, had it occurred to Justin that meeting with his man of business in any way slighted his bride.

Not that Elizabeth had given the slightest indication that she wished his company. Rather, the opposite. The duke wondered if he was indeed a coxcomb, rather than the man of the world he had long thought himself. A man of the world was hardly likely to be hankering after his own wife. Or to contemplate throwing her over his shoulder and carrying her off to some dark cave.

He could not kiss her, or converse with her, or toss her on the breakfast table. What the Devil did she want of him? And how the Devil had he managed to marry the one damsel in the kingdom who showed no inclination of falling at his feet?

Elizabeth at his feet was an intriguing notion. Justin sighed and took himself off, not to take the waters—among the various ailments the waters were said to cure was not unsatisfied desires of the flesh—but to visit Catterick's, which he had forbade his cousin, a gaming hell of considerable renown.

The club had provision for every kind of gambling

game, and a supper room, as well as an upstairs chamber reserved for the sole use of the gentlemen. Conversation there ranged from the pilfered antiquities found aboard the French ships captured by Admiral Nelson to a recent concert heard at the Pump Room, politics and opera dancers and horseflesh.

A relief to hear no female voices. Justin requested a glass of claret from a hovering waiter and walked toward the fireplace, where he had spied familiar golden curls. Nigel was sprawled in a comfortable chair drawn up to the hearth. His costume was even more eye-catching than usual, for he was dressed in solid black. "I take it Lady Ysabella has arrived," the duke remarked.

Nigel grimaced. "The whole household is in a flutter. Cook has already threatened to quit twice. What brings you here? That's a good girl you married, Saint. And no, I don't want one myself."

Justin sipped his claret. "Do *you* think I'm a coxcomb?"

Mr. Slyte didn't make the mistake of asking what had given the duke this odd notion. "Tell you what, Saint, sometimes I thank God that I'm a younger son. No title and no prospects. Except from Aunt Syb, who'll probably outlive us both."

The duke could sympathize. There had been a time when he wished to be a younger son himself. "How *is* Lady Syb?"

"In prime twig. I left her sitting in bed drinking a concoction of primrose wine mixed up with honey, brandy, and white of egg; and ordering the servants around. Fortunate it is I *ain't* in the petticoat line, the way Aunt Syb has me dangling on her string." Nigel's shrewd eyes rested on his friend. "I probably shouldn't mention it, but it looks to me like you may be dangling yourself, Saint."

"You're correct. You *shouldn't* have mentioned it." The duke's tone was so savage that Mr. Slyte cocked his bright head to one side.

"Ain't you devilish out of humor! I wonder if I want to know why. Don't go getting your hackles up! Tell you what, I'll loan you some of Aunt Syb's leeches if you wish to purge yourself."

"It's not purging I need." Justin swirled the ruby liquid in his glass. "I think she will drive me mad."

"Which one?" inquired Nigel. "You have a flock of females in your house. All you need now is for Lady Ratchett to come to town. If she does, you can stay with me. Aunt Syb would like the company."

Perhaps Lady Syb would tell him if he was a coxcomb. "Elizabeth," Justin said, then paused. How to best broach so delicate a subject? "Is very, ah, innocent."

Nigel brightened. There was nothing better for a fit of the doldrums than to encounter someone worse off. "Of course she's innocent. You want her to be innocent. God's teeth, Saint, the girl is your wife."

Reminded of teeth, Justin gritted his. "I mean that she is *still* innocent. The Devil, Nigel, don't make me spell it out."

Nigel would have loved to prolong the moment. However, St. Clair was his friend. "Well now, this is most extraordinary! Never tell me that you are, uh, sleeping by yourself? I see from your expression that you are." He beckoned a waiter. "Another bottle of claret. Or perhaps you should make it three!"

Chapter 11

"Towns are the destroyer of feminine virtue. Women are particularly susceptible to the fashionable fripperies and time-wasting amusement found there." —Lady Ratchett

While the Duke of Charnwood was being advised by his oldest friend on the ins and outs of courtship—though Mr. Slyte wasn't in the petticoat line, he *did* have a gaggle of sisters, not to mention a very worldly aunt, and therefore might be considered somewhat of an expert on feminine likes and dislikes—the ladies of his household were embarked upon an expedition to the shops. The chill weather did not deter them; they simply bundled up. Lady Augusta fetched a cloak of velvet trimmed with swansdown, and a cottage hat. Elizabeth donned a pelisse of fawn-colored sarsenet trimmed with mohair fringe, a straw bonnet, and Limerick gloves. Magda was persuaded to put on a Grecian cloak fastened on her left shoulder, and to abandon her sandals in favor of half boots.

The streets were crowded with people and vehicles.

Magda had to be pulled out of the path of a collier's cart, although Augusta would have just as soon let her be run down. Elizabeth would not have approved, however, and Elizabeth must be appeased. Gus's jaws ached from smiling. "A select part for fifty people. Dinner. Music. Dancing, perhaps."

She went on to consider who should be invited to this festive occasion, as well as who should not. Mainly because she wasn't listening, the duchess took all Lady Augusta said in good part. *Had* she been listening, she might have informed Gus that she didn't care a rap. Elizabeth stepped aside to allow a wheeled invalid chair to pass.

"But I don't see," continued Augusta, as she followed Elizabeth down the street, "why we shouldn't have cards. Everyone has cards. Perhaps you will put in a word with my cousin. St. Clair is unreasonable."

Magda paused to regard a print shop display. "Don't exert yourself, *petite*. The truth is that St. Clair doesn't want Gus to lose her pin money three times over under his own roof."

Augusta didn't care for this reminder of her estrangement from Lady Luck. "You are quick to defend someone you once called a brute."

"*Alors!* I was married to him. I may call him anything I please." Magda twinkled at Elizabeth. "As may you, *ma chère.*"

Elizabeth wondered what other things Madame de Chavannes had called the duke. "Maman does not approve of playing cards. She says that gambling is the national preoccupation, and that it dedicates people to becoming their own executioners."

"*Ma foi!* I didn't know your mama had met Gus." A pastry shop caught Magda's eye, and she paused to deliberate between a jelly and a tart. The ladies then moved on to inspect the food markets, where vendors touted fat chickens and flounders, oysters and cherries, hard onions and pea soup; and for those customers who lacked an appetite, goldfish and cutlery and lace. Elizabeth and Augusta weren't hungry. Magda selected a cheddar cheese. From there they proceeded to the fruit and flowers and confectionery shops on Pulteney Bridge.

All this time, Magda chattered gaily, a worldly frivolous gossiping kind of conversation of which Maman also would not have approved. Elizabeth mused that she seemed to enjoy many things that Maman disliked. Shopping. Parrots on the breakfast table. Bath itself.

Magda observed that the war with France and the resultant financial crash had marked a turning point in the city's fortunes. "Bath is past its heyday. It grew too fast."

"Speaking of heydays," murmured Lady Augusta, as they approached a milliner's shop. A discussion of whether to corset or not to corset followed, with Augusta pro, and Magda con. "You are sensible and levelheaded, Elizabeth!" Lady Augusta said at last. "Tell us what you think."

Elizabeth thought that Magda could probably tell her what constituted a revolting practice, and if women were known to slaver, or succumb to lust. "If Magda doesn't wish to wear a corset, then she shouldn't. She is surely of an age to do as she pleases."

"A hit! A palpable hit." Gus grinned. "Magda, Elizabeth says that you are an old crone."

"Don't gloat, *ma chèrie.*" Magda wrinkled her nose. "You are even older than I am."

Lady Augusta stopped smiling. "Then I should also be able to do as I please."

Magda shrugged and linked her arm with Elizabeth's.

"Your cousin does not agree. You will make Saint a very comfortable little wife, *petite.*"

Elizabeth struggled briefly against temptation. "As you did not?"

Magda's dimple danced. "Some women are not designed for marriage, *mignonne,* which is not to say that I would mind if some handsome rogue fell in love with me. It is above all things amusing, the game of hearts. And it is always good for a lady to have a gentleman or two dangling at her slipper strings. But as for anything of a more permanent nature, I think not."

Elizabeth was so fascinated she stepped smack into a puddle. "You do not wish to have a husband?"

Magda threw back her head and laughed aloud. "I have had several husbands. After poor Jules, I decided that to bid another husband *adieu* would be too much even for me. Instead, I shall confine myself to amours." She drew the fascinated duchess out of the path of a sedan chair. "I do not mince words with you. The gentlemen are very well, in their place. You are a married woman now, and you know where that place is!"

Elizabeth guessed that Magda referred to the bedchamber. No question that Madame de Chavannes had quelled any number of gentlemanly fires, without the least regret. She was not the sort of female to be married for her fortune, or any other reason than her luscious self.

"I never had a fortune!" twinkled Magda, for Elizabeth had said this last aloud.

Elizabeth flushed. "Well, then, for duty's sake."

"*Mais non.*" Magda patted her hand. "To wed for other than affection is the way of the world, *petite.* You would not wish to be me, I think."

Elizabeth didn't think it would be a bad thing to be a woman of the world. Better that than a maiden still. Did she remain a maiden much longer, the duke could simply have his marriage annulled rather than going to the trouble of obtaining a divorce.

Not that he was likely to do so. Was he? Elizabeth wished that her husband liked her just a little bit. "I'm not so sure," she said.

"The grass is always greener?" Magda smiled. " 'Tis a great deal of trouble, to be a successful flirt. One must never allow the gentlemen to become complacent. Better to play fast and loose. At one moment sighing for their caress, and in the next holding them at arm's length."

Madame de Chavannes still spoke in the plural, Elizabeth noticed. "In which category would you place bloodying a nose?"

Magda chuckled. "*Du vrai*, there have been stranger bedfellows than you and Saint. Where can Gus have gone? If she has found a game of cards, your husband will have both our heads." That suspicion proved unfounded. Lady Augusta was discovered doing nothing more exceptional than browsing through the multifarious articles for sale in a bazaar.

Elizabeth spotted a bookseller's shop, where novels, plays, pamphlets, and newspapers might be perused for the small subscription of a guinea. The ladies entered the establishment. Magda inspected a newly published collection of letters intercepted at sea during the Egyptian campaign, for although French headquarters had ordered all dispatches to be thrown overboard when capture threatened, the hardy British soldiers jumped into the sea right after them. Lady Augusta scanned a newspaper article about the vast number of *émigrés* in England, and the government's attempt to keep suspect agents in the country instead of letting them run free on the Continent. Elizabeth glanced at *Manners and Rules of Good Society* and refrained from flinging it across the room.

After all this exertion, it was only natural that the ladies repair to the nearby Pump Room. "I suspect the waters are said to be medicinal because they are nauseating," said Gus. "Take my advice and drink tea instead."

Elizabeth looked around with interest. Light from two banks of windows illuminated the interior of the large room, which was set round with three-quarter columns of the Corinthian order, crowned with an entablature, and over it a covering of some five feet. On each side of the room was a fireplace. In the center of the southern side stood the pump, from which the waters issued out of a marble vase. The room was thick with people, young and old, healthy and infirm, come to exchange scandals and quiz the appearance of others, and drink the waters for which the resort was famed. They all seemed to be talking at once, over the noise of the musicians, and not all of them in English.

Augusta twitched her nose and recalled the newspaper article. "Well, Magda, 'twould appear you have found some of your émigrés."

Who had found whom? Magda preferred to be the hunter rather than the fox. "You are very disapproving, Gus. 'Tis hardly the fault of the poor émigrés that the French Republic is eating Europe leaf by leaf, like the head of an artichoke."

Lady Augusta had a queer vision of herself as a bug on an artichoke leaf. "The newspapers have Bonaparte in Egypt."

Magda shrugged. "Do you think that he will stay there, fighting Mamelukes and Turks? By whatever means, the Corsican intends in time to encompass both the ruin of the present French government and the British Empire. He is an ambitious man."

The room was warm, and redolent with the scent of many bodies. Magda unfastened her cloak, thereby attracting the attention of several male passersby. "How do you know all this?" asked Elizabeth.

"I keep my eyes and ears open. *Pardon*, I must speak with someone." Magda smiled at two gentlemen who had stopped to admire her plunging neckline, and stepped around them to move into the crowd.

"Keeps her ears and eyes open," muttered Lady Augusta, as she followed Elizabeth toward a window, out of the way of the promenade. "She's probably an enemy agent herself."

Elizabeth was tall enough to look over the crowd. She saw Madga in animated conversation with a group of gentlemen. "Surely you don't believe that."

Perhaps she did, perhaps she didn't. *Were* Magda an agent, would her loyalty be to England or to France? "If you care to look out the window, down below you will see the King's bath."

Elizabeth glanced at a huge cistern where flushed patients of all shapes and sizes wallowed in hot water, packed as close together as the most accommodating of them all could wish. On one side a covering, supported by a handsome colonnade, shaded the bathers from the inclemency of the weather if not from curious stares.

Lady Augusta moved closer and glanced at Elizabeth's hand. "That ring belonged to St. Clair's mother. 'Tis the traditional wedding ring of the Duchesses of Charnwood. Magda never wore it. She had a simple golden band." Having exhausted her store of human kindness, she added, "I believe Saint picked it out himself."

The duchess put her hand behind her back. "You have known Magda for some time?"

"We grew up on adjoining estates, my brother and I with Saint's parents, and Nigel's family nearby. Magda's father owned a holding in the neighborhood. All that property now belongs to Charnwood. 'Twould suit Justin's consequence to own most of England, I vow." Augusta paused to smooth her gloves. "If I may presume to offer you a word of advice? Perhaps you have noticed that my cousin tends to be dictatorial. Magda was once able to manage him. Perhaps you may also be able to do so in time. But until then, you will not wish to offend."

Magda had managed St. Clair so well that he had divorced her. Elizabeth wondered if St. Clair's cousin wished to see him divorced a second time. "And so I should conduct myself accordingly. Allow myself to be guided by you, in other words."

Augusta overlooked the ironic note in that polite voice. "That will be as you wish. I do not mean to say that you should take Magda as your guide. St. Clair *did* divorce her, though he was ridiculously besotted at one time. I have always thought that she quite broke his heart."

Elizabeth eyed her tormentor. "Fiddle! You must read the same romantic twaddle as my maid."

Augusta opened her mouth to deliver a blistering set-down, then realized that she must not. Fortunately, Magda returned then, with a gentleman by her side. A gentleman so very handsome that even Gus stared at him.

It was difficult to say what precisely made him so appealing. If he was tall and broad and muscular, so were many other gentlemen. And if combined with that enviable physique he had a swarthy complexion, and unruly black hair that tumbled over his forehead, and strong white teeth that flashed when he smiled—

One thing was certain. No man could be trusted who had such amused dark eyes. Amused dark eyes that were fixed on her. Augusta gave him the coolest of glances, and looked pointedly away.

Magda was performing introductions. "Elizabeth, allow me to present to you Conor Melchers. You must beware of him, *ma petite*, because his intentions are only of the most dishonorable nature, and he has no conscience whatsoever in matters of the heart. Conor, make your bow to Saint's duchess."

The amused dark eyes turned on Elizabeth. "Your Grace," Mr. Melchers said as he raised Elizabeth's hand to his lips.

Before Mr. Melchers could say more, as he doubtless would have done, and something very provocative at that, an interruption occurred. The crowd parted to allow passage to an elegant woman wrapped about in sapphire blue, on her golden curls a village hat made of straw, twist and leghorn. Her delicate features were perfection, her eyes the brightest blue. Trailing after her was a weary-looking maid. "One *does* meet all one's acquaintances in the Pump Room," said Augusta. "Lady Ysabella. What a surprise."

Nigel's Aunt Syb raised elegant brows. "I don't know why you should be surprised. Since we're both in Bath, we were bound to meet. Not that you *should* be here, Gus. Were you mine, I'd slap you black and blue."

Lady Augusta tightened her lips against an imprudent comeback. Elizabeth hid a smile. Lady Ysabella was neither so old as Mr. Slyte had painted her, nor half so ill. And Gus was like to become sick herself, from the swallowing of spleen.

In point of fact, Lady Syb was no more than fifteen years older than her nephew and also, but only when it suited her, in the best of health. She was also as irrepressible as a force of nature, and had been known to flatten anyone so unwise as to put themselves in her path, including the Prince of Wales and several statesmen.

Madame de Chavannes stood in her pathway at the moment. Lady Syb regarded her. "I'faith, Mouse, I never thought you had more hair than sense."

Magda dropped a pretty curtsy. "*Bonjour.* I am happy to see you, too, Lady Ysabella. I trust you are well?"

"Who said anything about being happy? If you don't cover up your chest, you'll be the one drinking tar water for an inflammation of the lungs. 'The sight of a beautiful bosom is as dangerous as that of a basilisk.' Abbe Boilleau. 1673."

Elizabeth was amused to see Magda fasten her cloak. Lady Ysabella's blue eyes moved to her. "You'll be Saint's little wife. Or not so little, are you? Since these two feather-heads between them haven't the wit to introduce us, I'll do it myself. Lady Ysabella Ravensdale. I was a countess last time I looked. Have you seen my nephew? He is playing least in sight. Hello, Conor. You should not be clasping Saint's bride like that. You will all join me at the Assembly Rooms this evening. Nigel shall escort me there. Come along, Throckmorton! We have much to do." With a weary expression, the maidservant followed her mistress through the crowd.

Elizabeth had quite forgotten that Mr. Melchers still held her hand. Hastily, she pulled it away. "Nigel," commented Gus, "is probably hiding under the bed."

"She will drag him out, you'll see! And now we are to go to the Assembly Rooms." Magda twinkled up at Conor Melchers. "You will join us. Lady Syb has said so."

Mr. Melchers smiled lazily. "Sweeting, did you ask me, I would accompany you to the gates of Hell itself."

Magda dimpled. "And it amused you, perhaps. Else you would fling me to the wolves, I think. Besides, 'twill not be so bad as all that!"

Conor raised a skeptical eyebrow. "And if it is, then what?"

Magda twinkled. "I shall owe you a forfeit."

"Then I shall look forward with great anticipation to

this evening when I may collect my winnings. Until then, ladies." He bowed and strolled away.

If this was the sort of gentleman Magda kept dangling at her slipper strings, Elizabeth could only be in awe. "I don't dance," she remarked.

Magda clapped her hands together. "Let me guess. Maman did not approve. Come along, Augusta! Lady Syb is not the only one with many things to do."

Chapter 12

"A very fulfilling union can be formed by a man and a woman who enjoy each other's company, and can provide comfort and support through both the happy and difficult times in life." —Lady Ratchett

The Duke of Charnwood returned to his home in a somber frame of mind, as well as perhaps a little bit under the influence of the grape, for the gentlemen had imbibed considerable refreshment during their conversation, which had left His Grace more puzzled than ever, and not at all certain that he wasn't a coxcomb. He was not so cup-shot, however, that he did not realize the absurdity of applying to Mr. Slyte for advice other than regarding the drape of a jacket, or the tying of a cravat. Better he had spoken with Lady Syb. Lord knew he might have to yet. Now there was a sobering thought.

Chislett opened the front door. "Welcome home, Your Grace."

Justin regarded his solemn butler. "You look almost human, Chislett. Has some other disaster struck? I hope you do not mean to tell me that we have another house-guest."

The butler's thin lips almost quivered. "I was not aware that you were expecting further visitors, Your Grace."

"I'm not." Justin allowed himself to be divested of hat and coat. "However, neither was I expecting the ones I already have. Nor am I particularly grateful for them. Is that piano music I hear?"

The butler inclined his head. "It is, Your Grace." Again that strange quiver of the lips. "The ladies are in the drawing room."

The ladies were up to some devilment, judging from Chislett's odd behavior. Justin mounted the stairs. Not only piano music issued from the drawing room, but also parrot squawks. Justin paused unseen on the threshold.

Gus sat at the pianoforte, her fingers on the ivory keys. Birdie fluttered on her perch. Elizabeth and Thornaby stood facing each other on the Moorfield carpet. The duchess wore a determined expression. Thornaby looked as if he wished himself elsewhere. Magda paced back and forth in front of the instrument, in her hands a small book.

"*Retardante*, Gus! A slower tempo, *s'il vous plaît*. We are not teaching Elizabeth a country dance." She applied to the book. "The motion of the arms if af effential, at leaft, as that of the legs, for an expreffive attitude; and both receive their juftnifs from the nature of the paffions they are meant to exprefs.' "

So enthralled was Lady Augusta that she struck a discord. "'The paffions'?" she echoed.

"The paffions." Magda brandished the book. "Mr. Gallini says so. 'The paffions are the fprings which muft actuate the machine, while a clofe observation of nature furnifhs the art of giving to thofe motions the grace of eafe and expertnefs. Anything that has the air of being forced, or improper, cannot fail of having a bad effect. A frivolous affected turn of the wrift is surely no grace.' "

"My machine isn't being actuated," remarked the duchess. "What has all this to do with the minuet?"

"We are coming to that." Magda paged through the treatise. " 'It should alfo be recommended to the dancers of the minuet ever to have an expreffion of the fort of gaiety and cheerfulness in the countenance, which will give it an amiable and even a noble franknefs.' You must not look too forward or pensife. 'Twould be displeafing. And you must avoid that bathfulnefs which arises from low breeding, wrong breeding, or no breeding at all."

Gus played a sprightly arpeggio. "*You* would know about that."

"This is all well and good," interrrupted Elizabeth. "But while I am being gay and cheerful and not bashful, what the Devil am I to be doing with my feet?"

"We shall get to that, *ma petite*. The dance is not about your feet, but rather your attitude, expression, the graceful motion of your arms." Gracefully, Madame de Chavannes moved hers. "One measure of determining whether a man is truly a gentleman is by his ability to dance with confidence, stand well, enter a room gracefully, move easily without calling attention to himself. Yes, Thornaby, we know you are not a gentleman, but you are all we have just now, and it is incumbent upon us all to make sacrifices for the general good. Elizabeth, you are expected to have on hand a repertoire of light conversation, with which to pass the time while you stand and watch. The minuet is a dance for one couple at a time."

"I have the standing part of it down pat, I think," said the duchess. "Why must I dance at all? This does not seem like a good idea."

The duke had stood easily for several moments without calling attention to himself. Now he demonstrated the gentlemanly quality of his spirit by strolling gracefully into the room. "Excellent question. Why *must* Elizabeth dance, pray?"

Gus glanced at her cousin and switched to a lively march. "Because Lady Syb says so. We are all required to attend her at the Assembly Rooms. Along with Conor Melchers. I am surprised that you encourage him, Magda. Melchers is a rakehell. St. Clair will not approve."

Magda fanned herself with the little book. "Then it is fortunate that I do not have to answer to St. Clair."

Elizabeth was tired of Lady Augusta's constant troublemaking, and shy of her husband, toward whom she had been acting with not the slightest modicum of dignity and grace. "You know so much about rakehells, do you, Gus?"

Augusta struck another discord. Magda laughed. "Children! Play nicely together. Conor will debauch no one in the Assembly Rooms."

Justin's own brief amusement had fled at the mention of Conor Melchers. His cousin had been quite correct when she said he did not approve. Indeed, so much did he disapprove that he had briefly lost his powers of speech. He was also now entirely sober. "*Melchers?* Good God, Magda. The man is—"

"My oldest friend, other than yourself." Magda twinkled. "You must not fear that Conor will make a scandal, Saint. At least not a scandal of the sort you so dislike."

The duke's reservations were not allayed by reassurances from this source. His cousin's eyes were on him, however, and he would not give her the satisfaction of seeing him react. "Lady Syb requires us to attend the Assembly Rooms, and so we are having a dancing lesson. I see. You may enjoy the Assembly Rooms, Elizabeth. Maman would not approve of them. Perhaps the lesson might progress faster if I take Thornaby's place." The valet cast him a grateful glance.

Magda waved a careless hand. "We will be glad to have you, Saint. Thornaby was the best that we could find. *Hélas*, he is a perfect stick."

The valet flushed. Elizabeth frowned. "Unfair, Magda. You are the one who has had us standing here while you amused yourself reading to us from your treatise of the dance. I daresay that if we ever got around to dancing, Thornaby would be considerably more graceful than I."

Thornaby glanced at her, startled. Elizabeth smiled. "Thank you for your patience, Thornaby. I fear we are a trial."

"*Mon Dieu!*" cried Magda. "I am very rude. Of course you are not a stick, Thornaby. Merely you do not know how to dance. I shall teach you. You will like it of all things."

Thornaby greeted this suggestion with a shudder. It was quite sufficient that he saw to his master's clothing, brushed and shaved and trimmed him, cleaned his combs and brushes, and miscellaneous other chores. To be inveigled into dancing into the drawing room was the outside of enough. On the other hand, as regarded a certain wager, it might prove to the valet's advantage were the duchess to learn to dance. With the duke, of course. Which meant Thornaby must remain in the drawing room to see the thing done properly.

Magda watched the play of emotions on the valet's face. "*Voilà!* You will not care for the minuet. Perhaps a country dance."

Thornaby brightened. He already knew several country dances. An animated discussion ensued, involving the Fandango, Greenwich Park, Greensleeves, and Yellow Lace. Lady Augusta struck up a lively tune on the piano. Thornaby demonstrated his ability at the Scotch reel. Birdie squawked and jiggled on her perch. Elizabeth watched with amusement.

His duchess was a lady, whether or not she could dance with confidence or move easily without calling attention to herself. "I do not know why you should think I compared you to a chamber pot," said Justin. "I wish you would explain."

Elizabeth wished someone would explain to her why it was so difficult to hold a conversation with her husband, even in this moment when he was fully clothed. Now she had reminded herself of how he looked when he wasn't. Her cheeks burned. "If not a chamber pot, precisely, still a distasteful duty. I do not care to be that, Your Grace."

Justin winced. He had indeed said "duty." "Pray forgive my poor choice of words. I only meant that I had allowed certain matters to go too long undealt with. I am not usually such a cod's head, Elizabeth."

Nor did Elizabeth care to be considered an undealt-with matter. She turned thoughtful eyes on her spouse. "I don't believe I have ever heard you called a cod's head before."

"I do not think I care to know what you *have* heard me called." Slow going, this courting of one's wife. Cautiously, Justin took her hand. "Maman doesn't approve of dancing. I distinctly remember you said so."

Neither of them wore gloves. St. Clair's hand was

warm on hers. Almost as warm as when he had touched her in the bedroom. One butterfly somersaulted in her belly, then another, and then an entire performing circus troop went tumbling heels over head.

Elizabeth swallowed. What had the duke just said to her? "You told me to disregard Maman, as I recall."

Justin would have liked to disregard the other members of his household. Alas, he could not, no matter how dazed the expression in his wife's gold-flecked eyes, or the feeling of her hand in his. Concentrate on the moment, he told himself, and stop thinking untimely thoughts. "The minuet consists of a fixed sequence of figures. It is not difficult to learn."

Elizabeth dragged her own mind out of the bedchamber. "For you, perhaps."

"For you as well, if you will allow me to instruct you. There is Augusta's dinner party to consider. It will seem odd if you do not dance." Justin raised his voice over the hubbub of laughter and music and parrot cackle to request a more sober tune. Gus struck a resounding chord. Thornaby raised his arms above his head and snapped his fingers and shouted, "Heuch!"

Magda clapped her hands. "Bravo! Now we shall observe Saint."

All eyes were upon them as the duke demonstrated to his bride the minuet, which consisted of a salute to the partner, a high step, and a balance, and a number of turns executed with graceful movements and steps. Or ideally executed. Justin rapidly discovered that Elizabeth had not overestimated her abilities at the dance. Augusta grinned. Birdie whistled. Magda shook her head.

Thornaby moaned. Her Grace was a dangerous woman. The valet had already spent considerable time removing bramble scratches from His Grace's boots with a combination of muriatic acid, alum, gum Arabic, spirit of lavender, and sour skimmed milk. Now he realized that he must stock up on pumice stone.

Lady Augusta picked up the tempo. Birdie unfurled her wings and clacked her beak and bobbed back and forth on her perch. Thornaby recalled a certain incident involving one of his master's boots, and moved cautiously away from the bird.

Elizabeth glanced at the parrot. "Birdie wants to dance, it seems. Oh, blast. I've stepped on your foot again. It is very difficult to think of so many things at once."

What Justin was thinking at that moment had nothing to do with the minuet. In her efforts at concentration, the duchess had taken to nibbling on her lip. 'Twas a remarkably provocative sight to a gentleman who had yet to enjoy his own wedding feast.

Lady Ratchett had been right. Dancing did cause one to grow overheated. Elizabeth was flushed, and her hair was coming unpinned. Justin thought he would like to see his bride in a state of even greater perspiration. Or perhaps he would not, because they were in the middle of the drawing room. Not that the duke had anything against perspiring in his drawing room, but not before an audience.

A *plié* on the left foot flat on the upbeat, rise to the ball of the foot on beat one, straighten both legs, heels close together. *Plié* on the right foot on beat two, rise to the ball of the left foot on beat three, straighten both legs, heels close together. Keep both legs straight, walk forward on the ball of the right foot, then left foot on beats four and five—Elizabeth doubted she would ever get it right. Perhaps it was the prospect of dancing at the Assembly Rooms that exhilarated her pulse.

How hard she concentrated. How solemn she looked, as if what she undertook was something a great deal more serious than a minuet. Perhaps to her it was. Justin was reminded that he had never properly courted Elizabeth, or written her poems or sent her flowers, taken her for carriage drives in the park, stood up with her at balls. Not that he could have done the latter, because she didn't dance. Yet he could have flattered her a little bit. Indeed, he still might flatter her. "You shall never persuade me that you have not danced before," he said, then, "Ouch."

So much for grace and cheerfulness. Impossible to turn her feet properly and control her movements when engaged in conversation, even when that conversation was dictated by the dance. Elizabeth said, "I may need a few more lessons, perhaps."

Justin thought he would be happy to give his wife any number of lessons. Perhaps she might like to learn the German waltz, in which the partners stood face-to-face, her hand on his shoulder, and his hand on her waist. Her very slender waist. Perhaps she might dance with him in her very sheer nightgown.

Lord. Did he not turn his thoughts in other directions, he would succumb to an attack of the passions on the spot. Justin glanced at their audience as he executed an elegant right-hand turn. Magda looked thoughtful. Thornaby looked anxious. Augusta looked her usual contrary self. The damned bird looked like an animated rainbow. He returned his attention to Elizabeth, who was staring at her feet.

That glimpse of Magda reminded the duke of Conor Melchers, who was also to be present in the Assembly Rooms. Justin must make it clear to his wife that Melchers was not the thing.

"You must be on your guard," he said, as the dance drew them together. "For once, Augusta does not exaggerate. Conor Melchers is a rogue, a scoundrel, the black sheep of his family. You will not associate with him."

Magda said she must not take Mr. Melchers seriously, and Justin said Elizabeth must not speak with him at all. Nigel said Charnwood was a curst cold fish; Augusta said Elizabeth would not wish to offend. Magda said the gentlemen were very well in their places, and nothing was more amusing than the game of hearts. Maman said Elizabeth was to obey her husband in all things, but beware of the revolting practices to which gentlemen were prone.

Successfully, Elizabeth completed a double-handed turn, and sank into a curtsy. Magda and even Thornaby clapped. Birdie cried, "Biscuit!" Augusta struck a triumphant chord.

This one thing she had done right. As for the rest, it was all very bewildering, and made a person wish, like Mr. Slyte, to hide beneath the bed.

Chapter 13

"Music often draws a person to mix with much company as she would otherwise avoid." —Lady Ratchett

The Upper Assembly Rooms at Bath were most elegant, consisting of a central anteroom, charmingly octagonal in shape, from whence visitors might proceed into the ballroom to the left, the tearoom to the right, or the cardroom straight ahead. No sooner did the Duke of Charnwood step through the front door than he was accosted by several of his acquaintances, one of whom wished to contemplate the possibility that the Czar might sign an alliance with England; and another of whom had recently visited Sydney Gardens, and had an adventure in the Labyrinth, as result of which he was now embarked on a course of the waters in search of a cure; while a third lamented the sort of people one encountered in such places, a sentiment with which Justin could not argue, since he was present only on the orders of Lady Syb. Lady Augusta took immediate advantage of her cousin's distraction to vanish into the

cardroom, which had a musician's gallery, four marble
fireplaces, and a fine chandelier, walls containing frames
for portraits, and most important, cloth-covered tables
where whist was being played. Within moments of her
arrival, Madame de Chavannes was surrounded by a
group of gentlemen with names such as Edouard, Achille,
and Baptiste. Elizabeth stood beside her and listened to
animated speculation about the difficulties involved in
landing an expeditionary force in small boats along the
English shoreline, a seven- or eight-hour passage which
demanded long nights and thereby entailed all the haz-
ards of winter weather, for invasion by sloops in calm
weather wouldn't be practical; but at all events it wasn't
likely that the French would embark upon such a pro-
ject this year. The rooms were crowded with the fashionable and unfashionable tonight, for entrance was
available to all who could afford the subscription, with
the exception of those who carried on any occupation
in the retail line of business, or the theatrical, or performed publicly.

Or were *known* to perform publicly. Madame de
Chavanes was clad dramatically tonight in red and white,
amazingly low-cut. She looked up as Conor Melchers
strolled into the room, looking irresistibly sinful in a
dark coat and tight breeches that clearly had no need of
padding to broaden his shoulders or false calves to improve the shape of his legs. Deftly, Magda extricated
herself from her admirers. "*Mon cher.* I thought perhaps
you would not come."

Her gown could hardly have been more revealing.
Mr. Melchers was amused. Not that this was unusual.
Mr. Melchers was frequently amused, if not by his own
foibles, then by those of his fellow man. Or fellow woman,
for Conor was partial to the ladies and their foibles, especially those foibles displayed in the boudoir.

Though he was not in a ladies' boudoir at the moment, Conor had been very recently, and might have been still: where some ladies wore dampened petticoats to make their gowns cling closer, Magda eschewed petticoats altogether, with a most provocative effect. "I could hardly resist so charming an invitation. You are plotting, sweeting. I remember that look."

Magda smiled and took his arm. "How well you know me, *mon ami.* I wish merely that you will do me a little favor, and talk to Justin's wife. 'Twill be no great inconvenience. She is a good girl."

Good girls did not especially appeal to Mr. Melchers. He could not recall the last time he had spoke with one. "Why should I do that?"

"For the novelty, perhaps?" Magda dimpled. "Or because you love me, if for nothing else?"

Conor's lazy gaze moved over her. "Unkind of you to remind me. You owe me a forfeit, as I recall."

"*Zut!* You cannot be bored already, for you have just walked in the door. Go amuse yourself with the duchess. She will not know what to make of you. If Charnwood is a saint, then you are the devil, *n'est-ce pas?*"

Mr. Melchers glanced at St. Clair's duchess, who was trying valiantly to keep Madame's émigré admirers entertained. "Surely you don't mean me to seduce the chit."

Magda twinkled. "I think that might be beyond even you, *mon chou.* No, I wish you to distract her merely while I seek out Grègoirè."

Conor was relieved that he wasn't required to embark upon a seduction. Not that he had anything against seduction, as countless numbers of ladies could attest, but he preferred that the business be his idea. Curious, that Magda thought Charnwood's duchess proof against him. Or perhaps she did not. "Very well. Be off about your intrigues."

"*Petite!*" Magda beckoned to the duchess. "You will remember Conor Melchers. He will take you on a grand tour of the Assembly Rooms. Do not fear his reputation, not that it is unfounded, but because he will treat you with the utmost propriety, unless you tell him otherwise!" With a merry chuckle, she disappeared into the crowd. Or came as close to disappearing as was possible in light of her lush person and marked absence of petticoat and stays.

Startled, Elizabeth stared at Mr. Melchers, at the silver threads in his dark hair, the world-weary lines around his lazy eyes and mouth. Here was definitely a gentleman with a love of dissipation. Were a lady to wish to do wrong, this would be the gentleman to do it with.

She was gaping at him as if he were some queer exhibit. Conor quirked a brow. "Do I have a smudge?"

St. Clair had said she should not speak with Mr. Melchers. St. Clair, however, was nowhere in sight. Elizabeth could hardly go wandering about by herself. Moreover, she had never before had the opportunity to speak with a rakehell. "I have just heard the strangest conversation. Perhaps you can tell me if England is in danger of invasion by a handful of Frenchmen in fishing boats."

"You have been listening to Magda's émigrés. They are all talk and little substance. Shall we take that tour of the rooms?"

Mr. Melchers had a very nice smile. A nice, lazy, warm, intimate smile. Elizabeth had been thrown into very deep waters. Hesitantly, she took his arm. "Have you known Magda for a long time, sir?"

Conor was surprised the girl didn't go running in the opposite direction, so wicked had Magda made him sound. Not that she had exaggerated. Conor was living proof of the odd circumstance that a gentleman might be rendered even more intriguing by the practice of sin.

"It certainly seems like a long time. Your husband and I are also old acquaintances. How is it that St. Clair does not accompany you? Never mind, I shall entertain you in his place. Allow me to point out the oddities. See that ancient gentleman in the Bath chair?" He proceeded to entertain his companion with gossip of a somewhat scurrilous, and highly amusing, nature. She knew, of course, that here was where Prince Bladud cured himself and his leprous pigs by plunging into a reed-grown spring. The same Prince Bladud whose statue stood watching over the Roman Pool. Perhaps the duchess had a fondness for Roman ruins? Mr. Melchers would be pleased to offer her his escort. Or perhaps it was not an appreciation of antiquities that had brought the duchess to Bath, but concern for her health. Not that she should persuade Mr. Melchers that she had a predisposition toward gout, or rheumatism, Cold Humors or Hypochondriacal Flatulence.

His manner was polished, his smile wicked, his physique superb. Elizabeth could only admire Magda's choice in gentlemen. Not that Mr. Melchers would qualify as a gentleman. "I am in excellent health, I assure you. Tell me, Mr. Melchers, how do the Assembly Rooms compare to the gates of Hell? You look startled. I have not quite so proper a way of thinking as you had expected, perhaps?"

A surprising sort of female, Saint's little duchess. And not so little, because she could almost look him in the eye. " 'Tis not as warm here, certainly. You will notice the construction of the room. Heat from the fireplaces rises to the ceiling and escapes through the upper windows. Tell me, Your Grace, why do you not dance?"

Mr. Melchers was smiling at her kindly, as if he had a real interest in her answer. Elizabeth looked through the doorway at the minuet that was under way. "I do not have a proper sense of timing, as several people can attest. If you wish to dance, I believe Lady Augusta is in the cardroom. She is a very good dancer, and would be more to your taste."

Leisurely, Conor contemplated Charnwood's duchess, her long nose and strong chin and gold-flecked eyes. Her hair was pulled back in flattering ringlets tonight, and the bodice of her gold silk gown surprisingly low-cut. "Duchess," he murmured, "you might be surprised by what suits my taste."

Lord, but his gaze was warm. Elizabeth now understood what made up a heated look. The sort of look that was almost like a caress as it moved over her lips, her chin, her—

Blast. She tugged at her neckline.

"Don't fuss," said Mr. Melchers. "You will only draw attention to yourself. Beside, Duchess, your bosom is very nice."

How easily Mr. Melchers spoke of bosoms. Elizabeth narrowed her eyes. "Are you trying to shock me?" she inquired.

His mocking gaze moved to her face. "Perhaps. Did I succeed?"

Oddly, he hadn't. "You are an authority on the subject of bosoms, I daresay, Mr. Melchers. Therefore, I am not shocked. All the same, I am not accustomed to going about half dressed."

Conor nodded to a passing acquaintance. The lady regarded Elizabeth with less than favor. Sweetly, the duchess smiled. *Point to her,* thought Conor. "As I am an expert, I must inform you that you are only a quarter naked at best. I am surprised that Saint approves of his wife wearing such a dress. Do I see Magda's fine hand in this, perhaps?"

It hadn't occurred to Elizabeth that her husband

might not approve of her bosom. He certainly didn't seem to mind when Magda put hers on view. "Saint has not seen me without my cloak. I doubt that he would notice my, ah, bodice anyway."

Conor doubted that Saint wouldn't. Idly he wondered what Magda was about. "You are fine as fivepence, Duchess. Anyone who failed to notice you must be either blind or dead." He escorted her into the tearoom, which featured a two-storied colonnade on its west end, in the upper section of which the musicians sat. Corinthian columns surrounded the room at that level. From the coved ceiling, three chandeliers hung. "You have not answered my question. If the minuet does not tempt you, perhaps some other sort of dance might better suit your taste."

Elizabeth didn't think that Mr. Melchers referred to the sort of dancing that was done in a ballroom. She tilted her head. "First bosoms, and now dancing. Are you trying to get up a flirtation with me, sir?"

Conor smiled at her astonishment. "You do not approve of flirtation, Your Grace?"

Certainly Maman did not approve of flirtation. This conversation would have already caused her to grope for her hartshorn. "I don't know. No one has ever flirted with me before." St. Clair didn't count. Elizabeth knew without asking that Mr. Melchers would never refer to bedding a lady as though it were a nasty chore.

Conor paused to study her. "How can that be? Young women are fed instructions on the fine art of reeling in a male along with their mother's milk. Perhaps you have been locked up in a convent. Allowed no contact with the cruder sex. Until St. Clair rode up on his white horse and spirited you away."

"What a lovely notion. A pity it is so far from the truth. So far as I can tell, dashing knights on horseback

live only in the pages of my abigail's romantic books.
What I was fed along with my mama's milk—which is a
figure of speech merely; Maman would not have been
so crude—was an entire manual on propriety. You will
have heard of propriety, Mr. Melchers, although I
doubt it is a matter you've considered for a single moment in all your life."

Despite her severe words, St. Clair's duchess was smiling. Nor had she removed her hand from his arm. It was
second nature for Conor to notice such things. "You
wound me, Your Grace. And you will I hope forgive me
if I point out that, though my character may admittedly
be less than perfect, I have not been so very impertinent as to make such personal comments as you have
just done. Which is not to say I *won't*, but I haven't yet."

She had indeed been most impertinent. Elizabeth
flushed. Then she caught the mocking expression on
Mr. Melcher's face, and called him a rude name. "Oh,
blast!" she added, when he laughed aloud. "Now I suppose I must apologize."

"Never apologize, Duchess, and never explain." Conor
was enjoying considerably more than he had expected
this effort to aid Magda in her scheme. "I provoked you
to it, after all. And as I had anticipated, you are even
lovelier when you let down your guard."

"Moonshine! I am nothing of the sort." Elizabeth was
also enjoying more than she could have ever anticipated
her first conversation with a rakehell. "In truth, I meant
no criticism. I admire you, I think. To be not bound about
by restraints must be a very fine thing."

"It depends on the circumstances of the binding.
There, I have made you smile. Next, you will laugh for
me. And then—" Perhaps Magda wouldn't owe him a
forfeit after all.

The man was definitely, deliberately, wicked. Elizabeth

made no doubt it was most improper in her to be amused. "You are most provocative, Mr. Melchers. Still, I do not think that you would force a lady to do other than she wished."

In truth, Conor hadn't come across a great number of ladies who *didn't* wish. "Do you fear for your virtue, Duchess? I can hardly debauch you in the midst of the tearoom." He looked lazily around. "Or perhaps I could. There is that large cloth-covered table against the wall. I could lure you under it, perhaps. No one would ever notice, providing we did not disturb the teapot."

As he had intended, Elizabeth laughed, a surprisingly infectious, carefree sound. "I remind you that I am a married woman, sir."

For someone who had never engaged before in flirtation, St. Clair's duchess was getting the hang of the thing quick enough. Mr. Melchers wondered what else he might teach her, and when. "Ah, but I would be a paltry sort of scoundrel, would I not, to be discouraged by the minor impediment of a spouse?"

Chapter 14

"No woman even in the warmest flush of youth ought to be prodigal of her charms." —Lady Ratchett

The Duke of Charnwood was not enjoying his excursion to the Assembly Rooms, which appeared to be populated with a great many people he didn't wish to meet. Although the duke might have argued with Lady Ysabella about some more important matter—not that he would have enjoyed it, and not that he was certain he would win—in this instance he had thought Elizabeth might enjoy the outing. Perhaps she did. He had not seen her since their arrival, for he had been busy with other things, such as assuring his acquaintances that nearly all the monarchs of Europe waited for an opportunity to renew their attack on France, and that the waters at Bath were known for their miraculous powers in the curing of consumption and rheumatism, barrenness and gout, although mercury was generally more efficacious in the treatment of the pox; and extricating his cousin from the cardroom, and suppressing a strong desire to shake her till the teeth rattled in her head.

She was not grateful. "You grow odiously overbearing, Saint, and something of a bore! I had a excellent good hand."

"You were going to lose the rubber," retorted Justin. "I saw your cards. If ever there was a pigeon ripe for the plucking, Gus, it is you. Do try and recall that you have very few feathers left in your nest!"

Augusta seethed and sputtered with frustration. Justin ignored her sulks. At least this evening his cousin had indulged in nothing more serious than whist. He then plucked Magda from the arm of a tall aristocratic-looking Frenchman and inexorably steered his companions into the ballroom.

The ballroom was twice as long as it was wide, with a beautiful coved ceiling from which hung five superb cut-glass chandeliers. Splendid gilt-framed looking glasses placed at each end of the room brilliantly reflected more Corinthian columns, ornate swags, and a Vitruvian scroll. A lofty semicircular recess housed the musicians: a harp, four violins, one violoncello, two clarinets, and a tambourine. Justin escorted his reluctant companions to the three front benches reserved for ladies of precedence at the upper end of the room, where Lady Ysabella laughed as Conor Melchers murmured something in her ear.

Conor Melchers, damn the man. If Justin could tolerate rubbing shoulders with parvenus and cits, Melchers was something else again. The man had already made a number of scandals, although this had no noticeably adverse effect upon his dealings with the opposite sex, a surprisingly large number of whom were apparently attracted to lazy-looking gentlemen with shocking reputations. Now he made Lady Syb laugh with some improper sally, a circumstance that put Justin further out of charity with his hostess. "Hallo, Saint," said Lady Ysabella. "Nigel is dancing with your wife."

Augusta settled on a chair. "Brave lad," she said.

"*Zut!*" remarked Magda. "What an ungracious attitude. And after all our efforts. You must have lost at cards."

The ladies were in looks this evening, Lady Syb in a blue gown trimmed with bands of satin, roses, and rouleaux; on her golden curls a turban made of matching satin, fringed with gold. Magda wore her shocking red and white. Gus was more than passably pretty in a sea green gown that added color to her eyes. Both those ladies had not only spent the afternoon teaching the duchess dance steps but had also taken a hand in her dressing. The duke, who was neither blind nor dead, would likely have an apoplexy at sight of his wife's low-cut bodice, which was perhaps their intent.

Justin caught his first glimpse of his duchess as Nigel escorted her off the dance floor. He blanched. Any lower, and her bodice would reveal the top of her nipples. He hoped she would not bend over. And then he hoped she would. "Good God," he said.

"I thought you would not like it," Mr. Melchers remarked. "You may blame Magda, of course."

Magda twinkled. "You are a dull stick, Saint. Bosoms are all the rage. *Mais non*, you must not abuse me in front of all these people. Recall that yours is a great romance."

Perhaps instead of Augusta he would shake Magda till the teeth rattled in her head. Or better yet his wife. He had thought he could trust Elizabeth, at least, to behave with good sense. Clearly he had been mistaken.

And mistaken as well in following Nigel's advice (based on that gentleman's experience with his sisters) about leaving the ladies wanting more, about which he had been doubtful, because he had seen no indication that Elizabeth wanted anything from him at all.

"Here is our duchess, safe and sound," said Nigel, as he returned from the dance floor. "Although I do think someone might have warned me it was her first dance. No, don't apologize again. 'Twas only a small toe. Now she is going to assure you that no one's ate your bird, Aunt Syb."

"I do not know why anyone would *wish* to eat her. She is old and doubtless very tough." Lady Ysabella fluttered her jewel-inlaid fan, and cast Mr. Melchers a languishing glance. "Alas, to lose the succulence of youth is the sad fate of all things."

Conor languished right back at her. "Ah, but age is the best teacher of youth. If you will pretend to be old, Lady Ysabella, I will pretend to be a lad."

Lady Augusta snorted at this nonsense. "That bird is also very spoiled. Elizabeth had the creature at the breakfast table, and sleeps with her at night."

Came a brief pause in the conversation while everyone contemplated the duchess's sleeping arrangements, and Justin pasted an impassive expression on his face. "Actually," remarked Elizabeth, "Birdie sleeps with one of the maids. I was remarking to Nigel how well Augusta looks tonight."

"That's when she stepped on me," offered Nigel. "I was so struck by the notion of Gus looking less than waspish that I failed to pay attention to my feet."

"Shame on you. Gus *does* look very well. You will dance with her," said Lady Syb. Neither Nigel nor Augusta appeared particularly enthusiastic about this decree.

"Conor, you may partner Magda. Saint, fetch me some tea. You will indulge me in this, all of you. I wish to speak privately with Saint's bride."

No one argued with Lady Ysabella, particularly no one who figured prominently in her will. Therefore, Nigel merely bowed. Gingerly, Gus took his arm. With as much enthusiasm as if they went to meet Madame Guillotine, they stepped onto the dance floor. Magda and Mr. Melchers followed suit, albeit with considerably less gloom. St. Clair went off to fetch some tea.

Elizabeth gazed after them. Though Gus looked well this evening, Nigel outshone her in a green coat and kerseymere smallclothes, frilled shirt, and lace ruffles, waistcoat of pale pink silk with an overall pattern in rose, lace cravat tied in a design of his own devising, with ends floating free, and fastened by a diamond pin. "Nigel and Augusta make a handsome couple, do they not?"

Lady Ysabella patted the seat beside her. "That horse is troubled with corns. Nigel can't afford her, my dear. Do sit down, before I get a crick in my neck from gawking up at you." As Elizabeth settled on a chair, Lady Syb gazed out over the crowd. "Bath is overrun with all sorts of rabble. 'Tis what makes the city interesting. Hopeful mamas bring their daughters to public places like this in search of a husband. You already have one, lucky girl. Look at poor Gus, beyond her last prayers. I am almost tempted to take her in hand."

Poor Gus, indeed, in that case. Lady Ysabella had a very different view of Bath than did Maman. Probably Lady Syb had very different views on almost everything. Elizabeth watched the dancers and wondered what it would have been like to be raised by Nigel's aunt. "Lady Augusta dances well," she remarked.

All manner of emotions could be wordlessly conveyed

by the skillful manipulation of a fan. Lady Ysabella snapped hers shut. "Gus can do anything well, if she wishes. Unfortunately, she does not often wish. Let us return to you. It is my contention that all marriages would be better arranged by the Lord Chancellor than by the parties involved."

Did Lady Syb think her unworthy of Charnwood? Elizabeth felt cross. "Are *you* now going to tell me how I must go on?"

Lady Syb raised her eyebrows. "Should I?"

"If you must," muttered Elizabeth. "Everyone seems determined to preach and prose at me as if I were the greenest girl."

"If the shoe pinches," murmured Lady Syb. "One should never give advice to those who want it. Since you clearly do not want it, probably I shall. Unlike those other prosy people, however, I know to come in from the rain. Let me say merely that I sense a certain want of domestic comfort between you and St. Clair."

Was she never to live down that blasted bloody nose? "It was an accident. I assure you that I am not normally prone to violence."

"Pish tush!" Lady Ysabella waved a dismissive hand. "We are all prone to violence, given the right circumstance. Henry IV had during his lifetime some fifty-six mistresses, three of whom had been nuns. Smile at your husband, my dear! It will make a much better appearance to the world."

Elizabeth puzzled over these strange statements. Was she to think the duke kept mistresses in the double digits? Or was she to be relieved that he had only one? *Did* he have a mistress, damn and blast the man?

Not surprisingly, these speculations made her even more cross. Elizabeth reminded herself that she was a duchess, and therefore might behave like one. "I do not care to discuss St. Clair. Nigel calls you Aunt Syb. Is that another of his nicknames?"

"Thrust and parry." Lady Ysabella opened her fan. "Nigel has called me Syb ever since he was an infant and couldn't pronounce my name. He was a dreadful scamp. Still is, for that matter. I quite dote on him."

Elizabeth thought that Mr. Slyte also doted on his aunt, for all he said to the contrary. People, she decided, were altogether strange. Nigel bemoaned his Aunt Syb's whimsies and doted on her at the same time. St. Clair lamented Magda's arrival, yet made no move to oust her from his house.

"Is it true that Birdie has had her portrait painted?" she asked.

Gracefully, Lady Ysabella accepted this change of subject. She was still speaking of the macaw's colorful history when Nigel returned from the dance floor. "What have you done with Augusta, you scamp?"

"A hornet remains a hornet, no matter what you wrap around it," Nigel retorted, as the duke returned with Lady Ysabella's tea. "That female is beyond aggravating, Aunt Syb. I left her speaking with Melchers. Perhaps she'll persuade him to stake her to a game."

"Don't look so bloodthirsty, Saint," Lady Syb scolded, while Elizabeth reflected that Augusta was considerably less particular about whom she rubbed elbows with when it came to playing cards. "Gus is hardly in his style. Go fetch Conor to me, Nigel. I wish him to entertain me with scandalous gossip about our mutual acquaintances. Then you will dance with Magda. Saint, 'tis time for you to pay some attention to your wife."

The duke presented Lady Ysabella with her tea. She patted his cheek, and drew him closer to speak softly in his ear. Nigel winked at Elizabeth. "Saint ain't really that stiff-rumped, not underneath. He came into the title so young he had to act top-lofty to be taken seriously, and he's got in the habit of it now. You'll do us all a favor if you can persuade him there is more to life than duty and responsibility. *I've* certainly tried, but no one takes me seriously."

Elizabeth glanced at her husband's shuttered, aloof expression. He would dislike being talked about like this, almost as much as he appeared to dislike what Lady Syb was murmuring to him. "I don't think you want anyone to take you seriously, Mr. Slyte."

"Clever, Duchess. I beg you will keep my secret. 'Twould be most embarrassing were word to get out." Nigel glanced at his aunt. Energetically, she wielded her fan. "I'm going!" he said, and went.

The duke felt as if he were still in the schoolroom. So strong a peal had Lady Syb rung over him that his ears still burned. She poked him with her fan. He approached his wife and bowed. Prettily, Elizabeth curtsied, but didn't meet his eye.

Why the devil wouldn't she look at him? Must he stand on his head? Justin bit back his temper and led her out onto the floor. It was hardly Elizabeth's fault that Lady Syb had seen fit to read him a scold.

Nor was it her fault she wore that damned dress. He recognized Magda's work. Then he glanced at his wife's neckline—though he had tried very hard not to—and wondered how her nipples would look rouged. Not that he had ever seen her nipples. Perhaps they were so pink and perky that they didn't need rouge. Perhaps if they weren't rouged, she would let him rouge them for her. The duke gritted his teeth.

If his drawing room was hardly a fit setting for such thoughts, the Assembly Rooms were a hundred times worse. Justin searched for something to converse about other than nipples, rouged or no. He could hardly tell Elizabeth that he wished she would not display to the world charms that he had not yet uncovered for himself. She would be startled by this dog-in-the-manger attitude. Justin was startled by it himself. Even in his youth he had not been bit by the green-eyed monster. Perhaps this uncharacteristic jaundice was due to the frustration attendant upon his failure to bed his bride. 'Twas well known that prolonged abstinence was unhealthy for a man.

There could be no other reason for his surliness. Justin had no time for the gentler emotions. His first marriage had been made for love, or what he thought was love at the time, and never had he been guilty of a more ill-considered act. He said, "I have not seen that dress before."

Elizabeth was gratified. St. Clair had noticed what she wore. However, he did not seem to particularly appreciate the garment, because he was glowering at her. It seemed unfair, that glower; if the duke had a mistress, he would most likely have seen her in costumes more shocking than this.

Did St. Clair have a mistress? According to Maman, most men, if not denied it, would demand sex every day. The duke did not seem to be suffering from a lack of marital privilege. Or perhaps that lack was what caused him to look so very stern.

'Twas all beyond her understanding. "Thank you," Elizabeth murmured, and concentrated on the movements of the dance.

So much for doing the pretty. Justin had thought that Elizabeth might be pleased by his comment on her dress, might even favor him with one of her smiles. Instead, she displayed no gratitude whatsoever. Nor did she seem the least bit embarrassed by that damned neck-line.

Already she grew wise in the ways of the world. Justin would not have it. If anyone were to rip away the veils of his bride's innocence, it would be Justin himself.

He could hardly do so in the middle of the Assembly Rooms, however. He must be cool and self-controlled. "I understand that you spent some time in conversation with Melchers," he said, as he led her in a turn. "His friendship with Magda is to be regretted. Apparently I didn't make it clear that I do not consider that man fit to associate with my wife." Alas, the duke was not his usual self just then, else he would have realized that mention of his former spouse in this particular moment was perhaps not wise.

First he ignored her, then he glowered, now he scolded. Elizabeth had had more than she could bear. "*Which* wife might that be?" she icily inquired.

Chapter 15

*"A gentleman's right to chastise his wife
is indisputable."* —Lady Ratchett

The fire was burning, the candles lit, robe and slippers in their place. The dressing room was altogether cheerful, until the duke arrived. One glance at that irate visage was sufficient to alert Thornaby that the duchess learning to dance hadn't achieved the result he'd hoped. Discreetly, he glanced at the ducal shoes, and sighed. Definitely he must invest in pumice stone. Perhaps treacle and ivory black, to boot. He smiled at his unintentional witticism. "To boot," indeed.

The duke was annoyed to see his valet cheerful in his presence. "What the Devil's so humorous?" he snapped.

"Nothing at all, Your Grace." Thornaby didn't think St. Clair would find any humor in the condition of his shoes. St. Clair didn't appear in a frame of mind to find humor in much of anything, which didn't bode well for a certain wager. Thornaby helped his master out of his coat.

"Damned right," muttered Justin, although he would have rather argued. However, it would be very shabby in him to pick a quarrel with his valet, because Thornaby wouldn't fight back. Such familiarity was opposed to all the valet's notions of what was proper and what was not. Did a note of censure pass his lips, the man would probably go out and hang himself.

Justin deserved more than a note of censure. He was behaving very badly. Lady Syb had said so, graphically. "You are as busy as the devil in a high wind, Thornaby. Stop fussing before I box your ears."

Thornaby had indeed been fussing, rather as if he were a trainer preparing his boxer to step into the ring. He doubted the duke would appreciate the analogy. At least he had managed to wrestle St. Clair's jacket off him, his waistcoat and cravat.

Thornaby got no further. Came a noise from the next room. The duke scowled all the harder and strode toward the door.

The doorknob turned beneath his hand, but the door refused to open. He pushed at it. Still the portal remained firmly closed. If the duke had previously been angry, he was livid now. "Thornaby, this door is locked," he said.

Thornaby tried the handle. "It seems to be, Your Grace. Perhaps if you were to knock?"

Justin would be damned if he knocked at the door of his own bedroom. "Do I have a key to that door, Thornaby?"

Thornaby wondered who was the biggest pig widgeon, the duchess or the duke. "I believe the key is in the bedroom, Your Grace."

Of course the key was in the bedroom, else the duchess would not have been able to lock him out. Justin put his shoulder to the door, and shoved. It was a heavy door, and did not budge an inch. "Bring me my pistols, Thornaby."

Thornaby's question was answered. The duke was the biggest dunderhead. The duchess had only locked the bedroom door, which though not particularly intelligent of her, was hardly a capital offense. He cleared his throat. "Perhaps you might wish to reconsider, Your Grace."

"What I wish to do is throttle someone, and *you* are close to hand." Justin bared his teeth. "The pistols, and be quick about it, man!"

Thornaby did not wish to be throttled. He fetched the weapons out of the drawer where they resided, and opened the brass-bound mahogany case. On the green baize lining lay a pair of very fine flintlock dueling pistols with beautifully executed gold inlay on the blued locks, elegant French-style cocks, and browned Damascus barrels. The priming pans and touch holes were also covered in gold. Since the pistols had been made by Joe Manton, they also featured such innovations as hydraulic barrel testers, fast-firing recessed birches, and trigger springs.

Expertly, Justin dealt with powder, ball, and flint. He raised a pistol and aimed it at the door. "Oh, Your Grace!" moaned Thornaby.

The duke scowled at his valet. "Swoon and you're dismissed. Without a reference!"

Thornaby didn't swoon. Nor did he tell his master that he was behaving like a loony, though that was surely what he thought. A valet must have quiet unobtrusive manners, and employ delicacy when speaking of the gentleman whom he served.

The duke walked toward the closed portal. "Elizabeth! Stand away from the door."

A voice responded from the bedroom. "What?"

Justin sighted down the barrel of his pistol. "Stand away from the door, Elizabeth. Either that or open it. If you do not open it by the count of three, I am going to shoot off the lock. One. Two—"

The door opened. Elizabeth still wore her evening gown. Daphne had managed to accomplish even less than Thornaby in the matter of disrobing, due to no lack of maidly ability but because her mistress wouldn't cease fidgeting. Elizabeth stood still now. So did Daphne. The duchess's face was pale.

Justin walked into the bedroom. "How *dare* you lock the door against your husband?" he inquired.

Lock the door? Elizabeth blinked. Perhaps the duke was mad. 'Twould explain many things. If only someone had warned her that her bridegroom was prone to go off in odd humors. "The door wasn't locked. I dislike locked doors. Perhaps it was merely stuck instead." And perhaps it hadn't been, and St. Clair merely wished an excuse to wave that gun around.

Had the door been merely stuck, Justin was making a jack pudding of himself. The realization didn't improve his temper. "Where *is* the key, madam?" he inquired. Daphne scurried to fetch the key from the mantelpiece, and presented it to him. He took it from her and gestured with the pistol. "You. Leave."

Abandon the mistress? Daphne almost refused. Then she contemplated the duke's half-buttoned shirt and skin-tight breeches, his disheveled hair and the fire in his eye, and recalled the wager yet to be won. The abigail curtsied and hastily departed, her thoughts full of sultans and harems, and the odd fact that the concubine selected for the evening entered the sultan's bedchamber and crawled under the covers from the foot of the bed.

The duke frowned at his duchess, who still wore that

accursed gown. He placed the key in his pocket and slammed shut the door to the dressing room. "Now you will tell me, madam, why I shouldn't mind that Conor Melchers flirts with you."

One should remain calm when faced with a madman, Elizabeth told herself. Not that she had ever met a madman before, but St. Clair must surely qualify. "Why do you think Mr. Melchers was flirting with me?" she asked.

"Because he flirts with everyone!" snapped Justin. "The man is a curst menace. Look at Lady Syb!"

Elizabeth was briefly distracted. "Lady Syb?"

Justin was also distracted. Elizabeth was nibbling on her lip. The bedroom was warm and welcoming. Candles blazed on the mantelpiece. A fire burned in the hearth. The counterpane was turned back as if inviting him into the great mahogany bed. He looked from the bed back to his wife, who was staring at him as if he were a madman. "Is that pistol loaded?" she inquired.

Justin realized he was still holding the pistol, and set it down on the writing desk. Lady Syb had been right to scold him. He had lost control of both his temper and his emotions. "Turn around!"

Elizabeth looked startled, but obeyed. Justin began unfastening her gown. How could he have ever thought her but passably pretty? Half the bucks in Bath had been tripping over their shoelaces for a glimpse of her smile tonight. Or, rather, her cleavage. "I suppose I needn't ask how you came by that damned gown."

His hands were on her shoulders, sliding under her hair. Elizabeth clutched the gown to her bosom, and strove for nonchalance. "Do you dislike it? Magda vowed it was quite the thing."

Justin was gratified to hear her voice squeak. She was not entirely indifferent to him, then. "I dislike you making a display of yourself," he said, as he pushed the gown from her shoulders. And lovely shoulders they were. He wished Elizabeth would let go of that gown she was clutching for dear life.

If he did not wish her to make a display of herself, why was he taking off her dress? There was no doubt about it. He *was* taking off her dress. Elizabeth cleared her throat. "It seems to have grown quite warm in here," she said.

His fingers slid over her bare shoulders, paused to massage her neck. She was tight as a drum. Naturally she was tight; she was still untouched. Justin bit his own lip in an attempt at self-control. A hair shirt might have been more effective. Mortification of the flesh. The flesh, however, didn't want to be mortified. Justin removed his hand from his wife's soft skin and forced himself into thoughts of sackcloth and ashes and beds of nails.

He was staring at her. She could feel it, even though her back was turned. Her skin prickled where he'd touched it. Elizabeth's cheeks flamed.

Of course she was embarrassed. He was somewhat so himself. Gently, Justin turned Elizabeth to face him. His hands moved over her bare shoulders. She tensed and stared at him wide-eyed.

How deft were St. Clair's fingers, how skilled. How many gowns had he thus unfastened, Elizabeth wondered, as she clutched her own gown to her chest. Merely thinking about sex was sinful, according to Maman. Elizabeth was a sinner then, because she could not stop herself from thinking about matters conjugal. Perhaps the duke would kiss her now. How disconcerting to be standing half undressed in the middle of the bedroom wondering what would happen next.

Her skin was smooth and silky, her big brown eyes opened wide. She looked frightened as a fawn, and good enough to eat. What had they been talking about? Ah, that damned dress. Justin unclasped her fingers from the material, and let it fall to the floor. "For Magda to make a vulgar display of herself is one thing. You, however, are my wife."

Elizabeth was confused. If he was still talking about that blasted dress, she had thought it vulgar herself. But if he was talking about the exhibition she currently made, standing in the bedroom with her dress down around her ankles, it had not been *her* idea to take off her gown. Not that she was any more uncovered than she had been previously, because she still wore her petticoat and stays and especially her chemise. According to Maman, the chemise should be considered to be the sign of a lady's delicacy, a pledge of honor to shelter her from the gaze of unhallowed eyes. Blast Maman, anyway. And blast St. Clair. "Just why *did* you marry me?" she asked.

Justin contemplated his wife's shapely body, and wondered why so slender a damsel felt the need of wearing stays. Maman's influence, no doubt. He wondered also how he was to get her out of those stays without scaring her witless. Elizabeth was a maiden with delicate sensibilities, and therefore must be gently treated, lest he give her an eternal disgust of the marriage bed, which would be a very great pity, because he intended to spend a great deal of time in that bed with her, and not merely for the purpose of setting up his nursery.

Why had he married her? The question was impertinent, irrelevant, and unanswerable. Justin shrugged. "I do not immediately perceive what that has to do with anything. 'Tis not something you need to concern yourself about."

Elizabeth stepped away from him. "I suppose I am also not to concern myself that you and Magda eloped to Gretna Green."

Justin reminded himself to strangle his cousin. "I fail to see what that signifies. We were young and foolish. I would not marry for love again." He realized from his bride's expression that this had not been a wise choice of words. "You refine too much upon it, Elizabeth. People of our class wed for social advancement, security, wealth. You know that."

She had married for social advancement—or rather, Maman had—and St. Clair had married for wealth. 'Twas not unusual. Men of stature with dwindling fortunes frequently sought to revive their estates by marrying women of fortune, even women of lower social rank. Not that Elizabeth had seen any indication that St. Clair's fortunes dwindled. And not that this was the answer she had wished to hear. "Fiddlestick!" she said.

A good biddable girl with a proper way of thinking, Justin reminded himself. He had been promised a comfortable little wife. In this particular moment his good, biddable wife was glaring at him as though she wished to turn him to stone. Perhaps this was an instance where action would prove more effective than words. He scooped her up in his arms and carried her to the bed. Elizabeth gasped, and beat at him with her fists.

'Twas to no avail. St. Clair was much the stronger. He dumped his bride on the pillows and held her down while he went work on the corset strings. The corset was quickly discarded, along with her petticoat, leaving only her chemise. Elizabeth did not wish to give up her chemise. He caught her hands before she could box his ears.

Justin paused to calm himself. He was not displaying a great deal of finesse. Indeed, he was displaying none at all. Nor was he like to, if Elizabeth didn't stop writhing about on the bed.

Her cheeks were flushed, her bosom heaved. Her

hair was all a-tangle on the pillow. She looked lusciously abandoned, save for her expression, which was mutinous. "My dear," said Justin. "I do not wish us to live like cats and dogs."

Not? Then what the devil was he doing with mistresses and ex-wives and cousins all over the place? The duke wasn't bored now, at any rate. His expression was not toplofty, nor his countenance stern. Instead, he looked almost boyish, with his hair tousled, and his shirt unbuttoned, revealing his bare chest. It was most unfair of him to tempt her so.

Yet, why should he not tempt her? Were they not man and wife? Hard to remain coherent when so close to him. "You are squashing me. *Do* you have a mistress?" Elizabeth asked.

Justin was so startled he released her. Elizabeth grabbed the counterpane and scrambled off the bed. Justin propped himself up on one elbow. "*What* did you just ask me?"

Now that she had escaped the bed, she wished she were back in it. St. Clair was the most disturbing man. Elizabeth wrapped herself in the counterpane. "I asked if you had a mistress. An inamorata. A *petite amie.* You must know the meaning of the terms."

Of course Justin knew the meaning of the terms. He didn't think, however, that his wife should. Nor did he know how to answer her question, because naturally he had a mistress, though he hadn't thought of her in a surprisingly long time. "I'm shocked that you would ask me such a question. Why *did* you ask me that, Elizabeth?"

She had her answer. He had not denied the accusation. Though it was no more than she expected, her heart sank down to her toes. "Lady Ysabella made a reference to Henry IV. I wasn't sure if she was trying to tell me something or not."

Elizabeth wasn't to bother him with nonsensical notions. Her mama had said so. Elizabeth was supposed to be the sunny-tempered epitome of good sense. Not that Justin was demonstrating much good sense himself, or a sunny temper. He leaned back on the pillows. "Ah, the fifty-six mistresses. You may make yourself easy on that head. Come here, Elizabeth. I promise you I have never debauched a nun."

Nor was he going to debauch her. Elizabeth was no longer in the mood. Instead of approaching the bed, she retreated to the fireplace, and picked up a poker. "I don't think so."

How the Devil had things come to this pass? Justin supposed he could hardly blame his bride for arming herself with a fireplace poker when he had threatened her with a gun. He could disarm her easily enough, but what then? Chase her around the room yelling "Stop! Stay! Lie down! Roll over!" as if she were a hound? "I cannot do this," he said, and got up off the bed.

Elizabeth had been prepared to defend her virtue, or *pretend* to defend her virtue, which even she realized was a matter of cutting off her nose to be revenged of her face. Now she stared at her husband. He picked up his dueling pistol. That stern expression had returned.

He reached into his pocket, and pulled out the door key. Elizabeth lowered the poker. "Are you going to lock me in?"

Where did the girl get her nonsensical notions? Justin frowned. "Why should I do that?" She flushed, and looked at the floor.

Maman had a great deal for which to answer. Perhaps Justin would throttle *her*. He tossed Elizabeth the key. In catching it, she dropped the coverlet. Quickly, she snatched it up, her cheeks aflame.

She was such an innocent. He would have her remain

so. Instead of allowing reprobates to flirt with her and gaze at her bosom. No question but that Conor Melchers had gazed at her bosom. Only a eunuch would have failed to gaze at her bosom, and Melchers was anything but a eunuch. 'Twould be a cold day in the nether regions before Melchers gaped at her bosom again, had Justin anything to do with the matter. "Melchers is a rakehell. A man of convenient morals. A libertine. I trust I have made myself clear. We will not speak of this again."

Elizabeth understood that her husband had got on his high ropes, and also perhaps that he had got the cart before the horse. She thrust out her chin.

Lord, she was a lovely creature. Justin turned on his heel and walked out of the room. Firmly, he closed the door.

"Damnation!" said the duchess, and sank down on the footstool. A certain want of domestic comfort, indeed.

Chapter 16

"A cut is only excusable when a gentleman persists in bowing whose acquaintance a lady does not wish to keep up."
—Lady Ratchett

It was clear to everyone from Chislett to the boot boy that everything was not *le couleur de rose* between the Duke of Charnwood and his bride. Queer enough that St. Clair and his duchess had as yet failed to share the ducal bed; now it appeared they could scarce bear to be in the same room. Therefore, when Madame de Chavannes suggested a country outing, no one was especially surprised that St. Clair excused himself on the pretext of having urgent business elsewhere. "Spoilsport!" murmured Magda. "*Alors*, we will leave Saint to his sulks. And we shall contrive to be merry without him, *enfin!*" Lady Augusta also begged off, saying that she had an entertainment to plan out, and would do it much better if she weren't obliged to rub shoulders with *canaille*. Therefore, it was only Elizabeth and a couple of stalwart footmen who accompanied Magda on her outing, which wasn't precisely into the country, as she had suggested, but to a country fair. "I only stretched the truth a little bit, *ma petite*," she said, in response to Elizabeth's startled look.

The day was cloudy and overcast, the weather cool. The ladies were clad appropriately for their adventure, the duchess in a white muslin gown with a lace collar, pale purple pelisse with gold cord and gray fur trim, a matching bonnet with pink ribbons and roses, and half boots. Madame de Chavannes was less flamboyant than usual in a gown of chintz with long sleeves and a narrow flounce, a red shawl with a Greek pattern, a hat modeled on a Greek helmet, and high red morocco shoes. For someone who had fled the guillotine with only the clothes on her back, Magda was surprisingly well-dressed. "Gus says you are a foreign agent," Elizabeth remarked.

"*Vraiment?*" Magda dimpled. "Gus would see me burned for high treason just to amuse herself."

True, Lady Augusta was of perverse nature. Still, Elizabeth was not convinced. She looked at the people pressed around them, traders offering fabrics and trimmings and countless other products, merrymakers and pickpockets and thieves. The air smelled of animals and food cooking and unwashed flesh. "You cannot deny that you have friends among the émigrés. There might even be French spies in this crowd."

Magda counted on it. "*Zut!* You grow as suspicious as Gus. If there are Frenchmen among us, what of it? The émigrés gather together to lament their exile and curse the Republicans in Paris and do little else. Furthermore, I am not French."

Neither fish, fowl, nor good red herring. Elizabeth wondered exactly what Magda was, and her reasons for coming to the fair. Maman had not approved of fairs, which she condemned as gatherings of loose, idle, disorderly people where morals could be corrupted in a trice.

Corrupt or no, the crowd was merry. Hucksters and musicians strolled about. Elizabeth saw acrobats and rope dancers, equestrian performers, freak shows, and gambling tents. Had Gus known of the gambling tents, she would have overcome her fastidiousness quickly enough. Drum and fifes, pictorial handbills and banners advertised a puppet show. Elizabeth was staring entranced at a tightrope walker when beside her Magda said, "*Mon Dieu!* I am astonished. Conor is here also, *ma petite.*"

That Magda was the least bit astonished, Elizabeth took leave to doubt. She frowned. Magda twinkled. "Bonaparte is busy in Cairo executing rebels and dining in restaurants opened by the city's French citizens for the soldiers in their midst."

What had Bonaparte to do with anything? Elizabeth greeted the newcomer skeptically. With the air of a conjurer performing a magic trick, he presented the ladies with apples purchased from a fruit stall. Magda laughed and bit into her apple. Juice trickled down her chin. She wiped it away with a careless glove.

The crowd was thick about them, the air filled with noise. They paused to watch a dancing horse, a conjurer, and a puppet show, which incorporated some senseless dialogue between Punchinello and the Devil, and caused Magda to remark that Napoleon had even poisoned the dogs in Cairo because the beasts sounded a warning whenever French soldiers approached.

A blare of trumpets sounded. Costumed actors marched about on the balcony of the strolling players' booth, where a placard announced a performance of the farce, *The Whore of Babylon, the Devil, and the Pope.* Magda led the way inside the structure, which was built of stout wooden boards, and had two galleries in addition to the boxes and pit.

The farce was most amusing, and dealt irreverently with witches, necromancy, and regicide, the Papist church being the whore of Babylon, and the pope the Antichrist. Elizabeth forgot about her troubles for upward of a half hour.

The performance ended. Elizabeth and Mr. Melchers emerged from the players' booth to find that the weather had turned inclement, Magda and the footmen nowhere in sight. They had gone only a short distance when thunder crackled and rain began to fall. Said the duchess, "Damn and blast!"

"This way," said Conor, and took her arm. The crowd pressed close around them, some amused by the sudden soaking, and others less so. Animals milled, people shouted. A bedraggled harlequin tripped and fell flat in the mud. With a firm grip on her arm, Conor drew Elizabeth after him, using his body to shelter her from the worst shoving of the crowd.

What the devil was Magda playing at, leaving them alone like this? Though she had escaped Madame Guillotine, Conor thought he might have her head himself. There was no doubt as to how St. Clair would react to this tête-à-tête. And a tête-à-tête it would be, were that cart where he remembered. Not for any number of angry husbands would Conor get soaked to the bone.

Conor's memory did not fail him. Before them loomed a wooden caravan wagon with a high arching roof and door at the back, a contraption that would be drawn by a horse or mule, the driver perched in front on an outdoor seat. Neither horse, mule, nor driver were in evidence at the moment. Conor bent and scooped up a bedraggled black kitten that huddled beneath the cart. He pushed open the door and ushered the duchess inside.

Elizabeth looked around with fascination. The caravan was partitioned off at the further end to accommodate a sleeping place constructed rather like a berth aboard a ship. The other half served as a kitchen, fitted up with a stove, a closet, and several chests. Cooking utensils and crockery hung upon the wall. Strewn all about were hardware, tools, and strange metal items to mend and sell. "Someone lives here. We're trespassing."

"We'll leave a few coins as tokens of our appreciation. They'll probably wish to invite us back." Conor set down the kitten on the floor, took off his greatcoat, and shook it out. "Give me your pelisse, Duchess, before it's soaked right through."

It was only a coat, Elizabeth told herself. 'Twas not as if she were stripping naked in front of this strange man. She took off her pelisse and handed it to him. He shook out the garment and hung it up to dry. Elizabeth removed her bonnet and brushed raindrops onto the floor. The kitten pounced on the dangling ribbons. "What a wretched-looking little scamp you are!" she said, and picked the creature up.

"Here!" Conor tossed her a rag he found by the stove. "Dry it off with this. The creature is probably infested with vermin."

Elizabeth wrapped the kitten in the rag. It peered out at her with bright green eyes. Magda eyes, she thought. " 'Tisn't your fault if you have vermin, is it, you poor thing?"

Conor smiled, his amusement at this moment turned upon himself. Here he was, alone with a lady in the most private of circumstances, and she was far more interested in a bedraggled baby cat. He pushed aside miscellaneous objects and sat down on a chest.

If Elizabeth was lavishing all her attention on the kitten, which responded by purring, a strange rough hiccoughing little sound, she was far from unaware of her companion. She was defying her husband's wishes— nay, his stern instructions—in even speaking with the man. However, Mr. Melchers was here with her, where St. Clair obviously didn't care to be, and was smiling at her in a warm and lazy manner that suggested there was nowhere he would rather find himself. If he would be as charming to any other lady, what did it signify? At least at this moment Elizabeth felt like someone enjoyed her company, which St. Clair obviously did not. Nor did he desire her, or find her the least bit attractive, because what else could "I cannot do this" mean?

If Mr. Melchers had been going to proceed with his lessons in flirtation, and naturally he had meant to, the duchess's expression gave him pause. Her expressive face was somber, and there were shadows beneath her lovely eyes. St. Clair definitely didn't have a way with his wives. "Blue-deviled, are you, puss?"

Elizabeth set down the kitten, which promptly set out to explore. She might feel easier with Mr. Melchers than with her own husband, but she was not so comfortable as to ask his advice. Outside, the rain still came down in buckets. "This is very improper," she commented. "Being here with you like this."

"Not so improper as it could be." Conor glanced suggestively at the far end of the caravan, and the sleeping berth. "I was only teasing, Duchess. Don't jump out the door. In answer to your comment, the fair itself is hardly proper. Under the circumstances, one more little sin against propriety can hardly hurt. You see I do know the term, though I choose to disregard it. Do stop pacing the floor, and come sit here by me."

Elizabeth glanced around the caravan. In truth, there was no place else *to* sit. Gingerly, she perched beside Mr. Melchers on the chest. Curiously, she looked at him. "Are you really a rakehell?"

She was most entertaining, St. Clair's little duchess. Conor smiled at her. "I am beyond wicked, sweeting. Do you mind so very much?"

"I don't know why *I* should mind." Elizabeth regarded her water-spotted gloves, and pulled them off to dry. "Why does St. Clair dislike you so much?"

Conor watched the kitten attack a metal shaving. " 'Tis an old story, and not a pretty one. I will not tell it to you. You would think poorly of me."

"*More* poorly of you, you mean." Elizabeth met his lazy gaze. "Your reputation is hardly a secret. I've already been told that it is improper for me to even speak with you."

Who had told her that, Conor didn't wonder. "That is probably true. Still, bear in mind the rain. I suspect catching your death of cold is an even worse fate than being closeted alone with an incurable rakeshame."

Incurable *and* impenitent, thought Elizabeth. Maman wouldn't think death from cold a worse fate. Neither would St. Clair. Perhaps the two of them might get together and discuss her shocking misconduct.

How gloomy she looked. Conor tweaked her nose. "Poor Duchess. I'll wager that before now you've never done anything improper in your life."

Perhaps Elizabeth had not, but she was about to, as soon as she screwed up her nerve. Mr. Melchers was an encyclopedia, after all. Not that she wished her morals corrupted. She wished merely to know what it felt like to be kissed. And since it appeared St. Clair did not care to kiss her—Elizabeth closed her eyes, turned up her face, and said, "Mr. Melchers, would you kiss me, please?"

Here was a temptation, and one sufficiently alluring to wipe the lazy amusement right off Conor's swarthy face. He was sufficiently experienced in the way of the world, however, to realize that the duchess had none of the warmer feelings toward him. Therefore, after a brief tussle with his conscience, and very much against his inclination, he dropped a chaste salute upon her cheek.

Elizabeth opened her eyes and regarded him with disfavor. "That isn't at all the sort of kiss I had in mind. Not that I am certain what I expected, but—Oh, blast!"

Mr. Melchers was coming to some very strange conclusions about the relationship—or lack thereof—between the Duke and Duchess of Charnwood. "Has that gudgeon of a husband of yours never kissed you properly?"

Elizabeth was embarrassed by the question, as well as by her own forward behavior. Never would she admit that she'd never had a proper kiss. Instead, she picked up the kitten, which was playing with her skirt flounce. "Now it is you who are guilty of impertinence," she said.

Conor watched the kitten crawl out of Elizabeth's arms and up his jacket sleeve. "Impertinence, sweeting, is the least of my sins."

Even the profligate Mr. Melchers didn't wish to kiss her. "Am I such an antidote?" Elizabeth asked.

She looked rumpled, and rosy, and wonderfully cross. Conor felt somewhat annoyed with St. Clair himself. He lifted Elizabeth's hand, and brushed his lips over her fingers, and then over her knuckles, and pressed a kiss into the palm of her bare hand. Her mouth dropped open. "You are anything but an antidote, Duchess, and I am far from a pattern of the virtues. Merely say the word and I shall continue. Just be sure what you are about, because once started on that course, there is no return."

Elizabeth stared at her hand as if it didn't belong to her. "Goodness!" she remarked. "And no, you shouldn't continue, though I can't say I didn't like that, because it would be a lie. But St. Clair isn't a gudgeon, you know."

Conor knew nothing of the sort. And if St. Clair didn't properly kiss his wife before very long, then Conor would. The duchess definitely deserved kissing. She also deserved cherishing. Conor was very good at cherishing, at least for a little while. "Sits the wind in that quarter?" he remarked.

Her hand still tingled where he'd kissed it. With no little difficulty, Elizabeth pulled on her damp gloves. "'Persons of our station do not marry for love,'" she quoted, and met Conor's skeptical dark eyes. The man was entirely too discerning. "Have you never been in love?"

"Countless times." Mr. Melchers detached the kitten from his shoulder, where it was engaged in an inspection of his earlobe. "But I have never loved a lass enough to step into parson's mousetrap, nor have my pockets been sufficiently to let. *Now* why are you looking so down in the dumps?"

"St. Clair didn't marry me because he cared for me." Elizabeth took the kitten back into her lap. "And I don't like it much. Don't tell me that it is the way of the world, sir, or I may offer you violence."

Conor saw before him a young woman on the verge of rebellion. Perhaps he would encourage her. "I would never dare presume."

He had presumed a great deal already. Elizabeth sighed. "Truly I try very hard to do what is right, but sometimes it seems beyond me. I am not cut out to be a duchess, I think."

Conor thought otherwise. A pity she was St. Clair's wife. "You are cut out to be whatever pleases you," he said, and with an idle finger stroked the kitten's matted fur. "You merely need to decide what that is. Meanwhile, take that little fellow home to your husband. He will like it of all things."

Chapter 17

*"Nothing on earth is more abominable than to be nattering
always at the same thing."* —Lady Ratchett

While Conor Melchers amused himself flirting with
the duchess, and in the process amazed himself with
the discovery that good girls *did* appeal, and Elizabeth
was amusing herself with the notion that Mr. Melchers
might give her her first kiss; and Magda was, if not
amusing herself exactly, then engaged in a very stimu-
lating meeting with the mysterious Grègoirè; the duke
was engaged in an unexpected, and not at all amusing,
encounter of his own. This encounter took place in the
library, where Justin had withdrawn to brood in silence
about the habit he seemed to be developing of behaving like an ass, most recently exhibited in his refusal to
accompany his wife on her excursion into the countryside. In lieu of a hair shirt, he had brought the parrot
with him. "Biscuit," Birdie suggested.

"No biscuit," said the duke, as he watched the third
occupant of the library walk back and forth upon the

carpet in front of the *secrétaire*. "I am not certain that I understand what brings you here."

Sir Charles Ratchett paused in his pacing to study the duke. Tall like his stepdaughter, gray-haired and blue-eyed, Sir Charles remained in splendid physical shape, the result of regular sparring matches with Gentleman Jackson, exercise that had the additional benefit of relaxing frustrations resultant upon living with his waspish wife. If at home he dwelt under the hen's foot, Sir Charles remained a man of some influence in the world, however, and had been instrumental in the installation of a Semaphoric Telegraph, an ingenious apparatus devised to convey news of impending invasion, atop the Admiralty Office and a tower of Westminster Abbey. He had been involved as well in persuading the Duke of York that the defense of London was perhaps not most practically accomplished by providing the inhabitants of corner houses with hand grenades. Better, in Sir Charles's opinion, that the night cellars in the city be examined and all suspicious foreigners ejected. London was awash with émigrés, and spies lurked everywhere. For the apprehension of more than one such traitor, Sir Charles had been responsible. That he had a nose for such mischief, he would modestly admit. Were he still in Town—

Instead he was in Bath, where it was raining, and contemplating the duke. "I don't scruple to tell you that I am shocked, Charnwood. Lady Ratchett didn't raise her gel to be party to such goings-on. That Elizabeth should write to her mama—We may be glad I got to the letter first! I don't need to tell you that Lady Ratchett would find this business too smoky by half."

Justin, it may be recalled, was already out of charity with his wife, and with himself, and perhaps with the whole world. Therefore it did not sit well with him to now be raked over the coals by Sir Charles. "As for that,

I have a crow to pick with *you*! I distinctly remember
being told she was a good, biddable girl."

So did Sir Charles remember. He had been present
at that interview, during which he'd watched his stepdaughter being auctioned off as if she were a piece of
middling good horseflesh. He hadn't liked that business, not one little bit. However, neither did he like being
the target of his wife's sharp tongue, and Elizabeth was
no blood kin of his, for all she'd dwelt beneath his roof
since she was but a child. "She *is* a good biddable girl!
Unless she Takes a Notion, and she generally don't do
that without being given cause." He took another turn
around the room. "Tell you what, Charnwood, it sounds
to me like you muddled the thing. Not that I mean to
tell you your business, but if I was in your place, which I
freely admit I'm glad I ain't, I'd get rid of what's-her-
name. Confound it, man, it's hardly the thing to bring
along your previous wife on your honeymoon."

The duke was not accustomed to having his conduct
questioned, other than by himself. He gazed with great
disfavor upon his newest uninvited guest. "I did *not* bring
her along. I had no wish to ever set eyes on her again. I
still have no such wish. And once I determine what the
devil she's up to—I am not obliged to offer further explanations. You are correct, Sir Charles, it's *not* your place."

Charnwood distrusted his previous wife? Sir Charles's
nose for mischief twitched. He picked up the brandy
decanter and poured some for his host. "That's as may
be, but it's Elizabeth as has the bee in her hat." He sampled the brandy. Of course the duke kept a fine cellar.
Sir Charles wondered how much of it was smuggled.
"Females! They give a man no peace."

With this, Justin could hardly argue. He picked up
his own glass. "I assume Lady Ratchett doesn't know
that you've come here."

Lady Ratchett didn't know a great many of the places her spouse ventured, nor the people with whom he met. Sir Charles had a wide knowledge of London life, from the Court to the alleyways of Covent Garden and Drury Lane. "Not bloody likely," he observed. "Had she got that letter, she'd probably have keeled over on the spot. Or maybe not, there *is* the title. She was determined to settle for no less than an earl. I've been a sad disappointment to her along those lines, but I was the best that she could do. Devil of a temper, you know, and an adder's tongue. Not to mention that she's already nagged one man to death. Anyway, Lady Ratchett don't care for Bath, not that she's ever been here. Where *is* Elizabeth? Have you got her locked away?"

Justin remembered his wife's reaction to the bedroom key. "I do not like locked doors. Was your idea to lock Elizabeth in her room?"

Sir Charles contemplated his brandy glass. Had his temperament been less interfering and Lady Ratchett less choleric—But there was no use crying over spilt milk. "Lady Ratchett said 'twas the only way to cure the girl of thinking for herself. Mayhap I can talk some sense into her. Elizabeth, that is. I'll tell you this much, Charnwood: if I didn't think Lady Ratchett would fly into the rafters, I'd be of a mind to fetch Elizabeth home myself."

Justin took this to mean that Sir Charles had some fondness for his stepdaughter. A pity the man had the courage of a slug. He rang for the butler. "You will take Elizabeth nowhere, Sir Charles. At the moment, she is not in the house. Chislett, inform Mrs. Papplewick that we have another houseguest, and have her prepare a room."

Only by the merest twitch of a bushy eyebrow did the butler betray reaction to this announcement. "Very good, Your Grace." He bowed himself out.

Sir Charles set down his empty brandy glass on the *se-*

crétaire. "Very kind of you, Charnwood. No need, you know."

"Nonsense!" The duke smiled, somewhat ferociously. "For some reason, my wife has been writing worrisome letters. You will wish to see for yourself that all is well with her." How dare Elizabeth involve an outsider in this rumpus? Not that several outsiders weren't already involved. And not that those outsiders weren't at least partly responsible for the rumpus.

If all was well with the duchess, the same couldn't be said for the duke, who was exhibiting all the symptoms of an aggravated spouse. Sir Charles was all too familiar with those symptoms. He backed toward the door. "Very generous, Your Grace! Since I'm in Bath, I might as well have a look in at the Pump Room. Take a glass of the waters. Good for what ails one, what? And then when I come back here, Elizabeth and I will have a little chat!" He removed himself from the premises with alacrity.

Justin contemplated the brandy decanter. 'Twould be shocking to drink himself into a stupor so early in the day. Although he might as well, since he was clearly destined to have no peace, not ever again. It had seemed such a reasonable notion, to get married. People did it all the time. Especially people with titles and wealth that they wished to pass along to future generations. Justin had titles and wealth and a new bride. So how had it come about that instead of setting up his nursery, he was barking at the moon?

Birdie stretched out her wings. "Biscuit," she observed.

Justin got up from his chair. "We need to expand your vocabulary. Perhaps Magda can teach you to say '*Zut.*'" Again, he rang the bell and summoned a servant. "When the duchess returns, I wish to speak with her at once." The footman withdrew. Justin sat down again, Birdie on his shoulder, and prepared to wait.

* * *

No little time had passed when the duchess returned to the house in the Royal Crescent, along with the two footmen and Madame de Chavannes. Once the rain had let up, the little party reunited easily enough. Magda said nothing about Elizabeth's tête-à-tête with Mr. Melchers, though she eyed the kitten with approval, remarked that St. Clair disliked felines, and suggested that Elizabeth smuggle it into the house hidden in her pelisse. As a result both women were laughing when they entered the front hall. Chislett imparted the information that the duke awaited his duchess in the library. Magda winked. "*Allons, hop, ma petite!*"

She did not feel like hopping. Slowly, Elizabeth walked down the hallway. She had done nothing so very wrong, she told herself. And if she had *thought* about it, that could remain her secret, could it not? She knocked on the door.

Justin knew that knock. Or if he didn't know it, he could guess who stood in the hall. 'Twas about time Elizabeth returned. Birdie had fallen asleep on his shoulder, and the brandy was half drunk. "Enter!" he snarled.

Elizabeth walked into the room. She looked damp and mussed and so very desirable that the duke wondered where he was to find a hair shirt in London, because if he *didn't* find a hair shirt, he didn't know how he was to continue practicing restraint, Birdie proving next to useless in the mortification of the flesh.

St. Clair was glowering at her. Again. As usual. Birdie opened one yellow-rimmed eye and clacked her beak. Elizabeth remembered that her husband had said he didn't want her. "You wished to speak with me?" she said, coolly.

He wished to sweep everything off the *secrétaire* and have her up on it. Justin gazed at the young woman whom he'd last seen wearing a coverlet and holding a fireplace poker in her hand. Now she was wrapped in a pale purple pelisse that covered her from throat to toe. "Where were you?" he asked.

St. Clair was in no good humor, as was made clear by the expression on his face. Had she thought she would not leave the house without his permission? If so, he could think again. Elizabeth strove for nonchalance. "We went to the fair. Mountebanks and jugglers, equestrian performers, musicians and a puppet show. It was beyond anything, St. Clair."

Still, he scowled at her. Elizabeth knew she must look a dowd. She hoped she didn't also look as if she had been alone in a tinker's cart with a gentleman—or a not-gentleman—other than her spouse. Lamely, she added, "It rained."

His wife wasn't telling him the entire truth. Justin suspected he knew what the omission was. "You went to the fair with Magda. I suppose it was always her intention. Who did you meet there?"

He was glaring all the harder now. Elizabeth wondered what St. Clair would do if she suggested his face might freeze that way. "Answer me, Elizabeth!" he demanded. "Was Melchers present?"

Even Birdie was regarding her with suspicion. Elizabeth lifted her chin. "Yes, he was. Mr. Melchers is a most particular friend of Magda's. You *were* invited to come with us, St. Clair."

Justin wondered what would have happened had he taken up that invitation, and if by so doing he might have thrust a spoke in Magda's wheel. "Did you speak with Melchers?" he inquired.

Elizabeth had been mistaken. St. Clair was every bit as intimidating as Maman when he got on his high ropes. "Naturally I spoke with Mr. Melchers. To do otherwise would have been rag-mannered. Despite what you

say of him, Mr. Melchers has been all that is proper."
Even when she had asked him not to be.

Melchers was no more likely to be proper than a pig
was to lay eggs. Doubtless the scoundrel had taken advantage of the further opportunity to subject Elizabeth
to his rakish scrutiny. At least her bosom was properly
covered up today. The duke's gaze moved to that portion of her anatomy. It seemed more ample than he remembered it, and queerly bumpy. Doubtless it was the
brandy that made him think it moved. "You are quick to
defend him, madam."

"You are quick to judge me!" Elizabeth snapped. Justin
looked startled and she took a deep, calming breath. "I
am very comfortable with Mr. Melchers. He is the only
person I know who isn't forever ripping up at me. I will
not cut him even though you say I should."

The duke's reaction to this wifely defiance beggars
description. He might well have leapt right out of his
chair were Birdie's beak not so near his ear. He lifted
the parrot off his shoulder and set it on the desk. Perhaps
he should simply snatch up his wife and plop her on his
lap, toss up her skirt, and then—

"St. Clair!" said Elizabeth. "Why are you looking at
me so strangely?"

Just how *was* he looking at her? Hopefully not like a
lovesick pup, for that was how Justin had felt ever since
Elizabeth's steppapa threatened to take her home. Of
course, he would not admit such weakness, particularly
when the young woman didn't appear to like him above
half. If that much. And not that he would allow anyone
to take her anywhere. "I am afraid," said the duke, "that
I have made a terrible mistake."

St. Clair regretted marrying her. It was plain as the
nose on her face. Had she not suspected as much all
along? Why, then, did she feel so very horrid? Elizabeth

crossed her arms and hugged herself. In so doing, she squeezed the kitten. It mewed.

A bosom that not only moved about but made noises? Impossible! Gone now, all thought to explain that the mistake he had made was not in taking Elizabeth to wife, but in not taking his bride straight into his bed. "What the devil is *that?*"

Elizabeth unbuttoned her pelisse, pulled out the bedraggled creature, and snuggled it against her cheek. The kitten purred and licked her nose. Birdie waddled to the edge of the desk and cocked her head. "Biscuit?"

"*Not* a biscuit," Elizabeth said sternly. "This is a kitten. Its name is Minou. I'm told you have no great liking for felines, St. Clair. 'Tis a pity, because I mean to keep him. We are very fond of each other already, this little fellow and I."

Had the duke the benefit of modern psychiatry, he might have realized that his bride harbored a degree of resentment toward him. Lacking that benefit, he thought of the Taking of a Notion so recently discussed. Damned if he liked the way Elizabeth was cuddling that kitten. He moved out from behind the desk, snatched away the kitten, and held it at arm's length. Birdie waddled even closer. The kitten spat.

Justin's chill gaze rested on his startled wife. "Sir Charles has come to Bath, apparently in response to some message that you sent. He will wish to see you as soon as he returns to the house. Yes, he is also staying here. I appear to be running an *hôtel* for extremely annoying people. I must ask Chislett how many bedrooms I have left."

Elizabeth stared blankly, then her cheeks turned bright red. "But I didn't post it—Oh, damnation!" She picked up her skirts and ran out of the room.

Chapter 18

"Wherein you reprove another be unblamable yourself for example is more prevalent than precept." —Lady Ratchett

The duchess burst into the bedroom, where her abigail had finished tidying up and was rewarding herself for her efforts with a snooze by the fire. Elizabeth hurried toward the writing desk and rummaged frantically through its contents. Daphne jumped to her feet and barely caught the inkpot before it hit the rug. "Damnation! The letter isn't here! Did you put it out to go into the post?"

The only letter Daphne knew of was the letter to Lady Ratchett. The very angry letter in which Her Grace had denounced His Grace as "the most unamiable person of her acquaintance." "I would never, mum!"

"Someone did." Altogether frazzled, Elizabeth sank down in a chair. "Don't look so horrified, Daphne. Not Maman but Sir Charles is here, which is in itself very strange. Perhaps Maman is prostrate with aggravation. I wish I could remember exactly what I wrote."

Daphne remembered all too clearly. Also mentioned had been "the greatest beast in nature" and "biggest scoundrel unhung." Wondering how long Milady would remain prostrated, if indeed Milady *was* prostrated, Daphne set about tidying up the desk. Sympathy below-stairs in the Ratchett household was with Sir Charles. Milady was notoriously picksome and persnickety and no little bit of a shrew.

From the desk, Daphne moved on to tidy up her mistress, and divested her of bonnet and pelisse. The abigail was restoring order to the duchessly coiffure when a footman knocked on the door and announced that Sir Charles awaited Her Grace in the drawing room.

"Is Charnwood also present?" Elizabeth asked. The footman allowed that His Grace had left the house. Her Grace hoped His Grace hadn't gone in search of Conor Melchers. "Fetch Birdie to the drawing room," she said and walked to the door.

Daphne sank back down into her chair. Lord have mercy on them all. A sultan had the power of life and death over his harem, and could have a wife who displeased him tied up in a sack and tossed into the sea.

Sir Charles was striding up and down the Moorfield carpet when the duchess entered the drawing room. It was his habit to pace about when he was in the grip of some strong feeling, Elizabeth recalled. "Hello, Sir Charles. I have been to a fair. It was most agreeable." Two footmen appeared, bearing the parrot's cage, and placed it by the pianoforte. Elizabeth opened the cage door. "This is Birdie," she added, and placed the macaw on the floor.

Sir Charles doubted it was enjoyment that caused Elizabeth to look pale and anxious and worn to the bone. He stared at the parrot. Birdie ruffled her neck feathers and fanned out her tail. "I can't say I think much of the water here. Whatever were you thinking to write such stuff to your mama? Here, don't pucker up! I don't mean to comb your head."

Elizabeth was fond of her steppapa, though he remained somewhat of an enigma, even after all the years he had been married to Maman. "I never meant that letter to be sent."

"Then you shouldn't have written it!" Sir Charles allowed his cheek to be kissed. "We must be grateful that I opened it instead of leaving it for your mother to read."

Was her steppapa, like herself, grown tired of being bullied? 'Twas an intriguing thought. "I am more grateful than I can say—but how very odd of you."

Sir Charles did not inform his stepdaughter that he was in the habit of often reading mail not addressed to him, and then sending it on its way. Not that he had sent along her letter, heaven forbid. "I had a hunch. Which is fair and far off, miss! I have been speaking with your husband. Charnwood tells me you have been rubbing shoulders with rakehells."

St. Clair had been tale-pitching, and Sir Charles appeared all too ready to take the duke's part. In a less-than-ladylike manner, Elizabeth plopped into a chair. Birdie waddled around the room, inspecting various items of interest, and treating others to an application of her sharp beak. In that particular moment, Elizabeth didn't care if the parrot pecked the house down around them. "I am acquainted with only one rakehell, and he is everything that is kind. I don't see why I shouldn't rub shoulders with Mr. Melchers when St. Clair is rubbing shoulders with his former wife."

Elizabeth had Taken a Notion. 'Twas as Sir Charles had feared. Unfortunately, her logic was difficult to refute. "No need to fly into the boughs! We'll straighten out this tangle. The thing is, you've been kept too well wrapped in lamb's wool! A man of Charnwood's elevated station in life—Not that I've heard he was addicted to wenching—Still a lady overlooks a gentleman's, er, little peccadilloes—Oh, damn and blast!"

"I asked the duke why he had married me," remarked Elizabeth. "He said it didn't signify, and then he said he had made a terrible mistake."

This didn't sound encouraging. Sir Charles wrinkled his brow. "Charnwood married you because you're a good biddable girl with a proper way of thinking, who will think and do just what she should. Or so he was told!"

His stepdaughter regarded him with an unreadable expression. "In other words, I am expected to accept whatever my husband may choose to do with good grace."

Intensely, Sir Charles disliked these father–daughter chats. Not that he had ever had one before, because he wasn't truly Elizabeth's papa, but he disliked this one, at any rate. "I ain't going to scold you, Elizabeth, because it ain't my place, but from what I can learn of this business, your behavior merits the sternest reproof, or it would if your mama was here! If it seems a trifle queer to have his previous wife along on his honeymoon—and I will admit it *does* seem a trifle queer!—I am mystified as to why you must make such a piece of work of it."

Elizabeth was mystified as to why anyone should think she *wouldn't* make a piece of work of it. Mr. Melchers was supposed to be the rakehell, not St. Clair. Perhaps she had not made the situation clear. "I was not talking about previous wives, but ladybirds."

"You was talking about previous wives in your letter! I have it right here." Sir Charles reached into his pocket. "Or I did until I threw it in the fire. However, I remember exactly what you said. You was in the fidgets because

Charnwood's previous wife was in the house. You was also in the fidgets because no one had thought to tell you Charnwood *had* a previous wife. You may thank your mama for that. I told her you wouldn't like it above half."

Elizabeth wondered what Maman had told Sir Charles in return. "Matters have progressed. I find I can tolerate Magda. I can even tolerate Gus. I am not entirely certain, however, that I feel as charitable toward ladybirds."

For a startled moment, Sir Charles thought Elizabeth referred to his own tendency to dally elsewhere than in his own house. Then he realized she referred not to himself, but to St. Clair. "Good Lord, what matters the occasional ladybird? Everyone has one!" he said.

Did Sir Charles speak from experience? She almost hoped he might. "Fifty-six of them?" Elizabeth inquired.

Fifty-six ladybirds! A man would think he'd died and gone to heaven. "Think no more of it, Elizabeth. Ladybirds don't signify. 'Tis you who are his wife."

Ladybirds didn't signify? On certain matters the sexes felt far differently. "As to that," Elizabeth retorted, with a certain relish, "I'm not so sure I am."

Sir Charles regarded his stepdaughter with a *frisson* of foreboding. "Of course you're married. I saw you wed myself. True, it wasn't the ceremony Lady Ratchett would have wished, but it was legal all the same. 'Dearly beloved, we are gathered together here . . .' "

"Thank you, Sir Charles. I recall the ceremony very well." Elizabeth pressed forward before her steppapa could move on to the "wives, submit yourselves unto your husbands part." " 'Twas not my *wedding* I spoke about."

If not wedding, then what did the chit refer to? Not "procreation of children," egad! How could Lady Ratchett have raised a daughter so lacking in proper feeling as to force her steppapa to discuss that which he would rather not? At least Sir Charles was fairly certain that he would rather not. But needs must when the Devil drove. "Do you mean to tell me that you are—That he, ah, has not—"

"Yes!" Elizabeth blushed almost as mightily as her steppapa. "I am, and he has not, and so therefore I am not truly wed."

Definitely, Sir Charles disliked father–daughter talks. He reminded himself to avoid having one ever again. "And don't tell me that I should be *nice* to him," added Elizabeth. "Because I have been extremely amiable. Usually. Almost all of the time."

Sir Charles didn't wish to inquire into the particulars. "There must be some reason for this queer start. Are you sure you didn't do anything to give him a disgust of you, miss?"

This wretched imbroglio was to be laid at her doorstep? Elizabeth's temper flared. "I didn't do anything! Magda showed up on our wedding night."

"Heigh ho." Sir Charles could see how it was that a gentleman might find it a trifle unnerving to engage in amorous congress with his bride while his first wife dozed beneath the same roof. But in that case, why didn't he just send the extra female on her way?

"He says that he cannot," responded Elizabeth, to whom this question was addressed. "Magda hasn't a feather to fly with. She's just escaped from France. Moreover, St. Clair seems to think she's involved in some mischief, and wishes to know what that might be. I'm not sure that's not just an excuse, because he wants her to stay."

"France!" Sir Charles's notion of mischief was mightily a-tickle. "You didn't say she was an émigré!"

Elizabeth was startled by her steppapa's reaction. In

but a second he looked so suddenly alert that she had the oddest notion she'd never really seen him before. "Magda isn't an émigré, although she seems to know a great many of them. Gus is determined to make her out a spy." She went on to explain Lady Augusta's presence beneath the ducal roof. "We are getting off the subject. St. Clair doesn't like me, Sir Charles. The last time we, ah—That is, we didn't—He threw me on the bed and then said he couldn't do it, and walked out of the room."

Sir Charles had been on the verge of delivering a stepfatherly lecture on the subject of conjugal obligation and decorum. Now he snapped his mouth shut. The duke *couldn't?* How the devil did the man expect to get himself some offspring if he wasn't up to the task? Couldn't bring himself to the sticking point? Was flogging a dead horse? And what the devil did he *do* with those fifty-six mistresses, in that case? "How very extraordinary! Are you sure you didn't bungle the business, miss?"

Elizabeth rose to remove Birdie from the piano leg, which the parrot appeared to be courting, and deposited her on the jasperware urn. "I haven't had a chance to bungle anything! Perhaps it was stupidly done of me to write that wretched letter, but I was shocked that St. Clair had a previous wife, which is *not* unremarkable, and if anyone had seen fit to warn me, I might have behaved differently! But as for bungling, I am hardly to blame for what Charnwood does, or doesn't do, in our own bedroom!"

"Say no more, I beg you!" Sir Charles raised his hands. "There's something damned smoky here. I must puzzle over it. Perhaps all Charnwood needs is a little push."

Elizabeth felt like pushing Charnwood, right out of a window. She doubted that was what Sir Charles meant. "What sort of push?"

Sir Charles thought of the various females whose acquaintance he had made in the byways of Covent Garden and Drury Lane, not to mention various houses of civil reception, any one of whom would be better equipped to have this conversation than he was. Thanks to the tender ministrations of those females, Sir Charles knew what *he* liked, intelligence of which would definitely cause Lady Ratchett to have an apoplexy, but there was no guarantee that Charnwood liked the same. Upon further reflection, Sir Charles decided that Charnwood probably *wouldn't* like the same, being as he was a duke and therefore probably accustomed to more exotic fare. Not that Sir Charles intended to have that conversation with his stepdaughter, either.

He must tell her something. "Take off your clothes! Nature will do the rest."

Elizabeth was not so naïve as to think Sir Charles meant she should disrobe in public. "St. Clair didn't like it when I showed my bosom. Are you sure?"

Sir Charles wasn't sure that the duke's brains weren't in his ballocks. He regarded his stepdaughter dubiously. She wasn't chicken-breasted, but she did look downright missish in her simple white gown. She *was* missish, therein lay the problem. "You showed your bosom? I'll tell you what, Elizabeth, I don't think I should hear this stuff!"

Elizabeth flushed. " 'Twasn't like that! I showed it to everyone. At the Assembly Rooms." Sir Charles looked horrified, and she began to laugh. "Not like that! It was just a dress. A very low-cut dress. Maman wouldn't have liked it one little bit."

Sir Charles was a great deal more interested in Charnwood's likes and dislikes than in Lady Ratchett's, with which he had become all too well acquainted during the long years of their married life. The duke hadn't cared to observe his wife's bosom. How very queer of him. No wonder Elizabeth was in a taking. Sir Charles wondered what Lady Ratchett had—or hadn't—told her daughter about matters marital.

As he was wondering how to delicately phrase this question, voices sounded in the hallway. Said one, "*Voyons!* I am very hungry. It is almost time for dinner, *n'est-ce pas?*" Replied another, "How can you be hungry? You ate an entire plate of apple tarts!"

Sir Charles looked toward the door, as did Elizabeth, and the parrot perched atop the urn. "Try harder, there's the ticket!" Sir Charles said hastily. "I've told Charnwood that if this business between you ain't resolved I would take you home with me, and I shall! I don't wish to see you made unhappy by your mama's ambitions, Elizabeth." The duchess looked startled. Birdie fluttered atop the urn.

Magda stepped into the room, and dimpled at sight of the visitor. Gus followed, and frowned. Elizabeth performed introductions. "This is my steppapa, Sir Charles Ratchett. Lady Augusta Shadwell, St. Clair's cousin. Madame de Chavannes, his previous wife."

"Ah, but you must not hold that against me! I was an aberration, merely. This time Saint has got it right." Magda curtsied. "*Enchanté*, Sir Charles."

De Chavannes, was it? Damned if he'd ever seen a dress cut that low. At least not on a lady. If she was a lady. Sir Charles's nose itched mightily.

"Is something wrong, Sir Charles? You are twitching," Elizabeth asked.

"Perhaps he is allergic to the parrot," offered Magda. "Or your kitten. Where is Minou, *ma petite?*"

'Twas an excellent question. In the shock of her stepfather's arrival, Elizabeth had forgotten all about the cat. "I don't know. St. Clair took him away."

"Mayhap he drowned it," remarked Augusta. "Whatever were you thinking, to bring home a kitten? St. Clair does not like cats."

"*À bon chat, bon rat*," said Magda. "Mayhap he will drown you next."

Birdie fluttered her wings for attention and whistled. "Jack's Maggot," I believe," said Elizabeth, and picked up the bird.

A footman appeared in the doorway. "Dinner is served, Your Grace." The duchess led the way into the dining room. Birdie perched on her shoulder, Lady Augusta hovered at her elbow. "The invitations for our dinner party have been sent out! You will be most pleased."

Elizabeth did not look pleased, thought Sir Charles, but instead resigned. "Parrots at the dinner table?" he queried. "Lady Ratchett would not like that."

"We are very informal here." With an enchanting, twinkling smile, Magda took his arm. "You have just come from London, *monsieur*?"

Sir Charles admired the lady's décolletage, and the cameo that hung between her breasts. She twinkled at him. "You have noticed my Eros. 'Tis an invitation to *l'amour.*"

L'amour, by Jove. Sir Charles patted his companion's hand, and embarked upon an animated discussion of Frigates and Fencibles, Raftweather and the Semaphore.

Chapter 19

"A woman's honor lies in public recognition of her virtue, a man's in the reliability of his word." —Lady Ratchett

While Sir Charles and the ladies lingered over a repast notable not only for the presence of a parrot but the excellence of the fare, His Grace the Duke of Charnwood was being ushered into the drawing room of Mr. Slyte's house in Queen's Square. Nigel and his aunt were seated at a Chippendale card table, intent on a game of piquet. Lady Ysabella wore a dress fashioned from an India shawl, its wide border forming the hemline. Perched atop her golden curls was a frivolous lace cap, and on her nose a pair of wire-rimmed spectacles. Her nephew looked rather like a rumpled owl, for the cards were not falling in his favor and he had been running his hands through his hair. Both were drinking port, which was hardly a beverage for a lady, but Syb was a lady only when she wished.

She looked up as Justin walked into the room. "I am

one hundred twenty to your ninety-nine! Nigel has spent too much time with Augusta, Saint."

Nigel threw down his cards. "She's taken my last farthing. Next I'll have to wager the gold buttons off my coat."

"You shouldn't play if you're not prepared to come down with the darbies." Lady Syb rose from the card table and draped herself like an invalid upon a chaise longue. "Must I remind you that you're the one who wished to play for stakes? Saint, you look like a gentleman bent on carnage. No, you may not fling that chair across the room."

It was a temptation. Instead, Justin sat the chair down and leaned on it. "You may not be surprised to learn that I have yet another houseguest."

Distracted from thought of the ready rhino, or his lack thereof, Nigel picked up the bottle by his elbow, and poured his friend a glass of port. "Did I not predict it? Sometimes I astonish even myself. You can move in here with us, we have ample room. Although we may *not* have a cook much longer, does Aunt Syb not cease haranguing the poor woman."

"The 'poor woman' deserves haranguing. Imagine, boiled neck of mutton." Lady Ysabella shuddered. "I should have brought along my own chef."

"No, you shouldn't!" retorted Nigel. "Because then Cook would quit for certain, and I like boiled mutton well enough. I'll stake a button it's Lady Ratchett who's responsible for Saint's long face. Will you call my wager, Aunt Syb?"

Justin strode toward the table and snatched up the port glass. "Not Lady Ratchett has come to Bath, but Sir Charles. Elizabeth wrote a letter, although she says she didn't put it out to be franked."

"There lies exactly the peril of a household too well

run!" Nigel leaned back in his chair. "A lesson for you, Aunt Syb. If ever a letter was writ in this household, there's no chance it would go accidentally into the post."

"Before a letter might be written in this household, one would first have to give up his humbuggery long enough to apply himself to the task!" retorted Lady Ysabella. "Elizabeth wrote to her stepfather? That surprises me. I didn't know that they were close."

"I don't have the impression that they are." Justin took a turn around the room. "Sir Charles opened the letter instead of leaving it for Lady Ratchett. One wonders why. As opposed to passing it along to her, he then came here himself."

"Took French leave, did he?" Lady Syb took off her glasses and twirled them idly in an elegant hand. "I can't say I blame him. Geraldine was ever guilty of too much high-mindedness. It makes her very dull, and no little bit of a shrew. I'm surprised her daughter turned out as good-natured as she did."

Justin hadn't observed that his wife was especially good-natured. "Magda is leading Elizabeth into bad habits, I'm afraid."

"Which bad habits?" Lady Ysabella replaced the spectacles on her nose and peered at him through them. "Gaming? Consorting with low people? Frolicking in the flesh pots?"

Justin dropped into a chair. "Today they went to a fair."

" 'Tis you who are guilty of high-mindedness if you find fault in a simple fair," Lady Syb said sternly. "A consideration of your superior standing is one thing; but you must not allow yourself to become *pompous*, Saint!"

Justin returned her look. " 'Tisn't the fair with which I find fault, though I don't care for such stuff myself. Melchers was there."

"You astonish me, Saint." So startled was Lady Syb that her spectacles slid down her nose. "Conor at a country fair! Still, what is there in that to make you so cross? Magda and Melchers have a long history. Where you find one you find the other, eventually. No one should know that better than you."

"Magda may have Melchers with my blessing! It's Elizabeth I'm concerned about." Two pairs of bright blue eyes fixed on him expectantly. Nigel's gaze dropped to Justin's hands. He raised a brow.

Justin also regarded his hands, which were festooned with kitten marks. "Elizabeth brought home a cat."

Nigel's other eyebrow arched to meet the first. "As I recall, you don't like cats."

Justin got up from his chair and took another turn around the drawing room. "She named it Minou."

Lady Ysabella turned her head to watch him. "You haven't stewed that wretched parrot yet, have you? And no, I don't want her back."

The duke refrained from kicking a sidetable. "Elizabeth is fond of Birdie," he said.

"Sleeps with it, does she? I should probably tell you that Aunt Syb knows you haven't—Ah. Unless matters have moved forward?" Expectantly, Nigel paused. "I see from your ferocious expression that they have not. Don't eat me, Saint! Aunt Syb knows about these things."

Justin leaned against the mantelpiece. Lady Syb knew about a great many things. He only wished the nonconsummation of his marriage was not one of them.

Lady Ysabella cast a shrewd look in his direction. "Save your breath to cool your porridge, Nigel. This is beyond everything, Saint."

Why should he be made to feel guilty when it was his bride who was at fault? At least he thought she was. For the most part. Although he may have had a little bit to do with this pickle himself. "Elizabeth may have married me under duress. Lady Ratchett made it a habit to lock her in her room."

"Poor Duchess!" remarked Nigel. "Seems to me someone should lock up Lady Ratchett instead. Perhaps we might arrange a nice chamber in the Tower. Have you the proper connections, Aunt Syb?"

"Pish!" Lady Ysabella said sternly. "Elizabeth is hardly the first young woman to choose a companion for life under parental compulsion. I myself did so. The first time, at any rate. It is the way of the world."

It was also the way of the world for a gentleman to enjoy a wedding night. Justin caught Nigel's knowing gaze, and scowled. "I don't think she likes me much."

Lady Syb's frown turned on him. "It's not necessary that the chit like you, Saint."

"Am I to hold Elizabeth down and forcibly divest her of her maidenhead?" Justin left behind the mantelpiece to sprawl in a chair. "Since we are being frank! Thank you, but I would rather she didn't detest me for the rest of our lives."

"Then you do feel something for her," deduced Lady Syb. "How very unfashionable. I wonder why you feel you would have to hold her down? Not that I recommend doing so, since you seem to wish her to like you a little bit. Not during the initial encounter, at any rate. Later, perhaps—"

Fireplace pokers and pistols, rouged nipples and plump bosoms. There was only so much that Justin was willing to confide in Lady Syb. "She asked why I had married her. She also asked if I had a mistress. She said that Conor Melchers was the only person who wasn't telling her how she should go on."

Nigel snorted. "No. Instead he's giving everyone else something more to badger her about. Draw in your horns! I didn't say *you* was badgering her, Saint. Though if you was, it might be a good idea if you stopped."

"Lollpoop!" interrupted Lady Syb, albeit fondly. "Give us no more of your jaw. Impudence here does have a point, Saint. 'Tis perhaps disobliging of Elizabeth to enjoy Conor's company, but understandable all the same. Even the meekest of fillies will kick over the traces if she feels the sting of the whip too many times."

Were Elizabeth a horse and he the coachman—Sternly, Justin banished that startling thought. He opened his mouth.

Lady Syb forestalled his protest. "If you wish someone to like you, then you must be likeable, Saint. To refrain from censuring Elizabeth's conduct might be an excellent good start! The chit will have had quite enough of that already from her mama."

Justin did not care to find himself sharing a paintbrush with Lady Charnwood. "It is a wife's duty to abide by her husband's wishes," he said stiffly.

"Certainly, if those wishes are reasonable." Lady Sybil retorted. "As it is his to abide by hers."

St. Clair was regarding Lady Ysabella as if she had suddenly grown a second head. She was regarding him like a cat about to pounce on a plump mouse. Nigel cleared his throat. "Cards, anyone? I have several buttons left."

Several hours had passed, along with countless hands of loo, and no small amount of liquid refreshment as well, before the duke returned to his home in the Royal Crescent. Since the majority of those hands had been won by Lady Ysabella, who along with crowing about her winnings had been prone to philosophize upon a husband's duty toward his wife, the duke was out of patience with all of femalekind. Were it not for his newly discovered dislike of enforced abstinence, he might have joined a monkish brotherhood. Nor was he of a mind just yet to retire to his accursed dressing room, where Thornaby would be waiting to flutter over him. He retired to the library in search of something with which to divert himself. Justin was greatly in need of diversion. Perhaps he would embark upon *Plutarch's Lives*.

The fire had burned low in the fireplace, the candles in their holders. Shadows lurked in the corners of the room. From one high-backed chair issued a gentle snore.

Justin scowled. Even in his sanctuary, he was not to be left alone. He moved around the side of the chair, prepared to forcibly oust the invader. Not one of his uninvited guests, but Elizabeth was sleeping there. In her lap dozed the black kitten. On the floor beside the chair lay an opened book. A somewhat naughty opened book, Justin realized, as he tilted his head to read the title. She was full of surprises, this wife of his. She also looked enchanting in her simple white dress, her hair coming unpinned.

This dress, at least, met with his approval. It was high-necked and long-sleeved. Absurd to feel disappointed that he therefore could not view her bosom. Lord, he was in a sad condition Perhaps he should seek out a more accommodating female, and thereby relieve himself. Justin reached out and touched his wife's soft cheek.

Abruptly, Elizabeth awakened. She had been dreaming of St. Clair, and was startled to see him standing by her chair. *Had* he touched her cheek? Doubtless that gentle caress had existed only in her dream. "I wished to speak with you. I thought I would wait awhile and read, but I must have dozed off instead."

Chivalrously, Justin refrained from commenting on

the nature of the book which lay open on the floor. Elizabeth looked deliciously disheveled. Lest he succumb to the temptation to take her onto his lap, Justin seated himself behind the *secrétaire*.

Elizabeth straightened. The kitten stirred and yawned, then clambered down her skirts to drop upon the floor. Elizabeth watched her pet make its unsteady way toward the *secrétaire*, pausing en route to be delighted by the sight of its own tail. "Maman did not like felines. She said they are sneaky, and much too independent, and weave around one's ankles deliberately to trip one up. I am such a gudgeon. Until Katy brought Minou back to me, I thought you had taken him away to drown him, or worse!"

His bride had called herself a gudgeon. The duke was not disposed to disagree. He bent down and picked up the kitten, which was attempting valiantly to climb his boot, and leaving behind tiny needlelike scratches about which Thornaby would have a great deal to say. "If I'm to share my home with the wretched creature, it had to have a bath." He deposited the inquisitive kitten on his desk and regarded it with disfavor. "Lord only knows where it has been."

Were those scratches on St. Claire's hands? Katy had said he bathed Minou himself. Now he was even tolerating the kitchen's fascination with the table globe.

Elizabeth had misjudged her husband. She had behaved very badly toward him as well, brandishing a fireplace poker at him as she had. Although *he* had brandished a pistol first. The house was very quiet. She was intensely aware that they were alone together in the room.

Justin was acutely aware of his wife, who was fidgeting in her chair. What did it matter if she had spoken to Conor Melchers, other than that he had said she should not? Of course she should not go against his wishes, no matter Lady Syb's outrageous opinions on the subject, but the duke did not wish to think of that just now. Whatever had possessed him to barricade himself behind this infernal desk? He hit upon the brandy decanter as a solution to his dilemma, and poured them both a glass.

Warily, Elizabeth accepted the brandy snifter. One of the reasons St. Clair had chosen to marry her was because she was a model of good breeding, or because he thought she was. Elizabeth hadn't been behaving lately like a model of much of anything. Perhaps Sir Charles was correct, and she had somehow given St. Clair a disgust of her, and that was why he hadn't asserted his husbandly rights. If he disliked her altogether, surely he wouldn't have let her keep Minou.

If she had given the duke a disgust, then she must make things right. Elizabeth had no intention that Sir Charles should take her home to Maman, and therefore she must somehow persuade St. Clair to make her his wife in truth. But how was she to accomplish that? Sir Charles had also said she should take off her clothes. In the library? Elizabeth chewed her lip.

Lord, but she was lovely in the candlelight. Justin wished that he might take her in his arms. Yes, and why should he not? After all, she was his wife. Therefore, he took her hand and drew her to her feet. "I wish that you would call me Justin. Why do you look startled? It is my name, after all."

He was not altogether disgusted with her, then. "Thank you . . . Justin." Would he kiss her now?

If only he dared kiss her! But in this moment his bride seemed to trust him a little bit, and he did not wish to frighten her away. "We have had a great many misunderstandings between us, I think. Permit me to

clear up one of them. When I said I did not wish my
wife to associate with Conor Melchers, I did not refer to
Magda. It has been a very long time since I thought of
Magda as anything other than a curst nuisance."

Elizabeth was encouraged. "Magda is a trifle unconventional perhaps."

"Magda has an abominable inclination to meddle. If
I may say so, as I should not, I say so to my wife, and
nothing that we say or do together may be considered
improper, Elizabeth." Ruefully, Justin smiled, and raised
his hands to cup her pretty face. Elizabeth's eyes were
opened wide, her lips slightly parted. She looked infinitely kissable.

Well, then, he would kiss her. Surely he had sufficient self-control to kiss his bride without tossing up her
skirts and making love to her on the *secretaire.* For that
matter, why *shouldn't* he make love to his wife on the *secretaire?* Elizabeth was his wife, and this was his house. He
bent his head and—

"*Ah ça!*" Magda said cheerfully, as she walked into the
room. "I see I am *de trop.*"

Thus the moment was shattered. Magda strolled in
front of the fire, which outlined her figure nicely through
the lace of her negligee, to lean against the *secrétaire.*
Her expression was amused. Justin released his wife and
drained his brandy glass.

Elizabeth twisted her wedding ring. It seemed she
was not of sufficient interest to her husband that he
wished to embrace her—or *continue* to wish to embrace
her, because for one magic moment she had been sure
he did—in the presence of his former wife, who felt so
comfortable in St. Clair's house that she wandered
about the halls *en déshabillé* even more provocative than
the gowns she normally wore during the day.

Magda looked very much at ease in the library. She

had been in the room before. With St. Clair, no doubt.
A curst nuisance, indeed.

And then, as Madame might have said, *aller de mal en
pire*. Minou had gotten the globe twirling so madly that
he became quite giddy and tumbled off the desk. "*Bravo!*"
laughed Magda, and snatched up the kitchen in midair.
"This little fellow certainly looks better than when Conor
gave him to you, *n'est-ce pas, petite?*"

Chapter 20

"Be not curious to know the affairs of others, neither approach those that speak in private." —Lady Ratchett

Sir Charles found his host at the breakfast table, sharing a rump steak pie with Birdie and a small black cat. Before his fascinated eyes, the parrot snatched up the last bit of the pie. The kitten spat, climbed into the duke's plate, and began to lick it clean.

Damned if this wasn't the queerest household Sir Charles had ever visited. "Good morning, Charnwood!" he said, as a footman filled his plate with beef tongue and horseradish sauce, sausages and mashed potatoes, fresh bread and orange marmalade from among the selections on the sideboard. The duke merely raised a weary brow.

Sir Charles sat down at the table. Birdie fluffed her feathers, leaned toward his plate, and quivered longingly. Justin snapped his fingers: "No more begging, you wretched creature, or you'll go back into your cage." Birdie fanned her tail at him and strutted along the table toward the centerpiece. The kitten, sides bulging with his portion of His Grace's breakfast, pounced on the parrot's tail. Birdie snapped her beak and squawked. Minou hissed and fluffed up like a startled hedgehog.

The duke ignored them both and regarded his companion. "I trust you slept well, Sir Charles."

"Marvelous well. And you?" Sir Charles bit into a sausage, then paused midchew. In light of a recent conversation with his stepdaughter, this question might not be politic. Charnwood looked very much as if he had not slept at all.

As the duke refrained from comment on his nocturnal habits, the parrot ducked behind the centerpiece for all the world as if it wished to play hide-and-seek. Nothing loath, the kitten pounced.

The centerpiece tipped over. Fruit rolled across everywhere. Minou chased after an apple. Birdie caught a bunch of grapes in one claw and began to dine. St. Clair dropped his head into his hands.

The parrot he had already met. "A kitten?" Sir Charles inquired.

"Its name is Minou. Elizabeth brought it home. She seems determined to acquire a zoo." The duke lifted his head to cast Sir Charles an acerbic glance. "We won't speak of *how* she came by the kitten. Her mama would not approve any more than I do."

The duchess's steppapa did not wish to discuss her mama. Nor, in point of fact, did he wish to discuss the matter that he must. There was nothing top-lofty about Charnwood now. Rather, he appeared to be a man at the end of his resources.

Sir Charles seized the moment. "Since we find ourselves private, I have a crow to pluck with you, Charnwood."

Justin didn't know how private they could be considered, with cats and birds and footmen everywhere. "Thank you, William, James. We will serve ourselves." The footmen bowed themselves out of the room. The duke caught the apple, and the kitten, before they tumbled to the floor. "Perhaps you might care to pluck a parrot instead, Sir Charles."

Sir Charles looked at the parrot. Birdie blinked one baleful yellow-rimmed eye, darted out her wicked beak, and snatched a sausage from his plate. Sir Charles jumped. "By Jove!"

"Unruffle yourself, Birdie. It was merely a figure of speech." St. Clair plopped the kitten back down on the table. "What was it you wished to speak with me about, Sir Charles?"

"It ain't that I *wish* to, precisely." Sir Charles pushed his plate away. "Thing is, maybe I can help you out. Happens to all of us, you know. I've made a bit of a study of the matter myself!" He went on to speak knowledgeably about earth chestnut, and wild clary drunk with wine; black ants, deer genitals, raw oysters, and applications of camel fat. By the time Sir Charles had finished this little dissertation, the food had congealed on his plate, Birdie was perched on the duke's shoulder and grooming his hair, and Minou had fallen asleep in the sugar pail.

"I'll say no more!" Sir Charles put down his napkin. "Other than that if I fetch Elizabeth home, my wife will ring me *such* a peal. You'll see how that is, now you're a tenant for life! Take my advice, and we'll see everything fixed up all right and tight. Sometimes the ladies require a little effort, bless their hearts. Just where *are* the ladies, by the by?"

Justin was very curious about just what his own lady had said to prompt her steppapa's little lecture. Perhaps he would feed *her* raw oysters and black ants. "They have gone out. I believe they intended to visit the Baths."

"Excellent notion!" Sir Charles beamed, and pushed back his chair. Justin plucked Minou out of the sugar pail and thought nostalgically of the simple bachelor life.

Madame de Chavannes, at that same moment, was enjoying a Bath Bun, a sweet rich roll to which raisins, chopped lemon peel, and almond nibs had been added before baking. "Excellent!" she said, and brushed coarse sugar off her gloves. "Onward, *ma chere!* Did you know that during the Dark Ages, Bath was given the name 'Akesmanceaster,' which meant 'sick man's town'?"

Again Magda sought to distract her. Perhaps she contrived to send on vital information, but to whom? The Comte de Provence, marooned in exile, or the Duc d'Engheim? Bonaparte? The Directory? And what vital information had she unearthed in Bath, the ingredients in a Bun? Gus paused to look into the window of a woolen merchant. "I wonder why Elizabeth didn't wish to accompany us today."

If only Gus had proved equally reluctant! Magda wondered if the provoking creature would follow her even into the slums of Avon Street. "*Merde alors!* Now you accuse poor Elizabeth of getting up to some intrigue. She probably wished to stay home and play with her new pet."

Gus caught Magda's arm. The ladies walked briskly along a street of splendid shops. "I should never have let her go off with you alone. What were you thinking? Conor Melchers, of all people. The man is a libertine!"

"Attractive, is he not?" Magda shot her companion a

sideways, knowing glance. "Even you are drawn to him. Admit it, Gus."

Augusta snorted. "I am nothing of the sort. You must be set on leading poor Elizabeth astray."

Magda was relieved to see ahead of them the fretted pinnacles of Bath Abbey, the columned and pedimented colonnades of the Pump Room, the spacious paved courtyard where blue-coated sedan chair attendants awaited customers. *"Mon Dieu,* you grow protective. I thought you wished our Elizabeth to the Devil, Gus."

Lady Augusta paused to avoid a passing carriage, then hurried after her companion, who moved along as quickly as if she were engaged in a footrace. Or trying to outdistance someone, perhaps.

Gus wasn't about to be outdistanced. "Elizabeth can't be faulted for courage. A cat, of all things. And Saint will let her keep it. Saint does not like cats. It is all very strange."

The Baths lay before them. Magda led Gus toward the dark entrance and—since this outing had been her notion, if not Augusta's participation in it—paid the admission fees. "Not so strange as all that. Saint wishes to please his wife."

Gus followed Magda into the steamy, dungeonlike dressing room, where a female attendant waited to help them into canvas bathing costumes. "Why?" she inquired as she stepped into the stiff petticoat. "He hasn't wished to please anyone else that I can see. I still wonder why Saint married her. She's not at all in his style. I mean— Look at you!" A great deal of Magda's lush person was currently on view.

"It has been a long time since I was to Saint's liking." Magda thrust her arms into the brown linen jacket and waved away the bonnet that the attendant sought to put atop her head. "Tastes change, as you might discover for yourself, were you not so determined to be a thorn in everybody's side, *ma chere.*"

Augusta opened her mouth to protest this calumny, then closed it as the attendant plopped the chip hat on her head instead. "I am *not* a thorn," she said, when the woman was done with her. "And if I am, it is because there are so many restrictions placed on an unmarried woman. It is different for you. As a widow you may do as you please."

The ladies stepped out into the sunlight. On one side of the huge cistern, a colonnaded covering protected the bathers from the weather. Spectators and friends of the bathers lounged along the sides of the bath or on the gallery above. Several women sat in a semicircle near the bar, cup and saucer in either hand, listening to the musicians play. Also available were chambers in which a patient might immerse the afflicted portion of his body in hot water right out of a pump, and a steaming room where direct injections were considered of great service in violent intestinal complaints. In a niche stood a statue of King Bladud, erected in 1699. "It is not that I may do as I please," Magda said absently, as she stepped into the water, "but that I *do*. Imagine what this was like in Roman times. The bathing ritual lasted for hours. Can you not just see it? Everyone from military generals to shopkeepers mingling freely in the waters and conversing, playing games, relaxing. Traders displaying their wares, everything from fresh fruits to fine jewelry."

Lady Augusta contemplated her fellow bathers. Rheumatics, gout sufferers, people afflicted with rampant eczema and other unsightly skin diseases; fat women, thin women, obese and skinny men, all milling about and splashing each other and having a marvelous good time in the bath. The very hot bath, which she was sharing with them. At least they hadn't brought along their live-stock. "I hope the water has been changed since then. It doesn't smell much better than it tastes. I suppose those little floating copper bowls filled with scented oils and pomades are an attempt to purify the air."

"The baths are constantly fed by hot water springs that start beneath the earth, *ma chère*. Avoid the Cross Bath. Women become pregnant after bathing there."

Magda was teasing her again. Gus couldn't help her instinctive distrust of water that sprang out of the earth already boiled for use. She returned to the source of her annoyance. "Justin is a man, and can do anything he wishes. I would give anything to have the freedom of a man."

Magda wished she might have her own freedom, es-pecially from Gus. She waded through the crowd. "Olympe de Gouge was a French butcher's daughter who thought women should have the same rights as men. The National Convention escorted her to the guillotine. On what charge, you wonder? Treason, *naturellement*."

Was it truly treasonous of her to wish to control her own life? Justin would think so, at any rate. Gus dared not provoke her cousin further, not without some good reason, if she wished to keep her allowance and a roof over her head, which was why she had thus far, and with a heroic self-control, avoided the gaming clubs.

Men and women strolled around together in the baths. Although in theory the sexes were not to mingle, min-gle higgledy-piggledy they did, laughing and chatting in water that reached up to their necks. The men wore stiff canvas robes. The ladies' costumes were especially unbecoming. Some had attached handkerchiefs to their bonnets in an attempt to blot away the perspira-tion from their brows.

Augusta dabbed at her own brow. She had said she'd

never go into the baths. If only she had listened to herself. Amid the rabble—Gus's social consciousness hadn't been elevated one whit by the recent troubles in France—she glimpsed a familiar face. "Magda. Here is that Frenchman who seems to follow you everywhere."

Not only was Gus a thorn in one's side, she was also more observant than one might wish. Grégoiré was the reason Magda was in the bath today. "*Zut!* Many men follow me. You will tell me I might remedy the situation by putting on stays. I do not like stays, and I *do* like the gentlemen, and so—Perhaps you might consider putting off your own corset, Gus!"

Before Lady Augusta could point out that few of the females in the water were wearing stays, including herself, and had not consequently attracted hordes of admiring gentlemen, no doubt due to the rigid and definitely uncomfortable nature of the canvas costumes that they wore, Magda's émigrés were upon them, and all seemed to wish to talk at once. Augusta listened, and thereby learned that Napoleon had tried to level off the graves in a cemetery at Ezbekiya so he could have even ground around his headquarters, and the people had become so hostile that he had to abandon his plan.

Although Madame de Chavannes's various assets were not on public view, due to her stiff costume, she and her admirers still drew no little attention from the crowd. Among those other bathers was Sir Charles Ratchett, who had been waiting so long for the ladies to appear that he felt like a lobster cooking in the pot. Elizabeth's steppapa was no stranger—though he had never played it with a parrot—to the game of hide-and-seek. The name 'de Chavannes' rang a good loud bell in his mind. Madame was laughing, gay, and indolent, as if she had no purpose here other than to enjoy the waters. Sir Charles splashed his way through the throng.

Perhaps the lady's presence truly was a coincidence. Most likely, it was not. What remained to be discovered was whether Madame de Chavannes played a role in counterrevolutionary espionage, paid for by the British government, or whether she was one of the secret agents with whom France flooded the country in an attempt to provoke subversion and inflame invasion fears, or if she might be more innocent than she appeared.

The bath grew more and more crowded, and the ladies were briefly lost to view. After their sojourn in the waters, most of these bathers would adjourn to the Pump Room, and from there go to hear the daily service at the Abbey, during which they would see their lovers, make assignations, pass *billets-doux*. Sir Charles wondered if Madame de Chavannes would also pursue those fashionable activities. Then he wondered if she had a lover. Madame was a fine figure of a woman, even in that hideous bathing costume.

Augusta, who could have cared less that Napoleon's own ship *L'Orient* had narrowly escaped the fighting at Abukir, was distracting herself with thoughts of the entertainment she had planned. There must be cards at Elizabeth's *soirée*. The guests would be astonished if there were no cards. Saint would not wish his guests to be astonished, surely.

A sudden tingle ran down her spine then, as if she were the object of someone's intent view. Gus glanced around at the other bathers and saw Sir Charles bearing down on them.

She nudged her companion. "You have another admirer, I think."

"*Zut! Que difficultle!*" sighed Magda. With admirable dispatch, Grégoiré and his companions melted away into the throng.

Sir Charles was panting when he reached them. The

water was damned hot. "By Jove! What a surprise. Where's Elizabeth? Charnwood said she had gone out with you."

Lady Augusta would eat her ugly chip straw bonnet if Sir Charles was the least bit surprised to encounter them. How did Magda do it? Yet another conquest, and in this instance without even displaying her enviable *décolletage*. "Charnwood was mistaken. Elizabeth went off somewhere with her maid."

Magda was under no similar misapprehension concerning Sir Charles's interest. He had recognized her name. Sir Charles Ratchett was part of a group of intelligentsia of many nations, its prime concern to try and influence the political situation with France. Too late, now, to wish she had chosen one of the other titles in her repertoire.

Where a lesser lady might have shrieked with vexation, however, Magda merely raised her handkerchief and wiped away the perspiration beaded on his brow. "Well met, Sir Charles. We were discussing Bath Buns. Raisins, chopped lemon peel, almond nibs, coarse-grained sugar. They are very good. If you have not tasted one, you must."

Sir Charles caught Magda's hand and regarded her rather as if she were a Bath Bun herself. "Well met, indeed, Madame de Chavannes. You and I must have a little talk, *s'il vous plâit!*"

Chapter 21

*"An absence of vulgar behavior is often a sure sign of attach-
ment. It means that the suitor is trying to prove his good
manners and his concern for your comfort and reputation."*
—Lady Ratchett"

Bath abounded in sites of interest, Roman ruins,
lovely parks, and pavilions where one might revel in bu-
colic splendor to one's heart's content. In one such
public garden, Conor Melchers regarded his surroundings with a jaundiced, and distinctly bloodshot eye. His
dissatisfaction had nothing to do with the beauty of the
tree-lined walks and shady bowers, and everything to do
with the abominable nature of the hour. Rakehells cannot be expected to savor the benefits of early morning
exercise.

At least here in the gardens his ears were no longer
assaulted by the bawlings of newsboys, muffin sellers
and milkmen. Milkmen, by God. The last time Conor
had encountered a milkman was not because he'd risen

early, but because he hadn't yet been to bed. Furthermore, the blasted sunlight hurt his eyes.

Still, he was curious. It was one of his many besetting
sins. Mr. Melchers mused upon these various short-
comings as he strolled along a graveled path past an
artificial wallow, raised an eyebrow at a sham castle com-
plete with cannon, glanced thoughtfully at the entrance
to the labyrinth, crossed an elegant cast-iron bridge. Though
the gardens were far from deserted—Bath provided a
constant supply of new faces, at least some of which
were respectable, not that Conor cared for that—he met
none of his acquaintance, for which he was grateful, because he would receive no end of ribbing at being seen
in such a place at such an hour. Mr. Melchers was not
here of his own inclination, and if he didn't shortly find
the lady who had requested his presence, he was going
to return home and go back to bed.

He saw her then, pacing back and forth in front of a
half-circular stone pavilion at the very top of the princi-
pal walk. Hard to imagine garb more respectable than
that cottage bonnet and green printed pelisse. She had
brought a maidservant with her. For protection. Conor
began to be amused.

Daphne took one look at the gentleman walking toward them, and knew she beheld temptation personi-
fied. "As I live!" she breathed. "This is most—I mean,
what would Lady Ratchett say, Your Grace!" Daphne
had already been threatened with strangulation if she
mentioned the word "improper" one more time.

Elizabeth looked without favor upon her companion, who was turning out to be a positive chicken heart.
"You sound like Maman. Perhaps you would like to go
live with her. And I have told you already that I do *not*
care to be called 'Your Grace'!"

Definitely Daphne did not wish to return to Lady Ratchett. She pressed her lips tightly shut and thought of sultans, and harems, and how those ladies spent their time lounging in the bath, or peeling grapes, or warming the sultan's bed, and seldom set foot out-of-doors unless wrapped in heavy veils. But here was the mistress, having an assignation with an improper gentleman. Daphne knew an improper gentleman when she saw one. This was an improper gentleman worth being drowned in a burlap sack for, she thought gloomily, and wished that she might smoke a Turkish water pipe herself.

The duchess looked both worried and determined. Her abigail looked distressed. Conor disliked any female to be distressed in his vicinity. It was a reflection on himself. "Good morning, Duchess. I came as soon as I had your note."

Elizabeth wasn't sure he *would* receive her note, since she'd paid a street urchin to deliver it, not daring to entrust such a thing to any of St. Clair's staff. "It was very kind of you to meet me, especially in light of your condition. I recognize the symptoms. My steppapa was prone to occasionally overindulging in the grape, but this is the first time I have seen consequences so severe."

It was the first time she'd had an assignation, also, Conor wagered. The young lady was as jumpy as a cat on hot bricks. "I am not a kind man, Duchess, and the sun is very bright. Perhaps we might go inside while you tell me why you dragged me out at this curst ungodly hour. The rooster must still be abed."

Elizabeth led the way into the paved pavilion, which was supported by several stone pillars, and had within it a seat that commanded an excellent view of the park. "There is virtue in rising early, Mr. Melchers. As Mr. Franklin said, 'Early to bed, early to rise, makes a man healthy, wealthy, and wise.' "

"And as Mr. Kyd would have it, 'What outcries call me from a naked bed?' There may be virtue in rising early, but there is infinitely more pleasure to be had lying in late of a morn." Lazily, wickedly, Conor smiled.

It had not occurred to Elizabeth, when she sent her summons, that Mr. Melchers might have been entertaining a companion. "I wouldn't know," she snapped, then blushed brighter still. "Stop that! Magda has gone off with Lady Augusta to the Pump Room, and I wished to speak privately with you. We haven't much time."

Mr. Melchers was much too wise in the ways of the world, despite his somewhat befuddled condition, to think the young lady wished his participation in an amorous liaison, though had she wished such a thing, he would of course have been happy to oblige. "I would be delighted to be private with you, Duchess. However, we are not private at the moment, and I admit to a certain prudery about such matters. A witness, my dear, would greatly cramp my style."

Elizabeth took his meaning, and blushed all the brighter. "I did not ask you here to flirt with me, Mr. Melchers. I merely wished your advice. As for Daphne, I have no secrets from her."

"Ah, but *I* might." Conor winked at the maidservant. "You may go for a walk and enjoy the gardens, Daphne. Your mistress will be safe with me."

Daphne was doubtful that any female between the cradle and the grave was safe with this rascal. He even had her in a flutter, and she knew chalk from cheese. On one hand, she didn't wish to be shipped back to Lady Ratchett because she'd given offense. On the other, the duchess was as green as grass, and this lazy dark-eyed rascal could charm the skirts right off a nun.

Daphne wrung her hands together, so badly was she torn. "It's all right," Elizabeth said. "I will be perfectly safe with Mr. Melchers. If it will make you feel better, you may keep us in view."

"No, she may not!" inserted Mr. Melchers. "I have no intention of doing anything you do not wish me to, Duchess, but I heartily dislike chaperones. Go for a walk, Daphne, and come back in a half hour. I can do little damage to your mistress in that time. Or I *could*, but I won't. It isn't in my style."

He *was* a handsome devil. Still, Her Grace wasn't one to throw her bonnet over the windmill. Trying very hard to assure herself of the latter, Daphne set out to chase her own tail.

Conor returned his attention to his companion, who was twisting her wedding band. "It is a lovely ring," he said gently. "Are you in trouble, puss?"

"Trouble?" Elizabeth managed a wan smile. "You might say so. I don't think things could be in a worse case. Magda told St. Clair you gave me the kitten after I told him we have barely spoken. He was so very angry I thought he might drown us both. Now he's going about looking like a thundercloud. When he deigns to speak to me, which he hasn't yet, I make no doubt he'll read me yet another scold." She sniffled. "Or tell Sir Charles to take me home."

Unlike the duke, Conor had no special dislike of weeping females. Indeed, Conor had no dislike of females in any mood save those pertaining to leg-shackling him. He pulled a handkerchief from his pocket and held it out to her. "Sweeting, I'm not worth brangling about."

"No, you're not." Elizabeth blew her nose. "It has become a matter of principle. If St. Clair may have Magda, then I don't see why I should give you up."

Conor Melchers was somewhat more experienced than Elizabeth's steppapa in the matter of feminine logic. "Simple, puss! You have not yet provided the requisite heir. *Afterward*, perhaps—"

"Yes, I know you are one of the wicked! You need not keep trying to convince me of it," Elizabeth said, so crossly that Conor laughed. "I'm sure I would be pleased to provide St. Clair with his heir, but I don't know how I'm supposed to go about it when I cannot even persuade him to—That is—Blast!" She broke off, hugely embarrassed by what she'd almost said.

Not one of St. Clair's admirers, Conor revised his opinion downward still. The duke was a nincompoop. "If I am to help you, Duchess—and I think I am here because you want me to help you—you must tell me everything. Don't be embarrassed. 'Tis the way of us rakehells to be unshockable." There, he had made her smile. "In all seriousness, I am at your service, puss."

Elizabeth looked up at him. Mr. Melchers *was* a very kind man, no matter what he said. "Sir Charles says I must have bungled the thing somehow. I had hoped that you could explain to me what it is that I am doing wrong. What I've found in books isn't very helpful. I know how the business is done, because Maman told me, but I don't know—" She paused for breath. "I have truly *tried* to be amiable and accomplished, and sunny-natured, and to show good sense."

Conor reflected that the lady wasn't displaying particular good sense at the moment, which was fine with him. She added, "I can hardly turn to Magda for advice, since it is she who—Well, they did elope! Gus probably knows no more than I do, if as much. Damnation! It is very difficult to speak of this. Are you shocked by my boldness, sir?"

She was flustered and rosy and altogether enticing. Casually, Conor took her hand. "Rakehells are seldom shocked. I would be more likely to encourage you in wrongheadedness than to tell you not to flout society's rules. Back up a little bit, if you will. *What* did your Maman tell you? And I don't refer to sunny nature and good sense."

Elizabeth lowered her eyes and explained, as best she could, about lust turning even the most proper gentleman into a slavering beast, closing her eyes and clenching her teeth and wishing herself elsewhere. "Good God," said Conor at the end of this recital, "what hogwash. You might close your eyes and clench your teeth if the gentleman involved is doing his job properly; you might even curse and yell; but you definitely won't wish yourself elsewhere."

No? This was encouraging. Elizabeth had been right to try to get the facts straight from the horse's mouth. "*Is* it such a chore? St. Clair seems to find it so. He referred to bedding me as a duty. And said he'd made a dreadful mistake."

St. Clair had made more than one mistake, reflected Conor, as he shook his head. " 'Tis not a chore but a pleasure, Duchess. Perhaps you misunderstood."

Elizabeth contemplated her hand, which Mr. Melchers still held in his. "St. Clair doesn't lust after me. He hasn't slavered once. Perhaps it *is* my fault, as Sir Charles says. I did pop him in the nose, and though I didn't mean to, it may have put him off. I also cast up my accounts. Then Magda appeared, and I thought she was his mistress, because no one had bothered to tell me they had been divorced, which made me very cross. I accused him of having libertine tendencies. *Does* St. Clair have a mistress, do you know?"

Conor was fascinated by this glimpse into married life. "No, I don't. And neither should you, puss."

Naturally Mr. Melchers subscribed to a masculine

viewpoint. Elizabeth removed her hand from his to better twist her reticule. "Were you ever in love with Magda, sir?"

Here were dangerous waters. Conor understood what she really wished to ask. "I am not such a jingle-brain," he replied, ungallantly perhaps but with perfect truth. "I know the lady too well, you see."

St. Clair *had* been a jingle-brain. Elizabeth wondered if he still was. "But you are fond of her."

"Immensely." Conor removed the reticule from her grasp and set it down beside her on the bench. "Magda is one of my closest friends. Why do you ask?"

What was it about Madame de Chavannes that prompted such devotion? "St. Clair must have loved her very much."

Conor shrugged. "Perhaps he did, once. If so, he got over it. You refine too much upon it, Duchess. St. Clair is married to you now."

This practical comment went wide of its mark. Instead of reminding Elizabeth that her husband had cast off her predecessor, it reminded her instead that the Duke of Charnwood was a very powerful man who could cast off any number of unsatisfactory brides, among them herself. She fought against a renewed onslaught of tears.

Rakehell Conor might be, but he did not lack chivalrous instincts, and beside him was definitely a lady in distress. Therefore he drew her closer to him on the bench.

Elizabeth looked at him, damp-eyed. "What are you doing?" she asked.

Conor ran his fingers along the fine line of her jaw and tipped up her face to his. "Sweeting, I am going to kiss you," he murmured, and lowered his mouth to hers, and did.

'Twas not one of Mr. Melcher's better kisses, perhaps; he was very aware that in his arms was not one of his flirts but an untried miss; and he wished not to destroy her innocence, but merely to further her education a little bit. Feeling that he had perhaps done so, he released her. Elizabeth said, "Oh."

Conor's lips twitched. Though the kiss had not been one of his better efforts, he had anticipated a somewhat more animated response. "Elizabeth, do you not show a little more enthusiasm, you will do irreparable damage to my opinion of myself."

"Oh!" Guiltily, Elizabeth's eyes flew to his face. "Truly it was a very nice kiss," she said earnestly, "and I liked it very much. But—"

"But I am not the person you wish to kiss you." Hoist with his own petard. Conor had liked the kiss sufficiently to wish for a repeat.

Elizabeth flung out her hands in frustration. "No you aren't! Which just went to show the extent of my wrongheadedness, because I make no doubt there are few women in all of England who wouldn't want to kiss you, Mr. Melchers. Perhaps there is something wrong with me. I didn't feel the slightest tummy flutter. Although I am not certain—*Do* ladies feel lustful, sir?"

When Conor had wondered what else he might teach the duchess, he had not considered that he might not only receive a set-down in the process, but also wind up providing an explanation of the facts of life. He caught her hands before she could do one of them an inadvertent injury. "I most solemnly assure you that ladies *do* feel lust, indeed might even slather, if the circumstances and company are right."

Damnation, but she was in a dither! Why should that information make her wish to weep? Elizabeth wouldn't weep again, she wouldn't. She was made of sterner stuff.

Her lips trembled, her chin quivered. Conor retrieved his handkerchief and put it in her hand. Elizabeth flung herself onto his chest, and burst into tears.

She was but a child, Conor told himself, as he stroked her slender back. A lovely, slim-hipped, long-limbed child. Whose bosom, perhaps fortunately, was today not exposed to view. Had the duchess wished to snap her fingers under the nose of her spouse, there was no one better with whom to do it than himself.

Alas, Conor liked the girl too well to do her further harm. Patiently, he endured the storm. She subsided into hiccoughs. "Shall I cut out St. Clair's liver and fry it? Would you like that?"

Elizabeth drew back and sniffled, wiped the tears from her cheeks. "I don't ordinarily behave like this. Pray forgive me for being such a wet goose. Oh, blast! I've ruined your cravat."

"Doubtless my valet will cut out *your* liver and fry it!" Conor replied cheerfully as he set her bonnet to rights. "As for yourself, Elizabeth, I will forgive you anything."

"So you will help me!" Elizabeth blinked at him, then frowned. "But why?"

Conor twitched her bonnet back into its proper position. "Perhaps I am suffering an altruistic aberration. More likely, it amuses me to help you because I know Saint would hate it of all things."

Elizabeth hesitated at this reasoning. Still, one should not look a gift horse in the mouth. "Sir Charles said I should take my clothes off."

Sir Charles also was a jingle-brain. Conor marveled at the foolishness of his fellow man. "Eventually you must," he said gravely. "But first you must let St. Clair know that you *want* to be kissed. Your maidservant is hovering in the shrubbery. We will let her fret a little longer while we put our heads together and I will tell you what you must do."

Chapter 22

"Marriage makes our nation morally sound, as it encourages men to avoid certain illicit activities." —Lady Ratchett

The duke left his breakfast companions to the care of little Katy, and settled back in the library to await the ladies' return. At least someone was enjoying this sojourn in Bath, he thought savagely, as he gave the globe a tremendous spin that nearly tumbled it off the desk. When the ladies did at length return, and his bride was not among them, he swore a great round oath and demanded to know what they had done with her.

"*Zut!*" said Magda, to whom this query was addressed, while Lady Augusta started and stared. "What do you think, that we have sent her to her last accounts? Unfair, Saint! Elizabeth went off with her maidservant. Perhaps she wished to visit the shops. Perhaps"—she twinkled—"she wished to arrange for you a surprise."

"A happy one, I hope!" Augusta picked up the wax jack. "You have gotten in the habit of frowning, Saint."

The duke had any number of things about which to

frown, among them the discovery that Elizabeth had not
been present to rein in the other ladies. Doubtful that
Gus had sought out Catterick's at so early an hour.
However, the devious Magda could get up to whatever
mischief she was up to at any moment of the day or
night. "Sir Charles joined us." Magda touched her cameo.
"*Merde alors!* He is very interested in France."

Augusta snorted. "France, my foot. The man is interested in you. He was almost drooling. You should be
ashamed."

Justin wondered if he should warn Magda about black
ants and the like, then decided she was more than capable of dealing with a gentleman who wished her to smear
camel fat on his private parts. "I doubt that Lady Ratchett
would approve of Sir Charles drooling. Even on herself."

"*Donc!* The so-disapproving Maman. I would like to
meet her, I think." Magda leaned over the back of Justin's
chair, and murmured low. "I am not deceived. You do
not trust your bride, *mon chou*. Perhaps you have not
bedded her yet."

Damned if he wasn't blushing like a schoolgirl. "That is
none of your curst business!" Justin pushed back his chair.

Magda crossed her arms beneath her ample chest.
"*Ma foi*, how the times have changed! Poor Elizabeth.
Poor Saint."

Now Magda was flirting with Saint. It was most un-
seemly. Gus must try to interrupt them before Saint
throttled her. "Why is Saint poor? Has he lost his money
on the 'Change?"

"I have lost nothing. Your allowance is safe. Both of
you may go to the Devil." Justin left Augusta gaping, and
Magda chuckling, as he stormed out of the library,
mounted the stairs, and pushed open the bedroom door.

The chamber was empty. No Elizabeth sat in front of
the dressing table mirror, no Daphne brushed her hair.

No jealous Thornaby peered in the drawers of the tall-boy or inspected Her Grace's wardrobe, or bent to search beneath the bedstead for an errant ball of dust.

A sound caught the duke's attention. He paused to listen. Again came a slight wheezing breath. Did Elizabeth lie waiting for him upon the green and white counterpane? Had she only pretended to leave the house? He pulled back the bed hangings.

No Elizabeth lay upon the counterpane, but a small and very well-fed black cat. Minou was sleeping, and wheezing, on the pillow that should by rights have been the duke's. Justin regarded the kitten with disfavor. Not that the kitten could be fairly censured for the company it had kept. Conor Melchers, for God's sake.

Minou opened one green eye, sneezed at his visitor, yawned hugely, rolled over on his back, and went back to sleep. How comfortable the wretched creature looked, sprawled upon his pillow. It looked like a very soft pillow, moreover, if a little damp from kitten drool. As did the bed look much more comfortable than the cot in the dressing room.

Dukes should not sleep on cots. Duchesses should not sleep with cats. While Justin tossed on his infernal cot, the duchess would cuddle up with her infernal cat. Minou would stretch out against her slender body. Lick her soft warm skin. Explore beneath the coverlet where no man had gone before. Good God, now he was jealous of a cat.

Justin turned, kicked the tapestry footstool out of his pathway, strode purposefully out of the bedchamber. Bath was not so large a city that a man could not, with a little perseverance, track down his errant wife. And if he found her with Conor Melchers, which he half expected that he would, then Justin would have no choice but to call the damned fellow out. Justin had never fought a duel. He thought he might enjoy it very well. Ignoring everyone who attempted to speak with him—which included Chislett, Thornaby, and a footman known inexplicably as Knobs—the duke flung open the front door, stepped through it, and then slammed it shut. The skies were gray and overcast, which perfectly fit his mood.

A pity Beau Nash had forbidden the wearing of swords in the city. If Justin was wearing a sword, which of course he wasn't—indeed he wasn't even wearing a hat—he could skewer Melchers with his pig-sticker and watch him bleed on the pavement. Elizabeth would swoon. Justin would throw her over his shoulder, take her into the nearest semideserted alleyway, do his manly duty, and be done with it. The duke paused in his musings then, shocked by his hitherto-unsuspected blood lust. All the same, if anyone ever deserved skewering it was Melchers. As for Elizabeth—

It had seemed so simple, this choosing of a companion for life. One picked out a suitable young woman, contracted a marriage, settled down in matrimony with a minimum of fuss, and set about the production of the requisite offspring. 'Twas not an undertaking of such magnitude as to upset the easy tenor of one's life. Yet it had done exactly that. Justin would never have anticipated, a mere week ago, that this day would find him wandering around Bath in search of an errant wife. A wife whom he hadn't bedded, but wished to, very much. A wife whom he even thought he liked more than a little bit, even though she threatened to bring his comfortable world tumbling down around his ears. He was mad as Bedlam. Prolonged abstinence had unhinged his brain.

Through the heart of Bath walked Justin, past the Abbey and the Pump Room. Numerous fine shops tempted him to exploration no more than did a certain public garden, which is fortunate for a certain rakish gentleman's unskewered state. *Had* St. Clair gone into the gardens, visitors there might have enjoyed fireworks more spectacular than Pigeons and Chinese Tea, Maroons and Pots de Brin.

Steps near Pulteney Bridge led down to the river, where the duke paused briefly to gaze upon the water in search of inspiration or enlightenment. When neither was forthcoming, he followed the riverside pathway around the city to the south. Before him rose a hill as steep as any in Bath. At least this feat he might accomplish, and in the process perhaps walk off some of his irritability.

Alas, it did not serve. From the top of Beechen Cliff, Justin viewed the whole city of Bath, an enchanting vista of golden buildings spread out below him, with green hills all around. The duke was not enchanted. Somewhere in that city was his wife. She was hiding from him. When he found her, he would wring her neck. So caught up was Justin in his musings that he did not notice that the sky had darkened. He did notice, however, when the gray clouds opened and rain poured down on him.

It was in a dampened frame of mind that St. Clair returned to the city. Thornaby would fly into hysterics over the condition of his jacket and boots. Justin was none too pleased himself. He felt like a drowned rat.

He climbed the steps back up to the street. Pulteney Bridge was crowded with pedestrians and vehicles, inclement weather being no deterrent to the visitors who were determined to see and be seen by one another every day. Voices filled the air. Carriage wheels rattled, hooves clattered, pattens clinked on the pavement stones.

The duke was not interested in shoemakers, or plumasseirs, or linen drapers' shops. Neither ribbon nor silk netting, the multifarious articles for sale in a bazaar, nor a fan made of chicken skin caught his eye. What *did* attract his attention was Mr. Slyte emerging from a bookseller's shop with a paper-wrapped parcel tucked under one arm. Nigel looked like a coachman in a many-caped greatcoat. He wore a tall crowned hat and top boots, and carried a lime green silk umbrella in one yellow-gloved hand. "Hallo, Saint. I ate *la matelote au vin de Bourdeaux* today. You look like a drowned rat."

The duke was not in the mood for pleasant conversation. He shook himself like a damp dog. "Thank you for pointing it out. What are you doing here? I thought you had an antipathy to rain."

"Not so great an antipathy as I have to being disinherited." Nigel extended the umbrella as they strolled through the crowd. "Aunt Syb has been racketing about too much. The quacksalver has dosed her with steel and angostura bark in flannel next to the skin, and ordered her to stay in bed. She ain't happy about it. Threatened to cut me off without a groat again."

Justin stepped away from his friend. Between sharing Nigel's garish umbrella or becoming even wetter, he preferred the damp. "I am sorry to hear Lady Syb is ill. She won't dispossess you, you know that."

"To tell truth, I'd rather have Aunt Syb than all her blunt. You will not tell her so; 'twould spoil all her fun. I have been dispatched to fetch her a copy of *The World As It I*s. I am expected to read it aloud to her. The heroine foils a rape attempt by strangling a weakling lord, and an evil woman gets a sexual disease." The rain increased and Justin abandoned his aesthetic scruples to duck under the umbrella. "What are *you* looking so thunder-faced about?"

'Twas a good thing the duke wasn't wearing a cheese toaster, or he might have spitted his oldest friend. "Melchers gave that damned kitten to Elizabeth. It is sleeping in my bed."

Nigel tilted his golden head. "The duchess wants company. Damned queer of you to be here instead of there.

Let me guess. You rang a peal over her. Now she's in her tantrums, and you're in a snit."

Perhaps, in lieu of a sword stick, Jason might spit Nigel on his own umbrella. "I didn't ring a peal over her, and I don't know if she's in her tantrums because I can't find her. And I am not in a snit."

"Very well, a dudgeon, then!! All in all, reading to Aunt Syb about strangled lordlings and diseased women don't seem a terrible fate. It's no use to scowl at me. Aunt Syb says I am incorrigible. While *you* are turning into a curmudgeon. 'Twas only a kitten, Saint."

"I wonder if it is better to be a curmudgeon or a coxcomb. The fact remains that Elizabeth is playing least-in-sight."

"A *churlish* curmudgeon," Nigel amended. "Next you will say she goes beyond the line of being pleasing. What a lot of claptrap, Saint. Why should the duchess wish to please you? You haven't exactly been lavishing attendance on her. I don't suppose it occurred to you that she learned to dance for your sake."

"*My* sake?" Justin turned to stare at his companion. "What makes you say that?"

"It certainly wasn't to please herself! She's not good at it, you know. And if you don't, I do! She practically broke my toe. As to why she did it, Gus told her she'd put you to the blush if she didn't dance." The downpour had abated. Nigel folded up his umbrella and carried it by the golden ring at its tip. "If you can't see what's right under your nose, others can. Even Aunt Syb said you was a slowtop."

Had no one a kind word to say of him? Justin bared his teeth. "Was that before or after she disinherited you?" he asked.

Nigel twirled his umbrella. "Don't go getting your hackles up. You *have* been acting like a slowtop. It's not to be wondered if the duchess prefers Melchers, you're so wonderfully stiff-necked."

If he couldn't impale his oldest friend on his umbrella, perhaps Justin might strangle him instead. "*You're* the one who said I should leave her wanting more. It doesn't seem to have worked."

Nigel shrugged. His greatcoat settled about him like a hen upon her nest. "I don't see any indication you've given her anything at all, so my advice don't count. I don't like to see the duchess unhappy. I have a great regard for her, even if you don't."

Justin looked woodenly into the distance. "I didn't say I don't have a regard for her."

Nigel stepped aside to avoid a perambulating parson. "Maybe you should try telling *her* that."

"Maybe you should not bother yourself further in my business!" snapped the duke. "You and Lady Syb and Magda and Gus and Sir Charles may all take yourself to the Devil and leave Elizabeth and me alone."

"You forgot Melchers and Birdie and the kitten," Nigel supplied helpfully. "And you are providing far too much entertainment for us to go anywhere. We await the final act in your little melodrama. I'm sure you won't disappoint us." His eyes widened. "Oho. Unfair to introduce another character so late in the play, Saint." The duke turned to see what caused his friend to stare.

Among the traffic on Pulteney Bridge was a carriage painted canary yellow and trimmed with green and red. Justin knew that carriage as well as he knew the niceish hacks which pulled the vehicle. However, carriage and hacks and owner were all supposed to be safe in London and not clattering across the bridge to where he stood.

Perhaps it was a coincidence, he told himself. Perhaps the carriage maker had been so taken with the color scheme that he had chosen to duplicate it, in the teeth of all common sense.

The carriage drew nigh, slowed, came to a halt. In the window appeared a beautiful, pouting face, with a straight little nose, plump lips, and hazel eyes. Careless auburn curls tumbled from beneath a bonnet bedecked with pleated ribbons and bows. The lady was in the highest kick of fashion, as Justin well knew, since he had also paid for her wardrobe. "By all that's holy!" marveled Nigel. "Damned if you aren't about to out-rakehell Melchers, Saint!"

Skewer or strangle or mill his canister. Definitely the duke must deal emphatically with his oldest friend, who was so lacking in proper feeling as to laugh at him. First, however, he must deal with the occupant of the carriage. Perhaps he would mill her canister instead. Leaving Nigel behind, he walked toward the coach. A footman sprang down to open the door.

The lady wore a pale green pelisse with gold cord and gray fur trim, and carried a matching muff. On her lovely face was every evidence of delight. "St. Clair! You are glad to see me. Already you have grown bored with your dreary little wife."

The duke thought wistfully that he might like to become bored. He had lost the wife he wanted, and found the mistress he didn't want instead. Damned queer it was in him to not want Meloney, moreover. He had wanted her quite avidly a mere week ago.

His mistress would not care to hear of this change of sentiment. She was not only beautiful but hot-tempered, and not beyond throwing a dreadful public scene. Elizabeth would not like another woman yelling at him in public. Wherever she was.

Meloney waited. All the world watched. St. Clair climbed into the carriage he had provided for his mistress, and ordered the coachman to drive on.

Chapter 23

*"Passions run amok will break all the bonds of human
society and place, and make the world a wilderness
of savages."* —Lady Ratchett

"There!" said Daphne, as she pinned the last ringlet
into place. "The duke will be struck with admiration at
sight of you, Your Grace."

Elizabeth eyed her reflection in the looking glass. Her
provocative muslin gown was so sheer that her pink petticoat showed through, and she had left off her stays.
The low lace-trimmed neckline left an amazing amount
of bosom on view. Elizabeth had not realized she had so
much bosom. She looked positively wanton. Mr. Melchers
had assured her that St. Clair would like it excessively if
she looked wanton. He had also assured her that, did
she but ask St. Clair for it, she would definitely have her
kisses, although Elizabeth didn't know if she should trust
Mr. Melchers or not, because he had sounded amused.

He had also told her that St. Clair would be pleased
to know that Elizabeth liked him a little bit. According to

Mr. Melchers, a gentleman wished as much as a lady to know that he was admired. Elizabeth took a deep breath, and clutched nervously at her bodice. Daphne tutted. Carefully, Elizabeth lowered her hands. The gown remained safely attached to her shoulders. Elizabeth descended the stair.

Madame de Chavannes was already in the drawing room, as well as Lady Augusta, Birdie, and Minou. The ladies were engaged in renewed discussion about how London might be defended if Napoleon led his armies to England, while kitten and parrot were engaged in a game of hide-and-seek. Gus was pointing out, with relish, the farcical conclusion of the last invasion attempt, which had ended at Fishguard in Wales, when Elizabeth walked into the room. Gus's jaw dropped open. "Dear heaven! Why are you dressed like that?"

Magda's *décolletage* was no less scandalous, the cameo from which she was never parted hung around her neck. "Ignore her, *petite!* Gus is merely jealous. I told her already that she should purchase one of those false bosoms made of wax. *Quel dommage!* Saint will be sorry he did not come home."

St. Clair had not come home? Hopefully the duke would put in an appearance before Elizabeth lost all her courage. She perched cautiously upon a chair.

" 'Ladies dressing and behaving like handmaidens must not be surprised if they are treated as handmaidens.' I do not require a wax bosom." Gus moved to the piano and began to play a country dance. Birdie bobbed about in time to the music. Minou raced in dizzy circles in pursuit of his own tail.

Came a sound at the door. St. Clair had come home! Elizabeth stiffened, then lounged back in her chair in an attempt at nonchalance. Her gown slipped off her shoulder. She yanked it back up.

Not St. Clair walked into the room, but Chislett, with a note on a silver tray. With a bow, he presented the tray to Magda. All eyes were on her as she unfolded the note and read, then folded up the paper and tucked it in her bodice. "*Zut!* I must go out. No, you'll not accompany me, Gus. Do not press me further, 'tis a private matter. Chislett, I require my cloak." She swept out of the room.

No sooner did Madame pass from view than Lady Augusta sprang to her feet and followed. "Where are you going?" Elizabeth asked.

Gus paused impatiently in the doorway. "After her, of course. I'll wager anything you like Magda had that note sent to herself in an attempt to give us the slip."

Elizabeth wasn't entirely certain Lady Augusta hadn't contrived this entire business to give *her* the slip. "I'm coming with you."

There was no time to waste in argument. "Do as you wish, but hurry," Augusta replied, ungraciously.

Dusk had fallen when the ladies stepped outside. Even wrapped in a velvet evening cloak, Elizabeth was chilled. "There she is," said Augusta. "Hurry, before we lose her." Keeping to the shadows, the ladies followed Madame de Chavannes along the curve of the Royal Crescent to Brock Street, down the Gravel Walk, and turned into Union Street in time to see Magda admitted to a stately structure. Gus swore softly. "Catterick's."

It looked no different from any other building on the street, this gaming hell where many a lordling and lady had learned the consequences of playing deep and hard. Elizabeth wondered again at Gus's motives. "Do you really suspect Magda of being an agent for the French?"

"I suspect Magda of nothing and everything." Lady Augusta looked gloomily at the building's Palladian facade. "Saint told me that if ever I set foot in Catterick's, he would cut off my allowance for a year."

The air was damp and bitter. Elizabeth's feet, in her evening slippers, were turning numb with cold. "Magda will not thank us for following her like this. Perhaps we should go home."

"Magda isn't up to all the rigs, though she will not believe it. She has tumbled into trouble more than once." Gus drew her cloak more tightly around her. "We must go inside."

Would St. Clair thank her for keeping an eye on his cousin? Probably he would not. Nor was he likely to be delighted that his wife had entered a gaming hell. "Why must we go in?"

"Despite the fact that we agree on nothing," Augusta said stiffly, "I still would not wish to see Magda come to harm. It's too cold to stand here gawking. Come. I can't enter that place alone."

Elizabeth was fagged to death with worrying about what St. Clair might think. She picked up her skirts and stepped into the street. "I haven't seen any other indication that you care what St. Clair thinks. Surely he wouldn't really cut off your allowance for an entire year."

"I think I know my cousin better than you do." Augusta grasped Elizabeth's arm as they approached the front door. "Anyway, 'tis not because I fear my cousin that I need your company."

Odd to see a beseeching expression on Augusta's aristocratic features. Elizabeth trusted her no more in this conciliatory mood. "Then why?" she asked.

"If you must know, because I cannot trust myself! People play at games of chance in Catterick's. Faro. Hazard. Vingt-et-un. I like to gamble more than anything. I like to gamble so much that I dream about it. Once I start gambling, I do not stop until either the club closes or I haven't a shilling left, and sometimes I don't stop even then. 'Tis called gambling fever, and once I am over it, I wallow in self-loathing until the next opportunity presents itself, when I succumb to the lure of the tables once again. You will remind me that Justin will be very angry and cut off my allowance if I gamble. If that doesn't serve, then you will kick me, hard."

Monstrous, to be in the grip of such compulsion. Elizabeth drew in a deep, cold breath. "Very well. We will go in, and you will assure yourself that Magda is in no danger, and then we will leave. And if you make one move toward the tables, I will leave you there and tell St. Clair he is to cut off your allowance for the rest of your life." Perhaps this was not entirely what Mr. Melchers had in mind when he suggested Elizabeth show St. Clair some affection, but it seemed a great deal more practical than sitting moping in the drawing room.

The door was opened by a burly individual who resembled less a butler than a pugilist. He looked down his crooked nose at the ladies and lifted a scarred eyebrow. Elizabeth raised her own eyebrows and elevated her chin. "We are friends of Madame de Chavannes. I believe she has already arrived."

The butler recognized a gentry mort when he saw one. Gentry morts had no business in such a place as this. However, it was no skin off his nose if the silly twits gambled away their garters. He stepped aside and allowed the women to enter, and took away their cloaks.

A footman led the way up the staircase to a suite of rooms on the first floor. The establishment was furnished like a grand private home, with thick carpets, and marble fireplaces, richly upholstered furnishings, and comfortable chairs; green baize-covered tables and numerous potted palms.

One room was given over to deep basset, another to faro and E.O. In yet another, supper was being served. All the rooms were crowded with people engaged in every conceivable game of chance. Some of the more serious gamblers had turned their coats inside out for luck. Others wore eyeshades and leather guards around their cuffs. Luck was very much courted in this establishment, where five or ten or fifteen thousand pounds might be lost in an evening's play.

Augusta whimpered upon sight of a faro table. Elizabeth took a firm grip on her arm. "No! Not even a rubber or two of piquet. I don't see Magda. Where can she have gone? Perhaps she knew we followed her, and slipped out a back door."

Lady Augusta tried very hard to focus her thoughts on other than the temptations all around her. She moved toward the supper room, where chicken in mushroom and wine sauce was being served, along with an excellent claret and green peas. Gus glanced inside, then abruptly turned around and blocked the doorway. "Magda isn't there, either. You're right. We should leave."

Here was an about-face, and most abrupt it was. Elizabeth moved to look beyond Augusta into the supper room. Augusta moved also, to block her view. "Devil take it, Duchess!" said Conor Melchers, from behind her. "What are you doing here?"

"Mr. Melchers! You startled me." Elizabeth turned, and Conor caught her arm. He and Lady Augusta exchanged a look. "Why *shouldn't* I be here? What are the two of you trying to keep from me? If you do not remove yourself from that doorway, I will kick you, Gus!"

"Nothing to signify!" Lady Augusta said quickly, while Mr. Melchers added, "You must leave now, Duchess. I will explain everything to you another time."

Elizabeth did not feel like leaving. She jerked away from Mr. Melchers, and kicked Augusta in the shin. Augusta yelped and grasped her injured leg. Elizabeth stepped around her and entered the supper room.

Here, too, the appointments were lavish. Guests dined off the finest china and glassware. The room was crowded with visitors pausing to refresh themselves before resuming their pursuit of Lady Luck.

Among those visitors was the Duke of Charnwood. An auburn-haired beauty clung possessively to his arm. The woman murmured; the duke smiled. St. Clair appeared to be on considerably better terms with his auburn-haired companion than with his own wife.

The woman looked up, caught Elizabeth staring, stood on tiptoe to murmur into the duke's ear. Justin glanced at the doorway. His expression, upon seeing Elizabeth standing there with Conor Melchers in a gown so diaphanous that she might as well have been naked, was not indicative of admiration. He brushed off his companion and strode toward the door.

Mr. Melchers saw the duke approaching. "This is not the way I meant for you to get your husband's attention, puss."

Before Elizabeth could respond, St. Clair was upon them. Had he worn a sword-stick, the three people in the doorway would have been made into a human kabob. Lacking a sword-stick, he reached out and grasped his wife's bodice, and yanked it up as far as it would go. "Melchers, I require a word with you. Augusta, you will see Elizabeth home, at once. If you dare say so much as one word to me, I will wring your blasted neck."

Very little conversation passed between the ladies during their journey, on which they were accompanied by a footman from Catterick's, whose purpose was less to see that the ladies reached their destination unaccosted than to make sure that they reached the destination the duke had in mind, which was not the nether regions, where he might have fairly consigned them both, but his home in the Royal Crescent. Once safely

in the drawing room, Lady Augusta rang for refreshment, as well as for burnt feathers and hartshorn. The
women were alone, Birdie and Minou having already
been taken off by little Katy to bed. "I am so sorry,"
Augusta said. "I didn't know Meloney was in Bath."

Elizabeth was sorry, also, for a great many things.
"Who is she?" she said quietly. "Other than a demirep."

The duchess should have kicked Augusta harder. Gus
should have kicked herself. She sat down beside Elizabeth
on the sofa and took her hand. "Her name is Meloney
Smythe-Litton. She is a very dashing young widow who
has been in Justin's keeping for some time. Meloney is
not important. She is merely the favorite of the moment. You know how the gentlemen are."

If she didn't, she was finding out. How foolish Elizabeth
had been to think she could attract her husband's attention by putting on a pretty dress. Mr. Melchers would have
been kinder to inform her that she couldn't attract her
husband's attention if she ran naked through the streets.

Magda walked into the drawing room, followed by a
footman with a tray of refreshments, and another armed
with burnt feathers, hartshorn, and vinaigrette. "This is
a pretty kettle of fish. St. Clair is furious with Conor for
luring Elizabeth into a gaming hell."

"It's hardly Melchers' fault." Gus waved a burnt feather
under Elizabeth's nose. "We followed you there."

"And set the cat among the pigeons." Magda sat down
in front of the teapot, and began to pour. "What were you
thinking, to take Elizabeth into such a place, *ma chere?*"

Augusta accepted a cup of tea, and glowered. "What
were *you* thinking, to go there yourself?"

Magda shrugged and selected a macaroon, a ratafia,
and an almond cake from the pastry plate. "I go where
I please. *Pourtant,* since you are so determined to know, I
went to see Sir Charles."

Elizabeth sneezed, and pushed away Gus's burnt feathers. "Sir Charles?"

"It's not what you think, *petite*." Magda popped the macaroon into her mouth. "But your Maman would not approve."

Elizabeth stared at Madame, so lush and devious and stuffed with pastries. "You are not wearing your cameo."

Magda removed another almond cake from the tray. "The cameo was never mine. It has now gone on to where it belongs. *Ah ça!* We have more important things to consider. By morning all the world will know that Saint's bride found him in Catterick's with his *petite amie*."

So much for convincing the world that theirs had been a love match. "St. Clair is going to divorce me," Elizabeth said gloomily.

Magda patted her knee, leaving pastry crumbs on the thin muslin. "Things may be in a bad case, but Saint will not divorce you."

Elizabeth was in no mood for consolation. "How can you be so certain? St. Clair divorced *you*."

"That was because she had run off with Conor," Augusta volunteered. "Poor Saint had no choice."

"You are startled, *petite*. I can see it." Magda bit into the ratafia. "*Hélas*, I cannot help but think of poor Armand."

"Armand?" Distracted from the startling revelation that Magda had eloped not once but twice, Elizabeth stared. "Who is Armand, and what has he to do with this, pray?"

Magda licked her fingers. "Armand met his end in an *affaire d' honneur*. He was very jealous. As was *cher* Christienne. I was desolated, *naturellement*."

Aware of Madame's history with Mr. Melchers, Augusta was still confused. "You said your husband's name was Jules."

Magda surveyed the pastries remaining on the tray. "*He* was guillotined."

Elizabeth tugged at her hair in an attempt to concentrate her thoughts. "I don't understand. Both of them died in duels?"

Magda sighed. "They both died in the same duel. And all over a simple kiss. But that is far and far off! The question is, what are *you* going to do?"

Tugging had not alleviated Elizabeth's bewilderment. "Do about what?"

Magda threw up her hands in exasperation. "*Mon Dieu!* Will you just stand there and let them blow each other's brains out? Or perhaps you will be more fortunate than I and one will delope. Which will it be, I wonder? St. Clair is of course the more honorable, but Conor holds you in genuine fondness and for that reason probably will not blow out St. Clair's brains, in which case St. Clair will probably blow out his!"

Lady Augusta frowned and twitched her nose. "You are trying to tell us something, Magda? I wish you would not be so obscure."

"I am not at all obscure, *ma chérie.* You are not listening. Elizabeth would not like being a widow. She has not yet learned to like being a wife." Magda made another selection from the tray.

Nor did Elizabeth like being toyed with. "Magda, are you telling us that St. Clair and Melchers are going to fight a duel?"

"*Très bien!*" Magda bit into an almond cake. "They will meet at dawn. At Kingsdown on the outskirts of Bath." Augusta gasped and groped for her hartshorn.

St. Clair and Mr. Melchers would fight a duel. One of them would be wounded, if not worse. If not both. And all because Elizabeth had wished to show her husband some fondness. Said the duchess, "Damn and blast!"

Chapter 24

*"No circumstance, however trifling, which strengthens
the bonds of an honorable and mutual attraction should
be ignored."* —Lady Ratchett

The plateau atop Kingdown Hill commanded a lovely
peaceful view of noble trees and rolling green hills dotted about with farmhouses and sheep. Some five miles
in the distance in one direction lay the city of Bath, while
the opposite side of the hill looked eastward toward Box.
Along the hillside stretched a village. Several of the homes
there had been quarried from the local limestone rock.
The local pub perched so precariously on the slope that
it was secured by chains.

The pub was not open at this early hour, as the first
fingers of light inched their way across the sky, and
two carriages rattled along the road to the heights,
where a herd of grazing sheep were enjoying the
emerging view. The carriages drew to a halt. Mr.
Melchers emerged from one vehicle. He gazed unen-
thusiastically at the brightening sky. "This is damned

uncivilized," he said, for the second time in as many days.

From the second carriage stepped the Duke of Charnwood and Nigel Slyte. The duke looked murderous. This expression was due less to the earliness of the hour than to the circumstance that Mr. Slyte was engaged in reciting the twenty-seven rigid rules which governed a dueling event. It had been Mr. Melchers' prerogative, as the challenged party, to make the choice of weapons. Since Mr. Melchers had opted for fisticuffs, the duke was consequently unable to utilize either his excellent dueling pistols or a sword. If it was not at all the thing to settle an affair of honor in such a manner, neither was Mr. Melchers the thing. The gentlemen had dispensed with the nuisance of seconds. St. Clair stripped off his coat.

Nigel drew out a flask. "Whiskey anyone? It's damned cold out here. No? Then more is left for me. I see that you are anxious to bludgeon one another. You will please remember Broughton's rules. No hitting below the belt. Wrestling holds allowed only above the waist. No hitting or kicking an opponent who is down. I don't suppose I can persuade either of you to call off the business?" He paused. St. Clair and Mr. Melchers merely glared at one another. Nigel shrugged. Flask in hand, he arranged himself upon a boulder, and sat back to watch a mill. Though Nigel was not addicted to sport himself, he had in honor of the occasion scanned Mendoza's *Art of Boxing*, not that said art had stood the champion in particularly good stead when Gentleman Jackson grabbed him with one hand and beat him senseless with the other and took away his crown. Also in honor of the occasion, Mr. Slyte was dressed in funereal black.

"You're determined about this, then?" inquired Mr. Melchers, as he took off his own coat. "You might recall

that this won't be the first time I've given you your bastings, Saint."

"Tongue-valiant, aren't you?" retorted the duke, as
he unbuttoned his shirt. "*I* haven't spent the last twenty
years drowning myself in dissipation. No, I will give you
your bastings, and then you will take a fancy to someone
else's wife and leave mine alone."

"You are rapidly becoming a bore on that subject."
Mr. Melchers pulled off his cravat. "Your wife has a level
head on her shoulders. You, however, are a hidebound
chowderbrain."

Justin yanked off his own cravat and dropped it on
the grass. "Goble-cock!" he snapped, and raised his fists.
Mr. Slyte explained to an inquisitive ewe that this would
be no rough and tumble turn-up, but a scientific application of the manly art of self-defense. Short, choppy
blows delivered with the swiftness of lightning. A crush-
ing blow to the jugular delivered with the full force of
the arm shot horizontally from the shoulder. The gentlemen would stand up for a round or two until one cracked
the other's napper, after which they would all shake
hands and go home.

The men circled, trading insults. The words "knock-
in-the-cradle," "niddicock," "cabbage-head," and "fatwit"
were used. St. Clair was a proper man with his fists, Nigel
informed the ewe, and took another swig of whiskey,
while Melchers had a very handy set of fives. In height
and build and science they were excellently well-matched,
although their footwork might be complicated by the
presence of copious amounts of sheep dung.

"Shut up, Nigel!" snapped the duke, and jabbed. "I'm
sorry I ever saved you from drowning. I should have let
you fall through the ice."

"You *did* let me fall out of that tree!" Nigel pointed
out. "I still have the scar."

Mr. Melchers ducked, and circled. "And *I* still have the scar from when you hit me with that stick."

"I was looking for the Holy Grail. Saint was King Arthur, and you were Lancelot, and I was Sir Galahad." Nigel waved the flask. "Conor got the girl. Conor always got the girl. I never *had* a girl, which is probably a good thing, because Conor would have taken her away from me also. As it was, he locked me in the feed shed. I might have died there and turned into a mouldering skeleton if one of the grooms hadn't wished to tup the kitchen maid."

St. Clair swung a good roundhouse right and missed. Conor said, "You had Gus." Nigel shuddered, and drank. "Fighting hurts," Conor added, as he got in a good body blow. "You don't really want to hurt me, Saint."

"The devil I don't!" snapped St. Clair, and cuffed Mr. Melchers smartly on the ear. "You've been taking things away from me since we were nine years old. I'm sick to death of it!"

"You always had the best of everything. I wanted it." Mr. Melchers feinted with his left. "Interesting that you never made any effort to stop me taking things away from you until now. One might think you had a fondness for your bride."

"Fondness or not, I intend to keep her!" said the duke. Mr. Melchers' fist connected with his face. "Dammit, I think you broke my nose!"

"I knew I should have bet on Melchers," said Nigel to the ewe. "Look at that. Saint is bleeding like a stuck pig."

Conor lifted his hands. "I didn't mean to do it. 'Twas an accident, Saint."

"This isn't!" retorted the duke, and popped Mr. Melchers in the eye. Further fisticuffs ensued. By the end of the round, St. Clair's cork may have been drawn, but Mr. Melchers sported two black eyes and a split lip. "If I ever see you with my wife again," panted Justin, "I won't be satisfied with putting out your daylights. I trust I make myself clear."

"Clear as pudding," said Mr. Melchers. "You'll carve out my gizzard and serve it up to me on a plate. Here, take this handkerchief and wipe your nose. You are horn-mad, Saint."

St. Clair had reached out for the handkerchief. Upon receiving this provocation, he smote Mr. Melchers in the jaw instead. Mr. Melchers retaliated with a body blow. "Not below the belt, remember!" called out Mr. Slyte, who had by this time imbibed a great deal of whiskey and had one arm draped around the ewe. "No, Saint, you must not kick him! Damned if the two of you don't look like rustics! Yes, and smell like them also!" He began to laugh.

St. Clair and Melchers paused to look at each other. As a man, they rose, grasped Nigel by his arms, and tossed him into an especially large pile of dung. Nigel howled and came up swinging. The sheep paused in their chewing and moved closer to observe the three gentlemen rolling around the hilltop in a tangle of arms and legs.

Came the thud of hoofbeats, the clatter of wheels. Combatants and sheep alike paused as a third carriage rattled into view. A magistrate, perhaps, sent to break up the affair?

The carriage door opened. Elizabeth emerged. "Imbeciles! Jingle-brains!" she yelled. "Magda said you were going to blow each other's brains out. Instead I find you rolling about like children. Someone will explain before I blow out your brains myself. Get up off the ground!"

With alacrity, the gentlemen sprang to their feet, due not to the fire that shot from the duchess's fine eyes, or the acid that dripped from her tongue, but because of the dueling pistol which she held most awkwardly in her right hand. Nigel cleared his throat. "Duchess? The, er, gun?"

Elizabeth turned the pistol on him, and Nigel stepped back. "Stay right there, Mr. Slyte. I made Thornaby give the gun to me. Yes, it is loaded and no, I don't know how to use it, and if you do not stop this stupidity immediately I will blow *all* your brains out. Mr. Melchers did not take me to that gaming hell, St. Clair. Gus and I followed Magda there. Gus was worried that Magda was in trouble. *I* was worried that Gus might gamble, and I knew you would not wish her to. Mr. Melchers was merely trying to persuade me to leave before I saw you with your ladybird."

If this was true, then Justin might have cause to be grateful to Conor Melchers, galling thought. He glanced at his old foe. Conor was gazing at Elizabeth with overt admiration. "Magnificent! If you don't want her, I'll take her myself, Saint."

All thought of gratitude flew out of Justin's head. "Who said I didn't want her, you sapskull?"

Conor looked at him. "She did."

"Stop it!" Elizabeth was finding herself a tiny bit distracted by the sight of two gentlemen naked to the waist. Mr. Melchers made a fine figure, even with two black eyes, while St. Clair—Well. The duke was all that was desirable, even with dirt and bits of grass stuck about his person, and blood crusted on his face. "We were talking about your ladybird, St. Clair. Don't bother to tell me that I shouldn't know about ladybirds. Or that I am behaving badly, or I have sunk myself below reproach. *Or* that you will cast me off!"

"As I said, I'll take her," murmured Conor. "And my intentions are entirely dishonorable. Look at her. If your intentions are not dishonorable, you truly are a beef-wit, Saint."

"Shut up!" muttered the duke. "Why would you think I wish to cast you off, Elizabeth?"

Nigel had been too long silent. Furthermore, he had imbibed a great deal of whiskey and was consequently in a very merry state of mind. "It might have something to do with the way you yanked her dress up to her chin. Oh yes, I know about it. The whole world knows about how your wife caught you in Catterick's with your *petite amie* and you sent her home and challenged Melchers to a duel, which makes no sense to me, but then I wasn't there. Maybe if *he'd* yanked up her dress—But no, he'd be more likely to yank it down!"

"One more word," snapped Justin, "and I shall strangle you with your cravat. Perhaps I *have* been a bit high-handed, I admit it." Nigel tittered. "Very well, a lot! I still fail to see why Elizabeth would think I would cast her off."

"You cast off Magda," Conor pointed out. "Although it *was* after she had run off with me."

Elizabeth waved her pistol in his direction. "You told me you were never in love with Magda, Mr. Melchers. But you ran off with her. I don't understand."

Conor managed to look irresistibly wicked, even with two black eyes. "I wasn't in love, nor was she. It was something else. Saint will explain it all to you. And if he doesn't, I will." Justin growled. Conor raised his hands, palms out, and stepped back a pace. "You must not think Saint had his heart broken. Although he will not admit it because he is so full of starch, Saint was never more glad of anything in his life than to have someone take Magda off his hands."

The duke looked ready to chew nails. Nigel thought it time to intervene. "Tell you what, Duchess! Saint never tried to fight a duel over Magda!" he pointed out.

The duke did not in the least appreciate any of these

efforts in his behalf. "I will thank you both to be less busy about my business! Elizabeth, put down that gun."

The duchess, who had been about to do exactly that, raised the pistol again and aimed it at her husband's chest. "I am very tired of everyone telling me what I must do," she said. "Of being a good biddable girl, and a comfortable little wife, and all that other blasted poppycock. I am not feeling amiable, or sensible, and I do not *care* to be a model of good breeding, and to the Devil with propriety! You gentlemen expect that you may have your mistresses and your gaming hells and go about pounding each other and rolling about in sheep droppings and in general acting like lunatics, while I am expected to be as meek as a mushroom and ask permission even about the lowness of my neckline. It is utter idiocy, and I will not have it." Upon so saying, she yanked open her pelisse, and ripped the bodice of her gown right open. "So there!"

All three gentlemen stared at the lovely bosom thus displayed. Their expressions were unanimously bemused. Conor was the first to recover, perhaps because his experience with exposed bosoms had been the most varied. "I beg you, Saint, cast her off!" he said.

St. Clair glowered, first at Mr. Melchers, and then at Nigel, then his wife. He had thought she had a level head on her. Instead, she was acting like a Bedlamite. A Bedlamite with a lovely bosom. "Elizabeth, cover yourself. I dislike to have my dirty linen washed in public. You will stop at once."

Elizabeth's finger tightened on the trigger. "I didn't have dirty linen before I met you, Your Grace. I don't have dirty linen now, *you* do. Everything I have done was with the best intentions. You will tell me about your mistress, please."

He would do no such thing. "I do not have a mistress," Justin retorted, his own temper further exacerbated by the censure in his wife's voice.

"Yes, you do!" volunteered Nigel, cheerfully. "Maybe those blows you took to the head rattled your brain. Meloney, remember? Red-haired. Greedy sort of female, I always thought, but you must know what you like."

"What I would like is to place my fingers around your neck, Nigel, and squeeze until your face turns blue. Yes, Elizabeth, I know you have a gun. If you are going to pull the trigger, I wish you would do so, so that one of us might die, and the rest of us go home. Conor, you look like you are going to say something. I wish you would not, but I suppose that doesn't signify."

Conor shrugged. "I saw the lady myself. Lovely little piece."

"Then you may have her. I warn you, she's expensive."

Conor quirked a lazy eyebrow. "So am I."

The duke turned back to his duchess. "There. No mistress. Are we through now? Nigel will be drunk as an owl if he swallows any more whiskey. Conor and I are about to catch our death of cold. I don't know what you hoped to accomplish here today, but I trust you're satisfied."

Elizabeth didn't know what she had hoped to accomplish, either, other than preventing St. Clair and Mr. Melchers from blowing each other's brains out, which they had apparently decided not to do themselves.

Her anger faded, leaving her standing on the plateau with sheep and half-naked men standing all about her, a pistol in her hand and her own gown torn open to the waist. Elizabeth dropped the pistol. It discharged as it hit the ground, startling gentlemen and sheep.

The duke peered over the boulder behind which he

had taken refuge, and was pleased to see that his bride, while looking startled, had all her parts intact. She turned away from him. "Elizabeth, where are you going? I demand to know!"

"Demand and be damned, Your Grace." The duchess climbed into her carriage. "I am going home."

The door slammed. The carriage rattled down the hill. Mr. Melchers appropriated Nigel's flask, that gentleman being occupied with fending off the advances of a randy ram that had been attracted by his pungent scent.

Conor handed the flask to Justin. "I don't know as I've ever seen so nice a bit of cross-and-jostle work, with a muzzler to finish it!" he said.

Chapter 25

"Once a person has succumbed to the passions, there is no cure, and no redemption, except through death."
—Lady Ratchett

These interesting events, and their aftermath, took up no little time. Mr. Slyte had to be wrestled away from the enamored ram, and bundled into the carriage, and helped into his home in Queen's Square, under the disapproving eye of Lady Ysabella, who rose from her sickbed to demand to know why her nephew was not only drunk as a lord at this abominable hour, but also stank of sheep dung. She also wished to know why St. Clair was in a similarly odiferous condition, and with a bloodied nose. Upon hearing the explanation—from Justin, Nigel was in no condition to do other than hiccough and giggle—she informed the duke that he was cockle-brained, and bade him go on home.

The sun was well up in the sky when Justin arrived finally in the Royal Crescent. Chislett opened the door, and stared. "Your Grace! Oh, your poor nose. Sir Charles is in the library. He particularly wishes to speak with you. Perhaps you might wish to clean up first."

Justin raised an eyebrow. "Smell bad, do I?" Good!" He mounted the stairs.

Sir Charles was not alone in the library. With him were Lady Augusta and Magda, Birdie and Minou. Sir Charles was seated behind the *secrétaire,* Birdie perched on his shoulder. Gus sat stiffly on an upholstered chair. Magda leaned on one corner of the desk, playing with Minou.

She looked up as Justin entered. "*Alors,* I am pleased to see that your brains were not blown out. You are just in time to bid me *adieu.* My business here is done, and I find myself in a dreadful hurry to be off, *tu comprends.*"

St. Clair comprehended that Madame de Chavannes was dressed for traveling, in a lovely wine-colored carriage dress, with a fanciful bonnet on her head. "What business might that have been? Determining how you might interfere with me?"

Magda twinkled. "Perhaps just a little bit. Strange as it is in me, I have a certain fondness for you, Saint. *Voyons,* I needed a reason to be in Bath. When I heard about your nuptials, I decided I must meet your bride."

Sir Charles winced as Birdie nibbled on his ear. "If it's you who has been encouraging Elizabeth to Take a Notion, Madame de Chavannes, you are very much in the wrong."

Magda laughed and slid off the desk. "*Zut*! That will have been Saint. You must scold him for it. Come, Gus, we will say our good-byes privately, and leave the gentlemen to talk."

Was Magda an enemy agent, or not? Gus still could not decide. She paused in the doorway. "I wished to accompany Elizabeth this morning. Magda would not let me. I am glad that no one shot you, Saint." She left the room.

Justin did not wish to sit upon the furniture in his begrimed condition. He walked toward the fireplace. "There was never any chance of anyone shooting anyone. Save for Elizabeth. I don't think you wish to scold me, Sir Charles."

Sir Charles picked up the quill and tantalized Minou. "I don't even wish to scold Elizabeth. Was it you as tore her dress?"

"No. She did that herself. In an attempt to make a point." Justin plucked grass bits off his breeches. "It was most effective."

Sir Charles shook his head. "I must speak to her about this. Her mama would not approve."

"I believe that I do not approve of her mama." The duke detached himself from the mantelpiece. "If anyone is to give Elizabeth a rare trimming, it will be myself. Where is she, Sir Charles?"

"She said she was going home. I locked her in her room." Sir Charles tossed St. Clair the key.

Justin was frowning as he made his way to his bedchamber. By "home" he had thought Elizabeth meant his home, here. Instead she had meant to return to her wretched mama. His duchess must be very unhappy indeed.

He unlocked the door, and stepped into the room. Elizabeth, who had been sitting in a chair by the fireplace, stood up and eyed him warily. She had changed into a simple muslin dress. She had also put back on her corset. Her hair was drawn back severely. Her face was pale.

Justin put the key down on the writing table. "You may leave if you still wish to, after we have talked."

He fell silent, staring at the key. Elizabeth twisted her wedding ring, and fidgeted. The silence dragged on interminably until she cleared her throat. "I suppose it will accomplish nothing to tell you that I am sorry, St. Clair. I perfectly understand why you have taken me in disgust. I should have not done a great many of the things I did, especially as regards Mr. Melchers, but he seemed to like me, and you seemed so unreasonable. I might have acted differently had anyone told me about that old business. I don't know why Magda did not."

Justin moved closer. "Because she was meddling. I suppose I should be grateful to her for it, in a way."

Grateful to Magda, after all this bother? Perhaps the duke might be tolerant of Elizabeth also, when she was a former wife. "You will wish me to go home now. Had not Sir Charles locked me in, I would already have had Daphne pack."

"I wish you to go nowhere." Justin grasped her wrists. "Devil take it, Elizabeth, I am not accustomed to apologizing. Kindly give me a chance!"

Did her ears deceive her? Apologize? St. Clair? Elizabeth contemplated his dirty chin. "You don't wish Sir Charles to take me back?"

"Sir Charles shall take you nowhere," Justin said irritably. "You are mine, and I mean to keep you. Unless, that is, you truly wish to go. No, let me finish! I know they say of me that I'm starched-up, and I daresay it's true, but I know no other way to be. And it's also true that one of the things I liked in you was that you were so well-brought-up that you would never lead me the sort of maddening dance that Magda did. But I did not mean that you should try to be something that you're not, because I like what you are very well."

Elizabeth regarded him doubtfully. "You do?"

"I do now that I know you." Justin frowned down at

her. "And for that I must be grateful to Magda, because with me so starched up, and you being alternately awesomely proper and as provokingly prickly, I might never have *seen* you, had not Magda persuaded Conor to take a hand. She meant me to be jealous, and I was. It must have amused her immensely."

This grew more and more amazing. Elizabeth moistened her dry lips. "I thought you didn't wish me to know Mr. Melchers because he is a rakehell."

Justin's rare smile flashed. "Ah, but you have assured me that he was ever the gentleman where you are concerned. Which is not something I can understand in him, because I have been wishing to behave most *improperly* toward you for some time."

St. Clair was clasping her hands so tightly that her knuckles had begun to ache. Elizabeth didn't mind a bit. "You said you had made a mistake."

"I have made any number of mistakes," the duke said dryly. "I believe that particular folly had to do with my delay in, ah, asserting my husbandly rights. I wanted you dreadfully, my dear. But I did not wish to frighten you, or for you to take me in dislike."

As if she could dislike him. How uncertain he seemed, this proud man. Elizabeth remembered Mr. Melcher's suggestion that she should show her husband some affection, and took in a deep breath. "I do not dislike you at all. And I would like it very much if you would please kiss me, St. Clair."

Ever the gentleman, the duke obliged his lady, who promptly wrapped her arms around his dirty shoulders and pressed close to him. *This* kiss was all Elizabeth had ever dreamed of, and more. Her heart hammered, her butterflies turned quadruple somersaults, and she felt fizzy tingles all the way from her scalp to the tips of her toes. By the time he was done kissing her, she was di-

sheveled, and breathless, and her hair had come unpinned.

Lord, she was responsive. Justin wished to take her right
there on the rug before the hearth. With the greatest of
self-discipline, he moved his hands to her shoulders
and set her away from him. She looked startled, then
bewildered. "I smell like a sheep," he said.

Elizabeth wrinkled her nose. "I thought perhaps
Minou had an accident."

Justin touched a finger to her soft lips. "May we start
all over again? I will rid my house of all interlopers.
Magda has already gone. We will send Sir Charles back
to your mama, though he won't want to go."

Elizabeth couldn't blame him. She hadn't wanted to
go herself. "And Gus?"

"We will give Gus to Lady Syb. That will keep them
both occupied, as well as Nigel. Then we will be alone
together. Perhaps I will even dismiss all the servants.
'Elizabeth' is so very formal. Do you have another name?"

"My middle name is Ermyntrude. I don't think I
would care to be called that."

"Ermyntrude." Justin sampled it, thoughtfully.

Elizabeth swatted him. "Nigel calls me Duchess."

"The whole world calls you Duchess. I was thinking
of something more intimate. I believe I shall call you
darling, if that's all right with you." Came a silence
while the duke kissed his wife again. "And now before I
do my husbandly duty, I must have a bath. Don't look
down your nose at me. I know I used the word 'duty.'
This duty has nothing to do with chamber pots. It is my
duty to give you pleasure, as it is your duty to do whatever you please to me." He tugged the bellpull.

Footmen appeared with copper tub and pails of
water. Elizabeth watched the bath being prepared. The

footmen left the room. She started to follow. Justin said,
"Stay."

Stay in the room while her husband bathed? He would
have to take off his clothes. St. Clair wanted her to stay
in the room while he took off his clothes?

Elizabeth's knees felt weak. She dropped into a chair.
As Justin disrobed, he watched her, less in anticipation
of her reaction than in fear she'd bolt for the door.

Elizabeth didn't bolt. She wasn't capable of bolting,
even if she wished to, which she did not. What a very nice,
smooth, muscular chest had the duke. She had seen his
bare chest before, as well as Mr. Melchers', which was also
very nice. However, she had an opportunity to study
that chest now, as she had not in the field. As well as the
rest of him. Before her fascinated gaze, St. Clair pulled
off his boots. His hands moved to the fastening of his
breeches. Oh, my.

Elizabeth swallowed. She must say something. That,
or faint dead away. "Your poor nose. Mr. Melchers was
only trying to help us. He said you wouldn't like it if you
knew."

Justin paused, half in and half out of his breeches.
"Help us *how*?"

Elizabeth wasn't naïve enough to tell her husband
that a rakehell had kissed her, especially now that she
understood it hadn't been a proper kiss at all. "He said
that you would like it if I showed you some affection.
And that I should let you know that I admired you a little bit."

Justin raised an inquiring brow. "*Do* you admire me a
little bit?"

Damnation! How could a woman not admire a man
who looked like a Greek god? A very naked Greek god.
'Twouldn't be good for the duke if she told him just

how much she admired him. "Sir Charles said I should take my clothes off," Elizabeth said.

Justin was reminded of a certain lecture. Black ants and camel grease. "Just what *did* you tell Sir Charles?"

"That you said you couldn't do it." Elizabeth stared. "But clearly you can."

Clearly he'd better get into the bath before he made love to his wife still smelling like a sheep. Justin hopped into the tub so quickly that he splashed water everywhere. He didn't like Conor Melchers giving advice to his wife, but perhaps he was a little bit grateful to the devil, all the same. Perhaps he might even permit Elizabeth to speak with Conor, after all.

Whom was Justin kidding? His wife would speak to whomever she wished. He was grateful that, after all his prosing and posturing, she was speaking to him. Perhaps if he tried very hard, he might hear what she was saying now, instead of thinking of her lovely bosom, and how he would throw away her stays.

She was not only speaking, she had risen from the chair and was walking toward the door. Surely, after all his efforts, she was not going to leave. Astonishing, how one's heart could sink down to one's toes. Justin would not allow her to leave him. If necessary, he would chase after her dripping wet and naked through the house. "Elizabeth! Come back here!" he said.

She turned, key in hand, and inserted it in the lock, to the great relief of Thornaby, who was hovering in the dressing room, prepared if necessary to knock both the duke and duchess unconscious and lock the door himself. After the door was locked, she tossed the key onto the writing table. "You were saying, Your Grace?"

"Did I sound like a pompous ass?" Justin grimaced. " 'Twill be a hard habit to break. Nonetheless, I shall try.

In the meantime, you will put up with me. Won't you? I don't wish you to leave me, Elizabeth."

The duchess cocked her head to one side. "I believe, Your Grace, that you have just said that I suit you to a cow's thumb."

The duke, who was making an attempt to wash his back, paused in midscrub. "A cow's thumb at the very least. Where did that come from?"

"Mrs. Papplewick." Elizabeth circled the copper tub, just out of St. Clair's reach, and put her hands behind her back. "She was speaking of Magda, I believe. I also believe that I recall you saying you would not marry for love again."

Justin craned his neck and twisted in the tub. Elizabeth was still moving, and shedding garments as she went. First the gown was discarded, then the petticoat. Fascinated, he watched as she untied her stays. "I didn't marry for love the first time, although I thought I had," he said, a trifle breathlessly. "As for the other, I didn't want to love you, or expect to love you, but there it is. I do love you, Elizabeth. More than words can express. More than I will ever love anyone again. Not that I would ever think of loving anyone else, because I have already seen a pistol in your hand and do not wish to ever have another such fright. What are you doing now?"

Clad in only her chemise, the duchess knelt beside the tub and took up the sponge. "You were saying something about how I might do whatever I wished with you, Your Grace. I believe I will first wash your back. And then maybe I will shampoo your hair. And after that perhaps I shall climb into the tub with you, and we shall both slaver with lust."

Could one swoon from sheer pleasure? Hopefully not, because then one might miss what happened next. Said the duke, "Damn and blast!"

And so the Duke and Duchess of Charnwood had their wedding night at last, even if it was in the middle of the day, during which they progressed from the copper tub to the writing desk and at last to the ducal bed. The matter involved a goodly amount of kisses and caresses and other stuff which the reader will not wish to hear, but yet must be assured that the duchess did indeed close her eyes and clench her teeth, and wished herself nowhere else in all the great wide world.

Epilogue

"A roof to cover you, and a bed to lie; Meat when you're hungry, and a drink when you're dry; And a place in heaven when you come to die." —An Old Wedding Wish

The dinner party planned by Lady Augusta in honor of the new Duchess of Charnwood went without a hitch, despite the expectations of at least one of the guests. There were no errors of precedence, in arrangement of status and rank; no fault to be found in the ten-course meal—which included a *supreme de volaille aux truffles*, a sweetbread *au jus*, lamb cutlets with asparagus, a *fricandeau de veau à l'oseille*: stewed beef *à la jareiniere*; a Turkey poult, peas and asparagus; a marasquino jelley, a chocolate cream and *meringes à la crème*; two ices, cherry water and pineapple cream, and fruit; sherry, Madeira and champagne—although it was remarked that the great many-armed epergne placed in the middle of the table made it difficult to observe one's fellow guests.

After the meal, the ladies retired to the drawing room, while the gentlemen enjoyed their port, and refreshments were brought around. Although there were no cards provided for the guests' entertainment—and who could wonder at it, after the debacle at Catterick's—this was more than compensated for by the presence of musicians, who would not only soothe the guests with melodic strains, but provide dance tunes. Lady Augusta was noticed to be in looks this evening, dressed in a round gown of pale green silk, over the train a loose covering of black silk, and full black sleeves, on her head a cap of embroidered mull trimmed with tucks and lace. The Duchess of Charnwood, however, was the focus of all eyes in her gown of rose pink sarcenet with tiny puff sleeves, a narrow skirt trimmed with a double pleating of ribbon, and an amazingly low neckline, her hair parted in ringlets and bedecked with flowers. 'Twas evident to anyone with half an eye that the lady wore no stays.

If all the gentlemen present this evening admired the duchess's costume, at least one of the women did not. That lady was Elizabeth's own mama, who thought she had done a much better job of installing the principles of propriety in her daughter's head than apparently she had, because the girl had clearly left her chamber half dressed. "Elizabeth!" she hissed. "Cover yourself! A correct taste is ever the concomitant of a chaste mind."

The duchess smiled and tapped her foot in time to the music. "I find that my mind is not particularly chaste, Maman."

"And glad I am of it," remarked the duke, who had joined the duchess in time to hear this last remark. "If you do not cease to harangue my wife, I will see that you are locked in *your* room, ma'am." Lady Ratchett—who bore a vague resemblance to her daughter, had Elizabeth aged thirty years and taken to sucking on sour lemon drops—heaved with indignation and added her son-in-law the duke to the long list of things that she disliked.

Nigel Slyte was dashing in dark blue and light sage green, and a white striped Manchester dimity waistcoat trimmed with a small white fringe. To his arm clung Lady Syb, who had recovered sufficiently from her illness to don a petticoat and robe *à la Turque* of white satin, trimmed with gold foil, and a black fringe intermixed with gold. Upon her golden curls she wore a black velvet *bandeau* set with pearls, which boasted one white, one black, and two white and lilac feathers, and a large diamond pin placed on the right side. More diamonds sparkled in her ears. "I see you've overcome your dislike of Bath, Geraldine," remarked Lady Syb, as they joined the small group. "Or is it that you would be thought a poor thing indeed to fail to attend a dinner party held in honor of your daughter the duchess?"

Lady Ratchett turned an interesting shade of puce that clashed terribly with her gown of purple-blue satin.

Lady Ysabella smiled. "Yes, I am."

Mr. Melchers strolled up in time to hear this last exchange. "And we appreciate it in you, Lady Syb."

Lady Ratchett looked at this tall, broad stranger with dissipation writ all over his face, and amusement in his eyes, and promptly recognized a gentleman prone to nourish improper thoughts, and to encourage ladies to have them about him. Propriety was offended. She gave him a withering glance. Mr. Melchers quirked an amused eyebrow. Lady Ysabella patted his arm.

"Lady Sib is feeling better," Justin remarked to Nigel, who was observing this byplay with a bright malacious eye.

Nigel nodded. "She's decided to take Gus and me with her to London for the Season. I'd take to *my* bed if I thought it would do me any good."

Lady Augusta was indeed enjoying her last appearance as her cousin's hostess. However, she conceded that Saint deserved to be private with his bride. Not that he *hadn't* been private with her already: the duke and duchess had taken to spending a prodigious amount of time in their bedchamber, from which strange noises and shouts and groans frequently ensued. 'Twas most embarrassing. The servants went about pretending to be deaf as posts. A London Season would be interesting. Perhaps there would be gambling. Gus signaled to the orchestra to play a country dance.

The duke signaled to his servants. Two footmen appeared bearing the parrot's cage between them, followed by wide-eyed little Katy carrying Minou. "They have taken a fancy to each other," explained Justin. "Birdie begins to pull out her feathers if Minou leaves her sight."

Head cocked to one side, Lady Syb regarded the parrot. Head cocked to the other, Birdie regarded her. "*Zut!*" squawked Birdie, and turned her back, and fanned her tail. "That bird," remarked Lady Syb, "has gotten fat."

The duke and duchess exchanged glances. "Biscuit!" they said, as one.

"Pish! You have indulged her shockingly, the pair of you. I suggest you concentrate on indulging each other—" Lady Syb cast the duke a doting glance. "And leave the bird to Minou."

"Beg pardon, milady," said Katy, who was attempting to prevent the kitten from climbing onto Birdie's cage. "But it should be Minette."

Nigel eyed the kitten. "A feline Chevalier d'Eon! Will it reproduce?"

Lady Syb rapped him with her fan. "Since Birdie has fallen in love with your kitten, Elizabeth, I shall give her to you as a bride gift. However, you must allow her no more biscuits." Birdie squawked and swooned in the bottom of her cage. "Give it up, you feathermop, or I shall take you out of the cage and use you to dust the room. Yes, Geraldine, I know you disapprove. What a dreary life you lead."

Lady Ratchett turned from puce to plum. More than one observer expected to see smoke issue from her ears. It did not, of course. Smoking ears would not be lady-like. Instead she elevated her nose and turned point-edly away.

Now that he thought on it, so did Sir Charles lead a dreary life. At least that part of it he spent at home as opposed to interrogating mysterious madames who knew things they should not. Thoughtfully he said, "I believe I would like a kitten. Or perhaps two." Lady Ratchett sputtered and he added, "Locked in your room with only bread and water, madam! My time here with the duke has made me realize that I am your husband, and you must obey. Elizabeth don't obey *him*, but that's dif-ferent. You are a stickler for things being what they should."

Lady Ratchett subsided—a lady did not make a pub-lic spectacle—but with a fulminating glance that sug-gested the subject was not closed. Justin glanced at Conor Melchers. "Sir Charles will pay for that."

"Sir Charles has sufficient blunt to buy any number of garish carriages," Conor murmured. "He deserves to have a dashing high flyer in his protection, don't you think? Your wife is looking particularly fine tonight. I see you have allowed her to display her bosom. It's damned generous of you, Saint."

Justin glanced at his wife's bosom. Indeed, he had spent the entire evening alternately admiring her bosom and the look of his ring upon her hand. "Yes, you may dance with her. But at the first sign of drooling, I *will* carve out your gizzard." Conor was smiling as he led Elizabeth out onto the floor.

She eyed him curiously. "I shall never understand gentlemen. You and St. Clair might almost be friends."

Conor executed a step and closed. "We are. Almost."

The movements of the dance took them apart, and then back together. Elizabeth circled to the left. "I want to thank you for not—You know."

"Don't thank me, Duchess. Had you really wanted me to, I would have. Indeed, if ever you *do* want me to make your toenails twitch—" He winked. Deliberately, she stepped on his foot. Conor laughed aloud.

The duchess said no more but concentrated instead on the dance, which she completed without another misstep, and considerable amiability and gracefulness, and a very nice suppleness in her limbs. Mr. Melchers danced with confidence, as he did all else. And if any of the other guests thought it odd that the duke would allow his wife to dance with a rakehell, none of them were the least surprised when he reclaimed her immediately she left the dance floor. The rumor of a meeting between the men had been exaggerated, perhaps; although Charnwood was seen to treat his nose in a tender manner, and a fading bruise could be still seen around Mr. Melchers' right eye.

If the duchess's *paffions* had been aroused by the dance, it was not Mr. Melchers from whom she sought relief. She placed her lips close to her husband's ear, and said, "Mr. Melchers mentioned twitching toenails. Is there something you have not yet shared with me, Your Grace?"

Justin's own toenails quivered. With heroic effort, he contrived to remain composed. "Any number of things, my darling. I did not wish to leave you so limp with pleasure that you were unable to attend these festivities that Gus has arranged on your behalf."

Elizabeth looked around the room. "It is a very nice

festivity. Augusta has done well. Still, I believe I would like to retire to our bedchamber now so that you may teach me about toes."

That Lady Augusta's dinner party was a most charming affair almost all those privileged to attend later agreed. While some remarked upon the oddity that a macaw and a kitten were permitted to attend the festivities, and others thought it odder still that the duke and duchess abruptly abandoned their guests to their own devices and retired to the ducal bedchamber and did not reappear until the next afternoon, the majority agreed that the reason for their hasty marriage was more than adequately explained by their behavior. 'Twas a love match, after all.

For those who care about such matters, the wager laid belowstairs was won by Thornaby.

Lady Ratchett wouldn't have approved

God speed them well.

ABOUT THE AUTHOR

Maggie MacKeever lives in Los Angeles. She's currently working on her next Zebra Regency romance, which will be published in June 2004. Maggie loves to hear from readers, and you may write to her c/o Zebra Books. Please include a self-addressed stamped envelope if you wish a response.